I am

By

tom.d.featherstone

I am Tom is published by Books with Influence
www.bookswithinfluence.com

I am tom

Prologue	4
Chapter 1: THE END	10
Chapter 2: FRANKENSTEIN	20
Chapter 3: GREAT EXPECTATIONS	30
Chapter 4: REVOLUTIONARY ROAD	46
Chapter 5: THE INVISIBLE MAN	61
Chapter 6: STARDUST	71
Chapter 7: LONDON MEMORIAL	78
Chapter 8: MIDDLEMARCH	90
Chapter 9: BELOVED	103
Chapter 10: WUTHERING HEIGHTS	114
Chapter 11: WHEN WE WERE YOUNG	124
Chapter 12: LES MISERABLES	139
Chapter 13: A ROOM WITH A VIEW	151
Chapter 14: THE LORD OF THE RINGS	163
Chapter 15: ROMEO AND JULIET	175
Chapter 16: TO KILL A MOCKINGBIRD	183
Chapter 17: ANNA KARENINA	193
Chapter 18: THE ALCHEMIST	203
Chapter 19: JANE EYRE	212
Chapter 20: OF HUMAN BONDAGE	223
Chapter 22: THE CHILDREN OF MEN	232
Chapter 23: THE BEGINNING	241

For the 42%

Prologue

All that remained was the time he might spend searching for a matching sock. Sixty seconds, give or take. Had he been alert to what was coming, he would have grasped and kicked and screamed, like a sliding body on a listing deck.

For the time being, there was no reason to compute anything was amiss. All was well in his world. Not perfect, but whose life is? He opened the front door of their Wandsworth townhouse, pulling the worn brass handle towards him, simultaneously lifting and pushing up and to the right with the action of turning the key. He knew he needed to fix that door. Doors were above his DIY pay grade. Someone called John or Steve or Pavel would be called and remunerated at vast expense – reason enough to settle for the status quo and a stubborn door. It slammed behind him. It always slammed, even when shutting it gently. It was one of those doors. Inside it was cold, as if he were the first through the door after a fortnight's holiday. No waft of kids tea or thud of scurrying feet. Like a blind man unable to hear his own footsteps, something was terribly amiss. In years to come, if he emerged into the light again, the world and he would be very different. That's what Apocalypses do, change everything without warning, in an incandescent moment of mass destruction.

He thought later, it was like being shot in the back without warning. The whip of white lead spitting from the barrel, followed by absolutely nothing. What a disappointing way to die. One moment life beats out its metronomic tick and tock, the next you're gone. Lights out. Sayonara. Looking from the vantage of hindsight, he saw the bullet slice towards him in slow motion. He saw the gun, the puff of smoke, the recoil in her hands. No chance of ducking. Too little, too late, she would repeatedly chant with the callous intransigence of an on-message politician.

Before leaving for work that morning, he'd been abrupt with the kids bickering over the last portion of Cocoa Pops. Lightening the mood he'd ruffled his son's hair, kissed his daughter on the forehead. It was the last day of term and everyone was exhausted, no need to rock the boat. He didn't kiss Claire. They stopped kissing hello and goodbye a long time back. Once abandoned, the odd occasion either attempted to plant a peck became an awkward clash of faces. There was something contrived about it, something false. Valentine's Day had befallen the same fate a few years into their marriage. It seemed so trite, struggling for an appropriate card and suitably sincere words. They never celebrated their anniversary. Married on her Birthday, it naturally carried precedence in subsequent years. Memories of their fabulous wedding blanched in reality, like the oxidised patina on the engagement ring she never wore anymore. But they were as happy as any couple. Money was tight since he'd gone freelance. Too long he'd lived a nocturnal existence behind the night desk at The Guardian. The income drop had been a worthwhile price to retake his place in daylight society. She'd encouraged him all the way. She was good like that, she knew what made him tick.

Their social life was good. A great group of fellow parents met at school interspersed with the occasional meet-up with people from the old-days – her University friends, friends from the London Gang, before marriage and kids and Apocalypses. Claire hadn't been part of the original London Gang. A latecomer, she never quite shook her outsider status. First materialising as a friend of a friend at a party, nobody today can clearly remember who that friend was. Everyone remembers it was 1994, the year of the Gang's zenith. The year never to be recreated, even when the core ingredients were the same. Perhaps everything started downhill from there. Like trying to surpass that one album indelibly carving a rock band into music history – 1994 was their Bat Out of Hell; Breakfast in America; Dark Side of the Moon – never to be surpassed. It was the year The Shawshank Redemption and Pulp Fiction inked their place at the top of every dinner party list of best films ever. The year Four Weddings and a Funeral launched the actor Hugh Grant into an inescapable stereotype and underlined Britain's incongruous enjoyment of the antics of posh folk. The Gang all had post-university jobs, a bit of money and a lot of libido only marred by the inconvenience of the AIDS crisis. They hadn't yet assumed the responsibilities of senior management or marriage, mortgages, kids or needing to face Monday morning without a hangover. There was little concern for what life would look like when the curtain fell on their twenties. As the Nineties rolled on, their plots played out with the inevitable triumphs, calamities and twists of every transition from child to parent.

Claire flitted in and out, like a minor character in a psychological drama subtly primed for a disproportionate role in the story's denouement. No-nonsense glamourous, good-time-gal was her motif; petrol head; part-time tomboy; sex-kitten. Nobody seemed to know where she went or who invited her back, but she was always there when something was worthy of her patronage. Over the years, she dabbled in the clutches of a few of the boys, and rumour had it, at least one of the girls, before she eventually zeroed her sights on him.

He was taken aback by her interest. He thought her long legs, vacuum packed in denim, were out of his league. She was too pretty. Too headstrong. When she finally made her intentions clear, she claimed it had always been him she fancied. Excuses made and parked, some version of love unfolded between the sheets of mutual flattery, shared surprise at their latter-day coupling, and the desire not to spend Sunday nights alone when so many of the Gang had already paired off.

In the convention of pushing into their thirties, the Gang disintegrated in a flurry of weddings and self-certified mortgages. He proposed while on a weather-disappointed holiday to Dubai. Within the year, they married. Within the next, Jack was born. In the ensuing decade, the Gang produced a phalanx of children, most of the females predictably christened in the vowel heavy fashion of the time - Isabella, Zara, Tara, Georgina, Olivia, Antonia, Amelia, Ella. The host of male spawn seemed limited to a choice of Jack, Oscar, Ben, James or Sam.

For him and Claire, after Jack, came Clara. The picture-perfect scene of middle-class domestic ubiquity was set. Unseen, were the insidious spores germinating in their fabric. As year replaced year, their formerly enlightened sex life buffeted in the wake of child-rearing, financial pressure, a diverging taste in TV boxsets and stultifying resentment for this or that petty sleight. Carnal coupling tangibly morphed from impassioned to dutiful. From infrequent to rare. From a topic of discussion, to sore taboo.

Thirty seconds to go.

He trod carefully up the stairs, finding Jack and Clara huddled together on the landing, cuddling Bubs and Monk-Monk against the unseen terror. His hitherto half-formed inkling was rapidly taking shape like silently settling snow. He asked them where Mummy was, and then what was wrong. They answered neither. They both looked terrified. Bile rising in his gut, he reassessed his assumption of the suitcases he'd passed at the bottom of the stairs. The brain is such a fast worker. In a previous Nano-second, he'd computed Claire must have had a long overdue throw out of old clothes, the cases stuffed and ready for the charity shop. Now with a growing sense of loss of control, he arrived at a new clarity. It hit him like a heedlessly speeding scaffolding truck on a moonless winter's night. Discarded clothes go to the charity shop in black bin-liners.

She appeared from their matrimonial bedroom, dressed in the comfortable clothes she always wore on long journeys. He'd seen the look on her face before, though never so riven. His imploring heart raced for his brown Loafers.

Ten seconds.

His mind rapidly scanned for indiscretions moral, financial or otherwise capable of precipitating what was clearly not to become the evening he'd anticipated. A late convert to Sushi, he'd picked up a mixed tray from a new takeaway near his office. He had felt rather pleased with himself. She would be pleased. She loved Sushi. With wine and a little light banter, they might make it to bed without arguing and then who knows?

Beckoned into the bedroom out of earshot of the children, she explained without hesitation and the unswerving ruthlessness of a gangland boss to whom a code of honour had been fatally transgressed, "I am leaving you."

Sympathy did not feature. No grey area, no room for negotiation. Thirteen years erased with a single tap of the delete key. As the primary carer, she was taking the children. Going back to Ireland. He would need to continue to work and earn. She was miserable, she had been for years and wanted her life back. Her forty-fifth birthday hurtling over the horizon, she wanted to be with a man who appreciated her for who she was. He was four years older than her. Back then he'd called her his child-bride. It wasn't funny then, now the joke was sick.

Dumbstruck, he asked if it was Chris she was leaving him for, because, well, he needed to say something. He and Chris were good mates, he couldn't truly imagine he'd done the dirty on him. He knew as he said it, he shouldn't have said it, but Chris's way with Claire had always bugged him. Claire and Chris had a thing back in the day, but then Chris had a thing with most of the females in the Gang. Things were Chris's thing. And anyway, he had to say something, and the children were too close by for him to beg. After she'd gone he wished he had begged, told her she was the only one, that she couldn't leave. Instead, he tried to cry, but disbelief had his tears backed-up along with the words he couldn't summon. They would come later.

For the briefest of moments he imagined a look of pity on her face. Surely she wasn't going to go through with it? It wasn't the first time either of them had threatened to leave. Nope. It wasn't Chris, she said, it wasn't anyone. Adding for good measure, "it's just not you."

Tick, tock, zero. Boom.

Chapter 1: THE END

"Terror made me cruel"

Emily Bronte. Wuthering Heights

The silence following the slamming taxi doors was clichéd in its completeness. He stood alone in the hall, like a spaceman absentmindedly left on the moon with no chance of rescue. Like the moment before drowning when the distance between the sinking silhouette and the glint of sunlight on the surface outweighs the air left in the lungs. It was over. A living witness to his own death.

I am that witness. I am him.

My name is Tom. Three weeks ago, my wife left for Ireland robbing me of my two beloved children and every sense of what I thought I knew of the world.

"We'll talk in a few days," she said.

The children were both crying, clinging to me, their faces gripped in terror despite being too young to process the true nature of the threat. Unclasping their fingers from my faithful tweedy jacket with the black elbow patches and enamel 'Ibiza 2017' button badge I used to think so cool, Claire led them off the stage of my life like despondent actors from a failed audition. There was no curtain call.

It was a full week before I first found the courage and sobriety to speak to them. Now I phone them every day, Claire picks up the phone and I ask to be put onto the children. I don't ask her how she is or what she's doing, I don't want to know. I ask each in turn the same questions. How are you? What did you do today? What did you have for tea? Have you made any friends? How's Granny? I apologise for Mummy and Daddy being so silly, and tell them everything's going to be fine. What else can I say? Their answers are brief and functional and somehow disappointing. Last night Jack asked me how I was. He will be eleven before long, he gets it, well some of it, I suppose. I said I was fine, doing well. I didn't want to sound upbeat, but if I sounded down, he would worry. I feel so ashamed. I have failed them. We have failed them. I said I missed him, and I know he heard my voice crack and now I feel stupid for saying it. Claire would spit at me if she knew, say I'm using the children as pawns.

It's early summer and I feel like I am fading in the life of my children like a pet left locked up and unfed while its owners holiday abroad. I am broken and though long past rock-bottom, my descent shows no sign of slowing. I picture Jack and Clara in the family home in Dalkey, standing proud and detached looking out towards Dalkey Island, where the southbound railway from Dublin bends round the headland past Killiney towards Rathsallagh. It's such a lovely house - a cross between an Edwardian large family home and American clapboard with a wraparound porch, nestled on the cliffside, protected by Yew's and Oaks and unforgiving rocks facing off the Irish Sea. We spent dozens of holidays there as a family. We always dreamed aloud of moving there. We had been due to spend our summer holiday there in July, now I'm unwelcome.

On my Mother's orders, I've been to the doctor, he says I am depressed. He's probably right. But depression doesn't feel right for a guy like me. That stuff happens to other people. My glass comes half full. Perhaps it's the alcohol, I know I am drinking too much. Life is a vicious cycle of small ups being quashed by the next inevitable booze marinated disappointment. I don't look at social media anymore, I recoil from perfect lives. It would be a miracle to post something about myself. What would I say? Like the marriage vows I made to a god I don't believe in, I don't believe in eternal damnation, but I know what it feels like. My best friend Dyfed says I mustn't blame myself. Everyone says that. Easily said, easier still written. Take each day as it comes, is the constant refrain. Small steps, little victories. Blah, blah, blah.

My name is Tom, and until three weeks ago I thought my life was sorted. Now it is only questions and regret I didn't do whatever it was I should have done. The date on my passport puts me at forty-nine. That's a fact. Another fact is my close circle of old friends. Let's say there are ten of them – there might be a few more or a couple less. Like compiling a guest list for a significant event, it's not always clear where to make the cut. Three years ago, we were all married, or at least tied to a significant other by babies and homes. First Orla's marriage collapsed. Then Graeme's, but we'd all silently predicted that one. Only six months ago the rest of us had a discussion about how lucky we were to all still be married, statistically speaking that is. Now it's me, I had no idea I was for the chop. I've Googled the national statistic for divorce – it's 42%. That's insane, but it's what I was expecting. Everyone knows something like half of all marriages fail. And for some reason we accept it. Like statistics about childhood obesity, or knife crime or sexually-transmitted diseases in the over sixties, we hear a statistic and move on, because it doesn't affect us. If the numbers are true, I won't be the last, but for now, Audi's and Land Rovers on the drive and annual trips to Mark Warner resorts pronounce all to be well.

Of course word of my divorce is contagious, it spreads from mouth to text, to the big topic of discussion over a beer at the bar or a glass of red at yet another dinner party. One by one I meet people I know, and like announcing I have cancer, or won the lottery or am moving to Australia the news I impart is seismic. Well, it is to me. Despite their obvious sympathy and offers of support, I am no one else's problem.

I'm sitting alone at the bar of the Alma Tavern in Wandsworth. The barmaid is Australian or Kiwi, I can never tell. She could be nineteen or twenty-five. It's 4.30pm in the afternoon, my fellow clientele are all men on their own. Middle-aged men, old-men, easing their stories with alcohol. It's warm enough to be outside. Outside is where I'd normally be. If I was writing my online dating profile, which I'm painfully aware I may have to do, I'd probably say I was an outdoorsy person. Then I'd claim I could surf and ski and paraglide and upload action shots, only to disappoint the girls foolish enough to go on dates with me, as they realise I smoke, and drink until I can't remember. They would never go so far to find out I snore like a freight train - that's how Claire used to describe it. A freight train wasn't a direct criticism, but it was another black mark. Another lingering odour, minutely contributing towards suitcases in the hall and three one-way tickets to Dublin. I can't imagine my snoring has improved since she's gone. But then like a tree falling in the woods, who knows if I make a sound now?

"Tom.   Tom.   Is   that   you   Darling?"

I must have picked up my phone because a voice from it is shouting in my ear.

"Tom? Tom? Oh for fuck sake, I hate these things. Tom are you there?"

"Hello   Melissa."

"Ah, good. Right, I hear Fraulein has left you. Can't imagine what that feels like, so I'm not much use to you on the life support side of things. But happy to drink with you until we puke."

I refer to Melissa as my Commissioning Editor. She isn't really my editor as I'm freelance, but she and I go a long way back and the majority of work I do, I do for her, so I think of her as my pseudo-employer. Her sense of style might be described as Turner Prize chic, where nothing from her geometric haircuts to her multi-layered homage to Bedouin tent dressing makes any sense whatsoever. She combines this with an over-stated virulent hetrosexuality she wears on her profane sleeve, oversharing in excruciating detail at the most inappropriate times. She's been with her partner, a computer programmer called Richard for 'at least a million years,' though I've never met him I'm almost sure he exists. She calls him Dickie. I suspect she is the only person who calls him that.

"Do you want some work, or are you wallowing?" She asks.

"I'm wallowing. I won't be any good to you at the moment. Sorry."

"That is entirely understandable, my old cock. But don't wallow too long, I might find someone I like more than you."

"That would be par for the course right now."

"Thomas, you've taken a smash in the face. Go and fuck the barmaid of which ever sorry establishment you are sitting in. Or hire a hooker. Whatever floats your boat. But you've got to get back on the horse before long, or the horse will bolt, do you get me?"

I do.

But I also know I'm a long way off accepting conclusions.

"I'm just stunned by the whole fucking thing."

"Darling, I have spent my entire life searching for the floor of disappointment in others and have yet to reach it even in my advanced years. Even the ones we love let us down in the end. Not Dickie of course, I won't let him and he'd never give up his monthly blow-job. But as for everyone else, expect nothing. Everyone is out for themselves."

"I'm not sure you're helping."

"That's the point Chum. Nobody is coming to your rescue. So go and deflower some South West London daddy's girl, sort your shit out and I'll call you next week. Capiche?"

I thank her and tell her I'll be OK and try to inject a little lilt in my voice. I don't care about money right now, but I'm still conscious enough to know I am going to need it if I'm going to survive this. Which I'm assuming I am, while the alternative is probably closer than it's ever been.

On another day I would indeed attempt to follow Melissa's advice but I can't even get the barmaid to pour me a pint, let alone indulge in conversation and I fear the hookers would take one look at me and pay me to piss off or they'll call their Pimp.

What to do?

Another drink?

Another   pub?

Another nervous walk past the Thai Massage shop on the High Street?

I am rudderless. I've already drunk four pints and I know my decision making is subprime. I miss my kids so much. The guilt is crippling me. I decide it would be smarter to wallow in my grief in private and drain my glass. The barmaid has her back to me as I pull open the door and step onto the pavement. The sky's blue, but dirty blue and the heat has gone from the sun. I walk up the hill and step aside to let pass two apparently happy, healthy middle-class men in washed-out polo shirts and coloured shorts and deck shoes heading out for an early summer evening drink. A pair of pretty twenty-something girls locked arm-in-arm swish past me in a tornado of perfume and flowing skirts, and long, clean hair and dangly-earrings and genuine giggles. Oh, fuck it all.

Forcing open my bloody front door, I see my retro phone with it's thick cream-coloured wire, green plastic casing and rotary dial on the drop-leaf table in the hall. I'd bought it along with a vinyl record player now installed in the sitting room. I'd explained to Claire they were a cool throwback to when life was simple, a visible reminder of values and simplicity and form over function. She wasn't impressed. She views the world in black and white. Life isn't complicated to her, it's either yes or no, never maybe. To her, my pride in my antiques was nonsense when the modern world is designed to make life easy. I stare at the phone and wonder if I should call The Samaritans. No, that seems over-dramatic. Anyway, I'll have to explain the whole story from the beginning. I don't have the energy, and I know I'm quite drunk. Which is usually the moment before I get really drunk. Knowing I'm quite drunk is always the last thought I remember in the morning.

Sitting next to my old phone is the one picture of our wedding day that survived the cull and inevitable pyre that followed Claire's exit. It was taken less than an hour before Claire and I exchanged vows. All the members of the

London Gang are there, lined up like a sports team in our wedding finest, giddy at the prospect of the day ahead. We had no idea any of us would end up in the 42% of marital failure. Why would we? Nobody does.

Our collective successes and failures are both common and unique. Though dear to me, we could be any group of friends. We coalesced around a set of values, histories, geographies and one-eyed biases placing us in a specific demographic pot. What you might call a typical sample of life. Every group, no matter from where they herald, have similar compositions. It's too early in this tale to expect you to remember all the Gang names in case they pop up in the plot. I'll tell you anyway, then you can forget them until they show themselves again. As we stand in the picture the back row is the Adrenaline Junkie (Ade), the Quiet One (Graeme) the Straight-Talker (Peers), the Fool (Dyfed), the Dandy (Bic), the Rake (Chris), the Rabble-Rouser (Matt). The Fall Guy (me) is standing at front-centre flanked by the girls, the anything-boys-can-do-I-can-do-betterer (Orla) on my one side, and the Gossip (Gemma) on the other. Crouching awkwardly in their dresses and heels in front of us are the triptych from Bath University, affectionately known as the Bath Babes – the Tactile (Jess) a raven brunette; the Carer (Vanessa) a demure redhead; and the Suffragette (Rosie) an ash blonde. Van has taken up station, as they do in every photo, in the middle or the three - like a kaleidoscopic range of hair dye packets on a chemist's shelf.

I   dial   Dyfed.

Out of them all, he's my best mate, we met when we were seven at school and I haven't been able to shake him off since. Perhaps it's the other way round, but we have made more history in forty years than all we were taught at school about Kings and Corn Laws and why the Second World War was a consequence of the first. He answers immediately. I hear him getting off the sofa, knowing he is in for half an hour listening to my shit, rather than hanging out with Alice and his girls. But he doesn't seem to mind. True friends don't. He says all the things he is supposed to say. Just when I'm thinking I've heard it all before and I should drown in a bottle of red wine, he tells me I should write about my experience.

"Imagine yourself a year from now," he says. "A new house, a new girlfriend and a bestseller about to be published!" At first I dismiss the notion, as a kind but misguided yank of my chain. Then somewhere in my brain, cogs turn and my better judgement is overruled by what suddenly doesn't sound such a stupid idea. Admittedly, it's an entirely fanciful prospect, but I can't wait to get him off the phone. I wrap up our conversation with a brief summary to show I had been listening, thank him and hang-up. Pushing back the pile of papers on my kitchen table I send a bowl of shrivelled satsumas tumbling onto the floor. They can wait. I open my Macbook and click on the Microsoft Word icon. I write, *All that remains is the time it might take to find a matching sock.* Now I can't think of a second line, so I go to bed. Tomorrow I will write the first chapter, I'm convinced of it.

Here's the thing. I am a journalist and a writer. Following a year at The Portsmouth Evening news after University, I got lucky. For eight or so great years, I hustled between papers on Fleet Street and Canary Wharf, reporting on genocide in Rwanda, mass-rape in Srebrenica and other cheery subjects. I loved it. By the time I met Claire, I was a junior editor on the night desk at The Guardian, high on a different kind of adrenaline, second-guessing what the other Nationals were running, hanging on for the last second before calling 'off-stone,' setting the presses running. Writing for pleasure was a Busman's holiday I had never taken. A colleague had published a science fiction novel to critical derision, ending up as a runner-up in the Literary Review's Bad Sex Award over his trans-species love scene between a teenage runaway and an alien modelled on George Clooney. My colleague lost his luster and skulked round the newsroom with the monkey of failure on his back. I didn't want that fate. When I went freelance, I liked the freedom, but my mojo waned. Endless pieces on the tyranny of social media made a point, but the point was futile in the zeitgeist of the time.

I'm awake again.

It's daylight.

I still think writing a book is a good idea. After a coffee and two fags I'm working on my second sentence. This could be a long process. Everyone who's been through divorce says it's a journey. In writing stuff down, I realise I'm still in the rocky foothills of mine. Every time I think I find an answer to a question, it reforms into another question. There probably is no end, this is who I am now. I get that. The only victory will be to emerge alive, sane and accepting, and maybe having written a book. Beyond that, whatever will be, will be.

It's funny, but not funny-ha-ha, as I write and search for answers, I quickly uncover one of the biggest bruises I need to push. I remember the old maxim, success has many parents. If marriage is a 50:50 thing, I need to figure out my role as father of my own failure. It doesn't matter which party is the chicken or the egg, each has to take 100% responsibility for their half of the equation.

I email the first few pages to my friends Graeme and Orla because they are fellow divorcees and Dyfed because he's my best friend and well, he knows a thing or two about the ins and outs of marriage. Keep going they reply; so painful; it's so true! Dyfed says it's making him think about his own marriage. It turns out flattery is one of the best brakes of a downward spiral, no matter how exaggerated. It's giving me purpose. I never usually share my work before it's finished. Melissa, calls me a 'polisher,' always submitting my copy late. I take it as a nuanced compliment, even though she means it as a criticism. Perhaps now I want my words to be heard. A cry for help? Probably.

I'm told, victims of runaway wives make great second husbands. I'll probably never marry again, but I get the point. Despite its fulcrum in life's curriculum, we are not taught at school the what's-what of marriage. They say a dog is for life, not just for Christmas - but dogs rarely live beyond fifteen years. Perhaps someone should point out, fifty years of marriage is a lifetime under-estimated at incalculable peril. The presiding Priest says in every sermon; marriage takes hard work. How did I not hear his words? Perhaps I shouldn't beat myself up, so few of us listen.

My name is Tom. Your name is Tom. We are Legion.

Chapter 2: FRANKENSTEIN

"Nothing is so painful to the human mind as a great and sudden change."

Mary Shelley

It's three months since the Apocalypse and I'm sitting where I thought I'd never sit, at a Book Club. This is strange, I'm just not a Book Club kind of guy. Sharing oxygen and my inner thoughts with strangers, especially ones who are a tad outside my demographic, is my idea of hell. But I'm here because Orla made me. For the time-being I'll kid myself I am here to help further my own book writing, but I'm pretty sure I'm here to meet women.

The first thing I notice about Ian Korf is his knitted red jumper, despite the evening temperature being still in the low-twenties. Then, all at once I notice his trimmed black beard, pressed blue linen trousers, loafers, yellow socks, booming voice and aura of self-appointed authority. Oh, and his big nose. I instinctively take a dislike to him, but this is his show and I am way outside my comfort zone. In my new world, I'm trying to learn to not judge people on first impressions.

"This is Tom," Orla announces to Ian across the large wooden dining table set with bottles of mineral water, pads and pens, handwritten name cards and piles of books dotted down the centre like mini termite mounds, "who I told you about."

"Yes, Tom," he says, looking down at an A4 sheet of paper. "Well, we'll just have to do our best."

"Thank you for having me," I offer.

"It's very difficult changing the team mid-term," he says, "unbalances the equilibrium. We'll be kicking off a new book this evening, so I suppose it's as good a time as any."

It's the hottest summer I can remember for years. The Thames at low-tide looked at drought levels when Orla and I earlier ambled across Hammersmith bridge. I'd asked her what sort of books they read at Book Club. She said they'd just finished The Quiet American by Graham Greene which wasn't really her thing, but in the end, it was OK. Apparently Ian selects a classic, then a contemporary, and the third (that completes the terms cycle), is selected by a member of the Club who Ian deems to have contributed the most insights. Then they break for the school holidays. She'd explained Ian is the self appointed Foreman of the Book Club which he runs like a jury, seeking subjective consensus from the six men and six women members. There are mini-votes and breakout groups and if the decision is hung, a debate to break the deadlock. Apparently, he is an evening-class schooled Psychoanalyst who could have been Freud, had Freud not already taken the slot. Orla said sometimes she thinks the members are Ian's subject, more than the books they read.

"Shall we get a drink?" I ask rhetorically to Orla, moving towards the bar at the back of the room. A lone hipster with a sporadic ginger beard, tattoos and frighteningly low fat-to-weight ratio asks what we would like. I order a pint of IPA. Orla has a glass of Prosecco. We make slanderous observations under our breath as an assortment of disconnected people drift in, looking earnest and mostly old and not my kind of people. Orla looks at me with an empathetic warning shot to behave and I remind myself to be open-minded. Ian bellows a five minute warning as people shuffle round the table like guests at a wedding looking for their place. Orla says he moves everyone around each session. I notice a from-a-distance-pretty-woman looking younger than thirty-five, with boyish brown hair, a black shirt and black jeans, searching for her place. She puts her saggy handbag on the floor and pours herself a glass of water.

"Let's get going," bellows Ian. I take my pint glass and look for my name card. There isn't one so stand behind the only unnamed seat and wait to be told

I'm in the wrong place. Orla is on the opposite side at the opposite end, facing outwards across the river. To my delight, the girl in the black-shirt slots in on my right, her name card says Aude. On my left is a Heffalump of a woman in her sixties, pushing seventy with wiry, unkempt black and grey hair and black trousers pulled tight around her waist that seems way off where biology intended it to be. She is Veronica. I introduce myself in turn to both ladies and am told I am welcome, to sit down, to enjoy myself and not to worry about Ian, and isn't it a shame about Rory.

"Before we get going," announces Ian with faux bedside manner, his eyelids at half-mast and hands clasped in front of him, "we must pay tribute to our dear friend Rory who tragically is no longer with us." The man sitting opposite me lets go a derisive snort. Ian hesitates momentarily and reverts to his booming voice, "who can forget his wonderfully alternative appraisal of For Whom The Bell Tolls?" It appears nobody can, or nobody wants to speak ill of the departed. The man opposite snorts again. He's the only person with his name card turned inward, which he is caressing in the fingers of both hands. Everyone glares at him and he offers his apologies by way of saying "allergies" which doesn't feel like an apology at all. In fact, it feels like he's telling everyone to fuck-off. He's in his fifties, a good-looking, leathery ex-army officer type, with dark hair and olive tinged skin suggesting a blip in his Anglo-Saxon ancestry, which doubtless earned him merciless beatings at public school. He has a hardback blue notebook in front of him which he opens, makes a brief annotation, closes it again then slowly turns his name card to face outwards like he's patronising everyone in the room. Capital letters written with a shakey black marker reveal his name as Marcus O. A glance around the table shows everyone has an anonymous initial for their surname which I guess is important for honesty in any self-help group. Despite this being a harmless, anonymous Book Club, I'm getting the feeling I've fallen down a rabbit hole.

Ian stumbles over the conclusion of Rory's eulogy. He's no priest, but clearly feels the need to rally his flock after the death of one of their own, whose shoes, I've just realised, I am standing in. I stare at Orla diagonally across the table, sending her my you-stitched-me-up face, but she is staring out the window, sliding her fingers up and down a hank of her raven hair like she's waxing the bow of a violin. I love Orla. Despite being very close, back when we were carefree, before the bomb dropped, we hadn't spoken properly for years. To my shame, during my marriage, I allowed the bond we formed in the Nineties to atrophy and overgrow with new life. The odd text message and guilty phone-call made poor substitutes for what we once had, but true friendships, it turns out, can endure a hiatus. It was Orla I called when I woke the morning after Claire took the kids. I will always remember her sitting on the side of my bed, stroking my back, like a St. Bernard keeping me alive in a snowdrift of white linen.

I remember her telling me I had a long journey in front of me in her matter-of-fact Belfast twang. And I remember protesting I hadn't been there for her during the breakdown of her own marriage. That I'd been embarrassed, hadn't known what to say.

"Don't worry," she had said, "everyone is like that. That's why I'm here, because I know what this feels like." She gently told me I was having a breakdown, which was new news. I hadn't had a breakdown before. I had tried during night after night at The Guardian, but never quite managed it. I wasn't sure I was the breakdown type, but it sounded like a good escape from life.

In modern parlance, Orla would be described as a strong, independent woman. To put it matter-of-factly, she is Irish, beautiful, and mad. Mad Orla we call her. She doesn't have a problem with that, she lives up to it.

The man that really did it for Orla, was Chris. Yes, that Chris. The Chris I lamely accused Claire of running off with. She met him in Aix-en-Provence during her placement year from University. How Chris was furthering his oriental studies in Aix is anyone's guess, but that's Chris for you. Their romance was a hedonism of marijuana, Backgammon and daytime sex. When Orla introduced me to Chris in London, I could have disliked him, but his truculent intelligence made him frustratingly likeable. His modus operandi was lighting up a Marlboro Red in places he shouldn't. Marlboro Red are the heavyweight champions of the world when it comes to sticking two fingers up to your lungs. Chris stuck two fingers up everywhere. He was a smoking moth to the flame of No Smoking signs, dinners parties and railway platforms. A perennially unshaven son-of-a-bitch, his good looks hung from him like un-ironed designer clothes. Post-graduation and back in London, Orla struggled to recreate the magic of Provence. Chris has never married, a fact that still galls Orla. She was a serious catch in her own right. A catch Chris always ham-fistedly dropped, whenever the scent of Provencal lavender hung in the air.

"Before we move onto our next choice and I introduce you all to Tom, I know last time, some of you hadn't finished The Quiet American, has anybody got anything else to say on the subject?"

Nobody has, so to fill the void Ian looks directly at me for the first time, explaining a fierce debate had ensued at the previous meeting over the phrase the 'gathering gloom', which they all had agreed was lovely and evocative and alliterative and so very perfect as Graham Greene built the tension as Fowler and Pyle try to make their way safely back to Saigon. The question was whether the combination of words had originated elsewhere? Which it turned out they had, in We Three Kings, the Christmas Carol and a Moody Blues song. Marcus had labelled Graham Greene a plagiarist, Ian explains provocatively, hastily adding a chorus of opposing voices had argued copyright was impossible on such a small couplet. Surely Shakespeare had used it? Or Chaucer. Many had agreed it was the sort of phrase one might find in the New Testament, though nobody had actually read it.

"Well, thank you everyone," says Ian drawing a line under his own narrative, "I think that puts The Quiet American to bed."

With a little too much theatre, Ian holds up the new book selection, his arm extended like he's straining to read the small print on the jacket, while distancing himself from it's content. "Veronica has chosen our next challenge. It's quite different. We don't normally go in for such fayre, but given the deep waters we swam with The Quiet American, and I must tell you I have up my sleeve a corker by Amor Towles to get into next, this month we are going to try some, err, Trollope."

Ian looks pleased with his thinly veiled put-down. Veronica looks mildly crushed. "I just thought," she starts. "No, no, this will be good for us," interrupts Ian, attempting to row back from his besmirch. "She's sold squillions of books," says a new voice. An Anglo-Indian voice coming from a lady carded as Jenita, who looks tall though she's sitting down. Her face is pretty from one angle, then masculine when I look across again. She's already at the bottom of a large glass of white wine she seems urgently wanting refilled.

"I'm looking forward to it," says Aude.
"I've already finished it," says Veronica. Ian shoots her a glare, like she should be disbarred for procedure violation.
"My mother has read every one of her books," says another new male voice, "she swears by them." Marcus snorts again, I'm beginning to think he has some sort of tick. The new voice belongs to a dark-haired man, I guess in his late-thirties. Maybe early forties. He has artist written all over him. Actually he doesn't but you get my gist - man bangles, open-chested shirt, messy hair. Attempting to unhook his soft, brown leather man-bag from the back of his chair,

he stands up and reveals himself not to be wearing a belt to hold up his jeans which are, in turn, sliding dangerously down his protruding hip bones. Aude is staring at him. Come to mention it, so is Orla. Come to mention that, so am I, so I look away at his name card which says Oli O, which sounds like a brand of olive oil which amuses me and makes me feel better since my hip bones have not been seen in many years.

Ian asks Veronica to explain the premise of the book. She says *Oh*, and looking bewildered announces it is called *An Unsuitable Match* and she will read the blurb which tells us the book is about an older couple, who's children from their previous marriages object to them getting married. In trying to make everyone else happy, Veronica asks us, can they ever find happiness themselves? Then she adds, with another *Oh*, and the tiniest of squirms in her seat, the couple had known and fancied each other at school, so this was a sort of second-time-around thing.

"That all sounds plausible," says Ian, "I'm sure there is plenty we can all relate to. What about you Tom?"

Ian is now looking at me.

I am looking at Ian.

"Why are you here?"

"Why?"

"Why? What do you hope to get out of joining our little team? Not just to get drunk I hope?" He looks at my empty pint glass and flicks a look at Jenita who has managed to get her glass refilled by a long-armed waiter.

"Well, I've been going through some tricky times and my friend Orla has been helping me," I say, telegraphing a nod down the table in her direction, "she thought me joining would help."

Marcus let's go his loudest snort yet.

"He's writing a book about love and marriage and divorce," says Orla.

All   heads   turn   back   to   me.

"Have you written anything before?" asks Ian.

"Well, erm," I say, "I'm a journalist, so yes, but never a full book."

Ian asks who I work for and I say mostly The Guardian without trying to sound smug, or politically concerned, or as if I have some sort of elevated status. Ian says I must be able to write, as I'm a journalist. Surely their little Book Club is beneath me?

"There's a big difference between writing and constructing a story," I say, "I can write, sure, of course I can. But putting together a complete work of fiction is an entirely different prospect. I'm hoping I might find some inspiration here."

"So you're using us as fodder?" Asks Marcus coldy.

"I find inspiration comes from all around. Usually places I least expect it."

"It must be very cathartic," says Veronica.

"Everybody asks me that," I say, "yes it certainly is. Perhaps that is all it is. It's certainly helping."

"You must keep going," says Ian, "Hemingway said the hardest part of writing a novel is to finish it. You could share it with us when you're ready. Maybe as you go along?"

"Oh yes, you must," gushes Veronica.

"I'd like to read it," offers Aude, sounding like she might mean it.

"Well," says Ian firmly, repositioning himself back in the limelight, "we are honoured to have a true writer in our presence."

He scans down the table, holding up An Unsuitable Match, throwing his baited hook to the class. "So what are our views of this genre of novel?" Nobody answers, so he adds, "what role can it play in people's lives?"

"It's chick-lit," says Marcus.

"I'm not sure you can call it chick-lit anymore," says Aude

"Why not? Call it what it is," says Marcus.

"Joanna   Trollope   is   not   a   chick,"   says   Jenita.

"I am," giggles Veronica.

"It's women's fiction," says Orla with enough emphasis and Irishness to close off the conversation, until Marcus mutters something sounding distinctly like, 'women's problems.' In the moment Orla winds up to react, Jenita in an accent sounding more Indian than when I first heard her speak asks, "is it a Rom Com?"

"Rom Coms are for TV," barks Marcus.

"Cinema," corrects Vernica.

Ian jumps in saying he is less worried about the definition of the genre, but the style of the writing and how the beauty of reading is when you come across a thought or feeling or way of looking at things, that you think special, and there it is written by someone you've never met. He pauses for effect and looks upwards. We all stare at him as he flicks through his vast mental lexicon, selecting the appropriate words and forming his next sentence with which he looks pleased, and then says, "as if a hand has come out and taken yours." His words hang splendidly in the air until Marcus says, "that's what Richard Griffiths said   in   The   History   Boys."

"Oh, is it?" says Ian, blushing.

"The gloom seems to be gathering," says Orla, wryly looking out the window at whatever has been holding her attention.

"Yes, well," says Ian waving his copy of An Unsuitable Match at me. "This should be right up your strasse Tom, with your interest in love and marriage."

I reply I'm looking forward to reading the Joanna Trollope book, it will be an inspiration for my own efforts. I confess (to you, not Ian) I wouldn't have knowingly picked up a Joanna Trollope book unless kidnapped and chained to a radiator, and it was the only thing to read. It's just not my thing. I did read the Jackie Collins novels when I was young, but that was simply a search for the smutty parts when smutty parts were rare and coveted and only otherwise to be found in the underwear section of Mum's mail order catalogues.

The meeting fractures into small groups of earnest literary talk and hushed intrigue and excuses to leave early and relieve the babysitter or be back for the Ten O'Clock news, because isn't politics so exciting at the moment? Standing up, I notice the gold leaf inscription down the spine of Marcus's notebook is actually his name. The pretentious oaf has a personalised notebook. I review my earlier missive to not rely on first impressions, concluding first impressions are usually right. I still can't quite make out his surname exactly. It looks Greek and long with an oversupply of vowels, like exploding popcorn. He stands, deliberately hitching his trousers to reveal Dr. Seuss yellow and black striped socks.

"Thank you Veronica," says Ian loudly over the increasing volume of conversation, "for our new book choice." He summons us to hush with open Jesus arms, and closes down persistent small talk with an authoritative rat-a-tat of his large cupped hands. "Veronica is bringing cakes next time, if anybody else would like to bring along some nibbles, I'm sure the pub won't mind."

"Well, that was an interesting start," I understate, walking a step behind Orla across the same side of Hammersmith Bridge we crossed earlier.

"He's such a twat," she says. I want to say Ian, but I know she means Marcus.

"I'm glad I came," I say, "thank you."

"I'm embarrassed."

"Don't be."

"You know he's married to Jenita?"

"No? Really? Marcus?" I say. "In that case, yes, God he is awful. He treats her like he bagged her from the last days of the Raj."

"She's clearly not his first wife."

"Or his last," I say, as if I am suddenly the guru on all things marital.

Chapter 3: GREAT EXPECTATIONS

"We need never be ashamed of our tears."

Charles Dickens, Great Expectations

"Do you love Claire?" asks Dad.

"I don't know anymore Dad," I reply, waiting for him to clamber over the padlocked five-bar gate. He turns to offer me his hand as if I'm an invalid. I get a lot of hugs and hands these days, it's one of the benefits of being crippled by divorce.

"Did you?"

"Love her? I must have. I just can't really remember being in love"

"Well then, you didn't."

Hmm, thanks Dad. Invalidate my entire marriage with one swipe of your tongue, why don't you? He's onto something, I grant him but we're only just out of the gates, I need to stretch my legs first. We're walking down a cut grass avenue between two lines of Poplar trees. It could be Italy, but it's Hampshire and I'm glad to be out of the city. Red Kites circle above clusters of black crows scrapping in the thermals and pairs of wood pigeons sprinting from treeline to treeline. It's warm but morning dew sticks loose grass to my bare flip-flopped feet. Dad says this is private land but the owner Mary is never around and he's never met her. Technically, we're trespassing and I scan through the trees looking for human life and Groundsmen with shotguns and scary women called Mary.

"We'll be back on a public footpath before long," he says.

"Did you love Mum?" I ask.

"Of course! Still do. She's a bloody amazing woman."

"Did you love Grace?"

"No," he says, "not in the way you're getting at."

Dad left Mum and married Grace when I was seven. My abiding memory of Christmas during that time was my little sister Annabel and I swapping presents with Dad in the back of his Range Rover in a lay-by on the A3. He'd spotted Grace on a show predating reality TV, where members of the public were invited to cook with a celebrity chef in the days before chefs were celebrities. One normal weekday night, before he pulled the plug on our family, Dad pointed her out to Mum as they watched the show together. He'd said she was a woman he knew worked in an office a floor below his own. He'd seen her in the lift. What he didn't say was her TV appearances had given him reason to strike up a conversation. The result was a soap opera and my sister and I pulling crackers that didn't spark by the side of a deserted dual-carriageway while normal families gorged on festive cheer. Growing up, I liked to think being a product of a broken-home sensitised me to being smart about my choice of partner. It would seem not.

Grace, despite not living up to her name, had a playbook that made Dad happy. As far as I know she never cooked a meal or made a bed. She was the antithesis of a homemaker, spending Dads money in the manner she deemed best for him. To call her a gold-digger would be unfair, but to change a lightbulb she called in someone to fix the Gins, and someone else to fix the lightbulb.

Still, her chutzpah was oddly endearing, and she grew in our affections as Mum, who never remarried, swum in the opposite direction. Reinventing herself as an all-purpose Mother to all-comers, her kitchen became the go-to apothecary, graduating over the years from doughnuts and squash, to Nurofen and homemade sausage rolls as we discovered the wonders of underage drinking. Some of my friends had more open relationships with Mum than I did. I drew lines in front of the important things I should have discussed with her. Our relationship was close but unspoken. After Annabel and I both left home and about a decade after Dad left, she thought fuck-it, said sod-it and shipped out to Verbier to become the oldest chalet maid in town, baking cakes for chilled skiers in need of sugar replacement. I know there were men in her life, but I never knew them.

Mum is one of life's true angels. She had two idiosyncrasies when we were growing up. One, for reasons I never fathomed, was a violent reaction to calling the television a telly. The second was room searches. Once a month she turned my room over, searching for contraband that might stunt my growth. As a result, I developed an advanced tradecraft in secreting the accoutrements of teen-dom. A skill that would serve me well if I were ever to serve at Her Majesty's pleasure. Perhaps she was preparing me for all eventualities.. When Claire was gone, Mum admitted always finding her hard-work. She didn't elaborate further, perhaps she didn't need to. If men are supposed to marry a mirror of their Mother, the face looking back at me at the altar couldn't have been more alternate.

Grace had been sporting enough to die before managing to spend all of Dad's money. That said, her funeral could have featured in Hello! Magazine, under the headline, 'SOCIALITE BOWS OUT IN STYLE' – *relive her fabulous funeral, pages 7-19, and centre spread.*

"Sorry, Dad," I say, "but what the fuck? I know we've never talked about this properly. But, really? You didn't actually love Grace? Why did you leave Mum?"

"Darcey!" He shouts. "Come here you filthy beast." Darcey is Dad's adopted Cocker Spaniel of probable pedigree and indeterminate age. She is on the small side of Cockers, and is looking equally guilty as scared as she does what she is told.

"She's always eating shit," says Dad, "it's not normal."

"Grace?" I ask, stroking Darcey..

"Grace," he ponders, "Grace was like one long weekend in Vegas. She wasn't real life, but my god she was fun. Your mother was real life and I was a selfish prick."

"You said it."

"I mean it. I'm so sorry for all the trouble I caused you and Annabel."

"Trouble?! What about Mum?"

"And of course your Mother. She knows. She understands now, I think."

"She's just glad to outlive Grace so she can spit on her grave," I say a tad harshly. She wouldn't of course, Mum isn't like that, but I feel like saying it anyway. I'm still smarting at being told I didn't love Claire.

"Your mother would never do such a thing."

"I know."

"We all tell people we love them son." offers Dad gently, then launching a stick for Darcey to chase, "especially men during and after sex. It is a weaponised phrase. It shows you're not just there for the ride."

"I can't even remember saying it to Claire," I think out loud, "but then I can't remember...." I trail off, sailing too close to the wind for a conversation with my father, "maybe the memory is judiciously selective."

Darcey wants her stick thrown again. I can't remember throwing balls with Dad when we were kids. We must have, but he left when we were so young I think I erased him from all my childhood memories.

"Saying I love you is both aspirin and vitamin. It gives succour to your situation, and the preventative power of having said the required thing. When love is unrequited, we beg and wail; but I love you! Which is just a panacea to whatever 'but' is."

Wow. These are wise words from Dad I'm not entirely sure I'm following. It's wisdom nonetheless and like nothing I have ever heard tumble from his mouth, which is admittedly prone to bullshit. I've certainly never heard him spout on the subject of love. We had naturally drifted apart during his early years with Grace, but time and the eternal bond of the paternal heart had drawn us closer. Now Grace is gone, and, come to think of it, so has Claire, we've got no reason for distance. Annabel is less forgiving.

Like Mum did when he left her, Dad is now swimming in the opposite direction. Long retired from the bar, when Grace died he sold up and moved into a modest annex on a Hampshire estate and took to breeding gun dogs. Seeing him training dogs is like watching a different man to the one I knew. His aptitude for making them respond to his commands – often just the tilt of his hand, is a phenomenon to watch. As for love, he is always telling me which are his favourite bitches, and how much he loves them all. They're not pets, he likes to remind me - they are working dogs. Darcey is the only dog allowed in his house, I wonder if she'd perhaps prefer to be outside in the kennels.

"How old are you now Dad?" I ask.

"Seventy-something."

"Seventy-what-thing?"

"Does it matter?"

"Just curious. I can never remember. Did you know sexually transmitted diseases in the over-seventies is showing the biggest rise of all age groups?"

"If you can still get a rise at my age, good on you."

"Did you ever know anyone truly in love?" I ask as we pass through a gate in the fence secured by a hoop of rope.

"Antony and Cleopatra. Ha! Ha!" he says. "Can you imagine Burton saying to Elizabeth Taylor, I love you. I bet you bloody do, she'd say. What are you after? Egypt? A shag? Ha! Ha!"

"Be serious Dad," I say. We're in open fields now, the corn is high, but not as high as it should be. The summer is too hot, nothing is growing as it should.

"I'm being deadly serious," he says seriously. "When a woman first says it to a man. When she finally utters those three little words, he thinks; hell, I'm in this one now. Do you remember Jack Nicholson's in Terms of Endearment, when Shirley MacLaine said she loved him? He said, I was inches away from a clean getaway. That just about says it all to me. He was terrified of it being said out loud."

"Are you saying men don't want to be loved?"

"Men want to be loved of course. Still, a chap knows those words cross a line of tricky return. Once a woman says she loves you, the rules change. She has picked her alpha male, no matter how beta he is. She will defend her right to you. Her right to shag and nag. Her rights supersede all that have gone before."

"Uh-huh..." I say.

"The male when he says it, hands over the keys to the kingdom. Whether he be alpha, beta or a wet blanket. She is now the monarch - whether on the throne or behind it. She is the tunnel. He is the train. And she gets to say when and what travels on her track. I should know, I married Grace."

"Isn't that a tad cynical?" I ask.

"Yes, but I'm old," he says grinning. "Okay, sometimes love can be mutual. Take your godfather."

"Anthony?!"

"No, the other one."

"Jeremy?"

"Yes. Jeremy and Jane are like a dove-tailed joint. They just work together. Have you seen all the selfies they take these days?"

"No."

"It's horrific. In the old days they used to nobble every waiter to take their picture. Now they have a selfie-stick. When was the last time you went to their house?"

"God, I can't remember."

"It's a pictorial shrine to their life well-married. It makes me gag. But I've never seen them exchange a cross word. I used to say they were co-dependent, and I wasn't being kind. It's the closest thing to true love I've ever seen."

"What do they have, that the rest of us can't find?" I ask.

"I have no idea," says Dad, "where is that bloody dog?"

"Darcey," I call before he does. She bounds from the woods looking surprised to hear her name called. Who me?

"Too many men say I love you," says Dad, "without truly meaning it. Or we think we mean it, but if we really thought about it, probably don't. The worst kind is when you mean it, and she doesn't love you back."

"Mum loved you."

"Are   you   trying   to   make   me   feel   worse?"

"Of course not," I say.

"Does Claire like Marmite?"

"Yes," I say. I can't actually remember if Claire did like Marmite. I'm sure I can remember us eating it together in bed when we were first together, but I can't remember it passing her lips in later years. That said, she didn't eat anything in later years, I would eat meals with the children while she fussed around the kitchen, gorging herself on oxygen and wine.

"Does she like Peanut Butter? Country walks? Doing it with the light on?"

"Err, no and no and err, no."

"There you go."

"Go where?"

"On the right path," says Dad, turning purposely up the path flanking the church to prove his point. "There is a list of mostly tiny, inconsequential things you either have in common or not. It infinitely lengthens throughout your time together. It stands to reason the more things in the mutual column, the better. Birds of a feather don't flock together without reason. You might start out both liking Marmite, but over time interests diverge. You stop watching TV together. I bet Claire watched endless crap. I bet you only watched news and sport. Am I right?"

"Yeah."

"Well,   it   all   starts   with   Marmite."

"Seems   pretty   simplistic."

"Other   spreads   are   available."

Yeah, right Dad.

We pass through another gate and we're back at the line of Poplars.

"Listen son," he says. He never called me son, but then we'd never once discussed anything as sentimental as love either. "These are extraordinary times. Remember what Winston Churchill said?"

"Fight them on the beaches?"

"No," he says, "if you're going through hell, keep going." He has a way with words. Winston that is, not my Dad.

"Darcey you little fucker!!"

Right until the end, when Claire's name popped up on my phone, my heart rose, not sank. I wonder if it was anticipation of whether she was going to be nice or give me a bollocking. I wanted her to be nice. I wanted to be in love. Was it the fall of her hair, or the curve of her nose? She used to say, it was the white bits in my beard (when I had one), the width of my back. We never got a chance to know if the physical attributes that made us flutter when we first met would survive the sagging and greying of age.

We were once in the first flush, physically attracted to each other. Had we looked closer, we didn't have a great deal in common. But we didn't look, we didn't see a problem. Our family and social circle didn't audibly disapprove (though some had misgivings). We missed each other when apart, took genuine pleasure when contact was made. If the revolution came, we'd have fought on the same side. Our taste in breakfast spreads wasn't entirely opposed. We publicly ribbed each's different tastes. Like cats and dogs, Mars and Venus, our differences were a healthy sign of our normality. At least, that's how I figured it through. Was it love? If Dad is to be believed, for opposites to attract requires finding common ground on which to grow love. I'm not sure Claire and I ever had much common ground.

"Hey!"

Oh shit.

"You there, what are you doing here?"

A diminutive woman who must be in her seventies is marching towards us brandishing a metal hiking pole in front of her like D'Artagnan facing down Cardinal Richelieu.

"Walking," says Dad.

"This is private land," she says.

"Is it?" says Dad. "I had no idea."

"It says private on the gate."

"I didn't see that."

"Yes you did."

"No." He says, "I didn't."

"Are you blind?"

"Partially."

"Are you stupid?"

"Arguably."

"Well, it is private and it's mine and you need to bloody get off it."

She's five foot one at a push, slim and lined in her face, attractive with once blonde hair snaked into a bundle on top of her head with wisps breaking free and hanging over her green eyes. She's wearing baggy denim shorts to her knees and Le Chameau wellies and a once white fleece top that has aged less gracefully than its wearer. Dad is six foot two, physically it's not a fair match, but I suspect she knows to hit where it hurts.

"Are you telling us to get *orff* your land?" Teases Dad with a friendly chuckle.

"I am." She says parrying Dad's chest with her hiking pole.

"Isn't that what farmers say?"

"I am a farmer."

"What do you farm?"

"Well, pheasants mostly."

"You farm pheasants?"

"And ducks and six sheep."

"So you're not really a farmer."

"You sir, are not really a gentleman."

I jump in. "I'm so sorry," I say, "my father was just taking me for a walk. I'm going through a divorce." I seem to be oversharing my marital status with everyone I encounter. I'm beginning to worry if writing about it is turning it into a dubious badge of honour.

"What has that to do with me?" she says.

"Well, nothing" I say, "my father was just being kind."

"Well he can be kind on someone else's land," she says, then adding kindly, "I'm sorry for your loss."

"If you've been truly in love, where nothing else matters, you'd know. Isn't that right Mary?"

"Pardon me?"

"We were discussing love, Tom and I. Wondering if he was really in love with his wife."

She is looking bewildered.

"Who are you? And how do you know my name is Mary?"

"I live in the annex, with the Tottons," says Dad.

"Oh," she says, "you're him."

"Him?"

"The divorce lawyer."

"Ha! No, I'm an ex-lawyer who happens to be divorced. There's a difference."

"Well, I'm sure your poor ex-wife is better off on both counts."

"I'm sure she'd agree. What do you think Tom?"

I don't have an answer to that.

"Do you have kids?" asks Dad, nodding in my direction as if to say, aren't all bloody kids a pain, this one's forty-nine and still needing his Daddy.

"Three. Grown-ups. All very successful," says Mary, matter-of-factly.

"Are you divorced?"

"Pardon me?"

"Do you have a husband?"

"I'm a widow."

"Bad luck."

"Not really."

"Would you like to come round for a drink?"

Dad!

"Darcey, you F......" he shouts all of a sudden, "sorry, she's always eating shit."

"Dogs take after their owners," says Mary.

Touché, I think.

"Now bugger off, and no I will not come round for a drink."

"Suit yourself."

She turns on her wellied heel with a flourish of her pole, stomps five paces and wheels again, planting her pole in the ground, unlocking her left knee to ever so slightly extend her right hip towards its handle. I'm no expert in septuagenarians, but it looks to me like a move with a dabble of coy.

"I don't like annex's full of muddy dogs and ex-lawyers," she says. "You may come to my house to request permission to cross my land in the future. 8pm. Don't bring your dog, I have cats." And she's off again.

"Will I get a drink?" Calls Dad.

"If you bring your manners," she hollers without turning, waving her pole in the air like a tour guide in a crowd.

We're back in Dad's kitchen. Darcey has been left outside, her bark says she definitely wants to come in. "She reminds me of Felicity Kendal," says Dad.

"I was thinking Jenny Agutter. It seems she likes you, for some reason. Better watch out though, she's got kids."

"Why's that a problem?"

"Well, they all sound very accomplished."

"So?"

"It's a book I'm reading. It's about an old couple who's grown-up children don't like them getting together."

"I'm not an old couple," he says, "who's it by?" Dad loves books, I've always seen it as an endearing counterbalance to his bluster. As a child, after I'd read and reread everything Arthur Ransome and Gerald Durrell had put into print, he'd got me reading Dickens immersing me in the worlds of Sweedlepipe, Honeythunder, Pumblechook and Squeers. Our running joke throughout my life has been making up Dickensian names to people we encounter. The French Customs officer who confiscated four hundred cigarettes from Dad in Le Havre was known as Monsieur Chokerswipe. He christened my first girlfriend, who was blessed at fourteen with boobs only available to most women via an expensive trip to Harley Street, Little Miss.Rumbletop. The ticket collector who made him pay extra when we travelled home from a visit to Bath on cheap day tickets on a peak hour train was simply Mr.Colon. I wonder what we'll call Mary?

I tell him the book is by Joanna Trollope.

"Trollope? Why on earth are you reading chick-lit?"

"It's not...it's for a Book Club I joined."

"Book Club?"

"You remember my friend Orla? She made me join to get me out of the house."

"Lovely hair, great tits?"

"Yes, Orla. She's been a great friend. She got divorced a while back."

"You should give me her number," he says casually, chopping disgusting smelling dog food with the back of a fork.

"Dad!"

He opens the back door and puts the bowl of food out for Darcey.

"It's a funny old world," he calls from the back door, "you need to keep your pecker up son. You'll be back in the saddle soon."

"I know Dad, I just don't think I'm a very attractive prospect for anyone right now," I say quietly enough for him not to hear.

"There was someone," I say. "Do you remember Dyfed's cousin Charlotte? Lovely reddy-blonde haired girl."

"Yes, I have a vague memory," he says reappearing.

"We had a thing back in the day, I've always put it down to teenage lust, but I've never really believed that and you know that you said earlier about knowing? Well, I think I may have known all along."

"Careful son," says Dad, "one step at a time, there's no rush. Look where rushing got you last time. So what's next with Claire? You need to sort this out."

"I wish I could," I say. "She's not for turning."

"Don't   be   wet."

"I don't think I have much more fight left in me. If I fight it will damage the children even more. She's playing it perfectly – from her point of view. I'm running out of options. Neither of us want to fight over the kids."

"That's easy for her to say, from Dublin. Unfortunately it's not my area of the law. I will put you in touch with someone though. You can't not be with your children. My bloody Grandchildren."

"Thanks Dad," I say, "I know, I don't know where to start. You're right, I need to talk to someone."

Darcey is chasing her empty metal bowl around the flag-stoned kitchen floor with her nose, seemingly convinced there is more nutrition to be found in licking already gleaming metal. For reasons I have yet to fathom, Dad has taken his trousers off and is padding around in socks and a thankfully long shirt. This is a level of intimacy with my father I haven't known since I was a child, which feels equally endearing as awkward. He asks me about Mum and Annabel (who doesn't talk to him much these days) and my career and if I'm going to sell the house and says I'm welcome to crash with him whenever I like. I tell him I'd just spent a week with Mum and how I could see her visibly wilting under the stress of watching her forty-nine-year-old son in such a state. How she'd fed me nursery food and taken me for walks in the bluebell woods behind her house in West Sussex that Dad has never visited.

He opens the dishwasher which looks like it's been over-stacked by itinerant removal men, saying, "Do you need money?"

"No," I say. "Yes. Well, yes I could do with some help, I'm not working much at the moment, for obvious reasons."

"I'll give you a number to call," he says, picking sticky grains of rice from a pyrex dish that hasn't cleaned. "You can tell them I'll put some money on account for you to get you going. They know me. I'm good for it."

"Thanks Dad, I appreciate it. I'm writing a book."

"A book?"

"More a collection of essays really. About love and marriage."

"And divorce?"

"And divorce."

"Well, it's about time, you are a bloody journalist, even if you are writing for the Commies. You'll never make any money out of it."

"That's not the point I say. It's helping me figure stuff out."

"A catharsis?"

"That's what everyone says."

"How's your drinking?" He asks.

"Pretty good thanks."

"You need to get your shit together, boy. You've got a lot of mountains to climb. A book's a good idea."

"Everyone says that, too," I say, "I read somewhere you should write drunk and edit sober."

"Does drinking improve your writing, or blind you to the quality of what you write?"

"I think it improves it."

"I doubt it," he says. "Though, to be fair, I once won a case after a very, very long lunch."

"Were you at lunch with the Judge?"

"No!" he says, "that would be entirely inappropriate. Though I may have been sleeping with her."

"Dad!"

"Darcey!!"

Chapter 4: REVOLUTIONARY ROAD

"No one forgets the truth; they just get better at lying."

Richard Yates

According to a story I'm reading on my phone, when certain female members of the animal kingdom blur the distinction between flirty and hungry, they have sex with their partners, then commit matricide. Apparently Octopuses, Tarantulas and Praying Mantises are all proponents.

I tell Orla this exciting news and she says, "really?"

"In humans," I say, "the phenomenon is generally limited to Sharon Stone films."

"Is that what it says?"

"No," I say, "I made that bit up."

"Why do men get all the bad press on midlife crises?"

"Women have them too."

"Isn't that the menopause?"

"Not just the menopause," she says, "it can be just mid-life, like you guys."

"Yeah, but you don't go out and buy brown-leather jackets and Porches and shag secretaries."

"We're cleverer than that, we have our own version. But you're right, the female mid-life crisis is less well known."

"Perhaps like rare cancers or the search for extraterrestrial life, it suffers from a lack of funding and research"

"Women can be beasts when they decide they're unhappy," says Orla. "Beasts."

"No shit," I say. "I'd never thought about the female mid-life crisis before. There is a Nobel Prize on the subject waiting out there for someone. Claire hated being on her own when the kids were young. When I was at work, or sleeping off a night shift."

"I was the same," says Orla. "It felt like Nick was never there."

We're walking across Wimbledon Common, there is still warmth in the sunshine, but it has an edge to it I can feel in my chest, like I've eaten a strong mint. We talk about the impact on Mums of a decade of sleeplessness, the anxiety, thankless meal preparation and loss of body confidence. I know, being one of the last couples to marry, the smug nonchalance of our further-ahead-friends, compounded Claire's feelings of inadequacy. Shinier, newer cars cut her up at the school gate. On the odd occasion I managed the school run, I understood what she meant. Winsome women with figures regained minutes after childbirth, beamed and brayed in figure advertising lycra.

"I think those days played havoc with Claire's mind," I say.

"Yeah, but all Mums go through that. It didn't mean she had to break up your marriage."

Looking back now, I can see I was in my own paradigm, I took the brunt of her erratic moods and nagging and drinking as proof of her weakness of character. I built a sub-conscious rap sheet of her crimes in my head. I developed a profile of her like a criminal psychologist. She fitted a pattern. I anticipated the next point of conflict – a match I wanted to attend, or a weekend away with the boys. I focused on her negative traits and neglected to see the huge effort she made to fulfil apparently menial tasks; the drudge of meal-planning, shopping and cooking; the cleaning and infinite washing cycle. Those were her jobs after all. If she paid anyone to help her, a cleaner or decorator, I viewed it an unnecessary waste of money. I worked my arse off bringing home the bacon, she spent it on sugary bribes, chicken nuggets and yet another pair of shoes for the children. When she went back to work, to bring in some money and keep her sane, I heedlessly saw the added weight of responsibility as part of the new equation.

"You are a great Dad," says Orla, "you know that. Your children adore you."

"I'm not sure I was a great husband though. I tried, but I don't think I was scratching the surface. I used to bring her tea in bed, take Jack and Clara to the park to give her time out. We tried to orchestrate romantic evenings, date nights. Oh, but the tiredness. And the constant talk of the children. And blah, blah, blah. Oh, it's all bollocks."

In the Spring of 2011 Claire and I went to New York as a special treat. We both knew it was an expedition to suture some of the wounds of our marriage. She had always wanted to see New York. I'd been once before for work, but never 'done' the City. Emerging from the terminal at LaGuardia we were immediately mugged by Snoop Dog's taller brother, grabbing both our suitcases and throwing them in the trunk of his car, assuring us he offered the cheapest rates to Manhattan. Considering it churlish and possibly life-threatening to refuse we got in the back and he chatted happily all the way about Oprah and Obama and how he planned to visit London once he'd fleeced enough tourists. Like any good guide he pointed out the sites, of which there are none on the way into town from LaGuardia. Claire said it was nothing like the movies, and then we crossed the East River onto the movie set that is Manhattan and her face lit up like a child passing through the gates of Disneyland. Snoop dropped us on Fifth Avenue, assuring us our hotel was just around the corner and demanding one hundred and twenty dollars. Too great a coward to negotiate, I handed over all the cash I had withdrawn safe in the knowledge it would last us a good few days.

I had picked our hotel off the internet due to its 'boutique' status on Fifth Avenue. We wheeled our suitcases up and down the block three times before discovering the launderette between Starbucks and the shop selling anything you could imagine as long as it had 'I ☐NY' printed on it, was in fact the door to our hotel. I can't say the pictures I had perused online were lying, but the cameraman had a way with angles. The whole place was immaculate, but tiny. The bedrooms were stacked three per floor like a game of giant Jenga. The walls of our room felt sucked in by life reducing humidity, like we had stumbled into an Alice in Wonderland experience. It wasn't that bad, as long as you hadn't brought a cat to swing. Unpacked and with little choice or room to do anything but sit in very close proximity or have sex, we headed out in search of oxygen and the whole tourist thing. We walked in Central Park among the circus of characters and all the marvelous normalities and eccentricities of humanity. We got all sombre at the World Trade Centre memorial, then Snoop's cousin drove us downtown in a yellow cab and we had supper in a stripped-wood bistro in Greenwich Village, which was like having supper in pretty much any city, except the portions were bigger.

Once the oops-we-drunk-too-much-on-our-first-night-argument was out the way, we loved every minute, easing away our bruises in a deep bath of New York. And then Dyfed came to town.

Dyfed was on a planned stopover from South America, on his way to Cape Town. Claire moaned he would interrupt our romantic break. I couldn't fault her there, but it was pre-planned, and we were all going to spend the night with our ex-pat friend, James Parker. In my pre-wedding picture on the table in my hall, James is next to Dyfed who is grinning insanely, looking determined to milk every ounce of mischief from the day ahead. His wife, Alice, isn't in the picture. She wasn't from the Gang, he had fished her from a different pond. The thing I always admired about Dyfed and Alice is how comfortable they were in their own skins, and with each other. If Alice ever knew a goose, she never said boo to it. She was timid, tidy, punctilious, and pretty. Not pretty-pretty, but pretty. To paint a picture of Dyfed, think of Peter Duncan the TV presenter from Blue Peter. Remember him from those days when wholesome children created things with their hands, before destroying things digitally became the norm? Square-jawed. Cheeks slightly sallow, eyes sunken a smidgen too deep. Nondescript brown hair in league with gravity, no bounce or curl. That's Dyfed.

When they met, Dyfed was a Senior Artworker at a central London advertising agency, and Alice was a Dentist. Strictly speaking, she was a dental assistant, but such technicalities were trivial. Her splendidly opulent boss let her blur the lines between helpful-passer-of- instruments, with facilitator-of-basic-procedures he couldn't be bothered to perform. In her mind, she was the dentist. Early in their marriage, speculatively answering an advert in The Evening Standard, Dyfed reinvented himself as a salesman of state-of-art medical equipment, travelling globally, attending conferences and closing multi-million deals with health authorities and cash-rich private practices. The outcome of his unbelievably successful career pivot was a life of considerable wealth. Moving into a five-bedroom house in two acres, all was very, very good. In no particular order, kids, dogs, chickens, widescreens, Botox, exotic holidays and a wine cellar suitable for Louis XV followed.

Seven years in, their three children moved en masse from the local state school to a Prep School, apparently counting Prince Charles its most famous alma mater. The school car park was akin to a HR Owen showroom. The ten-upmanship of Bentley and Aston owners trumped Range Rover owners and trounced anyone with a car from Germany, or heaven forbid Japan. There were no Korean cars. Helicopters landed on the cricket pitch. Class allocation was the school's version of a postcode lottery. Lowly children of well-paid, nondescript professionals shared paint pallets with the offspring of minor celebrities and major stars. Social engineering, bribery and attendance register tampering was endemic. Children's party invitations naturally followed. Gasps, modestly suppressed at the magnitude of this pile or that, grew audible when little Caspar's sixth birthday necessitated a half-sized pirate ship to dock in his garden, complete with Captain Hook, Peter Pan, The Lost Boys and half a dozen, inappropriately busty Princesses dressed like Victorian street walkers.

Alice and Dyfed were the cats and the cream. They became best buddies with the almost-as-glamorous sister of a well-known TV presenter. Stardust swirled. Glitter lingered in their hair and deep-pile carpet long after basking in whichever party rained it upon them. I'm going to tell you now, their life was perfect – just so you know it's bound to go tits up in the next few chapters.

The spring mercury was rising when Dyfed, Claire and I got the subway from Penn Station in Manhattan under the East River and out to Port Jefferson via Queens. The Subway was pretty much like any other city underground, except the carriages were made from unpainted brushed steel giving the feeling of travelling in an industrial oven. Our fellow passengers were a perfect tapestry of New York. A black woman with Donna Summer hair and glasses, standing reading a book in a black skirt so short it showed her black under shorts and a suspender belt, unclipped a long way north of knee-high pink socks emerging from yellow walking boots; an ill-disguised serial killer searching for a victim small enough to conceal under his heavy coat in Spring; an old Jewish guy in a big black hat whispering into a phone so small it was invisible in his bony hand; a gnarled old woman who I didn't hear speak, but imagined only spoke in profanities. Opposite us was a short chubby Hispanic man in a vest holding both hands up to the rail, giving us a forensic view of his armpit hair, and him the perfect fulcrum to launch a double footed kick to my face, should he take offense to an Englishman riding the carriage he had patrolled ever since being turned into a troll by the crazy Witch with her elbow locked around a pole pretending to do Sudoku.

The crowd thinned as we headed out of town. The troll swung off to harass a group of plain-clothed school children on a field-trip, gathered round something making them shriek with laughter. Finding our confidence to speak and betray our origins, we talked about our soon-to-be host, James, or Bic, as he is known, who was already on his second wife.

"What was his first wife called?" I asked Dyfed.

Dyfed thought about it and said, "Ha! I can't remember! She was fit, I remember that. Do you remember her going away outfit at their wedding?"

"The all in one white jumpsuit?"

"That's the one," I said.

"What's so special about that?" Asked Claire.

"It was unbuttoned to her navel," I said. "I remember the look on Bic's Mum's face."

"Was that the wedding all the grannies did snow angels on the dance floor to Snow Patrol?" Asked Dyfed.

"No," I said, "that was our wedding."

There had been so many weddings during that run of summers either side of the Millennium, the memories have homogenised. We sat in silence until Claire asked a few stops later, "how come Bic hasn't got any kids?"

"I'm not sure," I said. "I don't even know what he does really. But he must do it well, whatever it is."

I was referring to his holiday house on Long Island we were heading to, I'd seen the pictures. It was something else. We were the last people on the carriage as we pulled into the haven of Port Jefferson, with its white stucco pillars and tasteful brickwork. Turning left onto the platform, I scanned through the windows for the troll. He was nowhere to be seen, but I knew his beady eyes were watching us from somewhere. Probably the roof.

Bic greeted us at the station gate and we hugged awkwardly. As we drove in his black Cherokee jeep, we reacquainted ourselves with small conversation. Perhaps because Claire was in the car, we reined in our male jubilance at the prospect of the night ahead. Bic turned into a gated complex and steered through the manicured perfection of a paint-by-numbers community. His house was indeed spectacular, except it had neighbour's by cheek on one side, jowl on the other. I remember thinking, houses like that should be in open space with vistas and wandering Buffalo. The wraparound porch faced, on one side onto a lovely man-made waterway. The other three sides sat opposite neighbour's identical equivalents, giving it the feel of an extremely posh Butlins. Nevertheless, it was Bic's pride and joy and he threw a hell of a party for his friends from across the pond.

Joined by various neighbour's with a very short distance to travel, we drank into the night. Gin and tonics, bangers and mash served to a soundtrack of Britpop, reminded everyone Britain shall ne'er ne'r be slaves. Indulging in increasingly to-the-point transatlantic ribbing, we all managed to keep on the right side of the special relationship.

A woman called Karyn was there. She was all-American and a midwife. She had overseen the birth of thousands of children, she said. The mental image was not to be lingered on. She also had no husband, three kids and Dyfed's attention for much of the evening. She did that jeans and boots and perfect hair thing American women do better than any women in the world. Despite Dyfed's best efforts to deploy his British accent into her inconspicuous undergarments, she made her excuses and left the party when it was still in full-swing. Dyfed looked disappointed. Anyway, he had to get a cab back to the city for an early flight to Cape Town.

I woke the next morning beside Claire. As focus returned, I felt rather chipper. I couldn't recall doing anything stupid the night before. There had been no serious altercations with the Americans – no need to apologise to Bic for anything. Silently awake, I mentally joined the freckles and moles on Claire's bare back into constellations. She would open her eyes soon. All was well.

Except it wasn't.

Apparently, I had been an arse all evening.

I had been extremely rude to the Americans.

I had flirted outrageously with that midwife woman.

And I had snored all night.

Bugger.

I asked myself what Jack Nicholson would have done in such a situation. Somehow, I couldn't raise his grin. The one that says, who-me? The grin that leads to passionate love-making followed by an open-topped drive down the coast road in Ray-Bans and a smug smile.

I offered to make tea.

We flew home later that day. On balance, I thought it had been a successful trip. We'd reconnected in and out of the bedroom. We'd shared some new experiences. Talked a lot. And though I may have been a tad flirty with Karyn the Midwife, the female of the species had no concrete reason to want to kill me.

Except, I have a confession to make, Dyfed didn't get a cab back to the City.

"Mate, mate," he'd said, beckoning me into Bic's book-lined study.

"What?" I said

"It's on with Karyn. The midwife babe."

"She's gone."

"I know she's waiting for me to go over."

"Dude," I said - Dude is the substitute word for 'mate' when you're trying to tell a 'mate' not to be a 'dick' - "Don't be a dick."

"I know," said Dyfed, "but she's gorgeous. And gagging. I can't not mate. She is my dream-woman."

"Dude," I said. "Claire is out there. If she gets a whiff of this you are toast. Alice will have shredded all your suits before you make Heathrow."

"I know," said Dyfed, "just help me get out of here without any suspicion. I have found my calling and it's called Karyn."

"Dude?" I said.

"What?" he said.

"You're having a mid-wife crisis."

The fact we were hiding and whispering in Bic's study made trying to suppress our laughter all the more funny. When Dyfed laughs his whole face goes crimson. When he really belly-laughs, his whole body follows suit. At any moment he may have exploded like Violet Beauregard. Still we laughed. Still he didn't explode. Still we went through with the deception of asking a little too loudly how Dyfed should go about getting a cab back to the city.

Having made a number of bogus phone calls he scuttled to Karyn the midwife's house. All night they painted the stars and stripes together. At the time, I didn't feel guilty about my part in the deception, I guess none of us is perfect. In truth, Dyfed has something of a reputation among those in the know. I didn't ask, but I suspected Karyn wasn't the only port to which he called on his trip round the world.

I imagine he felt pretty-shitty on the flight to Cape Town. Still, by the time he'd washed his guilt in the icy cold Atlantic and returned home, all would be forgotten. I didn't tell Claire. She was good friends with Alice. Alice would be waiting dutifully at home, living up to the gilded conventions of her adopted lifestyle. Baking and child-rearing and being homely. Of course she would.

I'm sorry Alice. Sitting here now, writing these words, I'm wondering what I could have done that night. What I should have done. The solidarity of gender is a strange thing. They call it the battle of the sexes, but is it really a war? Men versus Women? I am complicit in helping Dyfed screw Karyn and screw up his marriage. But was it already screwed? Okay, I tried to stop him with words. Should I have tackled him to the floor, taken away his wallet, threatened to shop him to Alice? These are worthy thoughts, but he's my best mate and that comes above all else. By that equation, as his mate, I really should have blocked him at the door, but I didn't. Because we don't. It's no different for women. They are plotters and schemers like us guys. Perhaps we really are at war.

It's the August Bank Holiday weekend. Summer is drawing to a close. Claire has come over to see friends and take away more of her things. I've got the children for three wonderful days then they will go back to Ireland and start at their new school in Dalkey. Jack told me last night, when they play with the local kids, he and Clara pretend they are Swedish (Claire's Mum is Swedish), allying themselves as Norseman or Celts or anything but English. I get the logic but it's another nail slammed into the lid of my familial coffin. Before long I will have a different coloured passport to them.

I said to Jack, "you may be a quarter Swedish, or an eighth, and you are living in Ireland, but it doesn't make you any less English. I understand why you are doing what you are doing, but trust me living behind a lie never works out in the long run. It's better to be honest."

Jack and I both realised in the same moment what I'd said and he asked what had to be asked.
"Were you and Mummy a lie?"
And I said, "no of course not. Things just didn't work out, that's all. Are you Okay?"

Jack told me he missed me in the most grown-up way he could muster, but his voice was weak and hesitant like when he's trying to bunk a day off school with a non-specific illness, except I know he's not putting this voice on. Both Jack and Clara try to sound cheerful whether we are together or on the phone. Like parents trying to protect children through a divorce, children try to protect their parents. I am terrified by the damage we are doing to them.

"They've taken the dinosaur away!" I say.

"What dinosaur?" asks Clara.

"The big brontosaurus darling. It always used to be here."

We're in the Natural History museum surrounded by herds of European schoolchildren trying to escape their fraught teachers. The main exhibit I always remember from my childhood has been replaced by some gigantic prehistoric fish hanging from the ceiling. I tell the children about a film I cherish in my memory - One of Our Dinosaurs is Missing,describing how two Nannies kidnap the Brontosaurus and drive around London with it on the back of a truck. They don't seem too keen to see it.

The day got off to an iffy start with an argument about who would sit in the front seat of my car. Clara won and Jack sulked in the back seat. It's odd not having Claire in the car, the children safely strapped in the back. It's unbalanced and in my mind, horribly poignant. Claire's absence feels a vivid sign of the failure we have put upon our children.

We don't stay in the Museum long. Clara coos at the dusty stuffed animals, until I tell her they are real stuffed animals and she doesn't like it anymore. We have lunch in a French cafe in South Kensington and I'm thinking everyone is looking at us and can tell I'm a single Dad. I imagine their whispered conversations, conjecturing about where my wife is. Whether I'm the one at fault, had an affair.

I ask the children if they want to go to Harrods. They don't.

Jack wants to go to Hamleys, and I say I don't want to drive into town.

Clara asks what Hamleys is. I tell her it's the biggest toy store in the world, which it probably isn't, but she has a hissy fit anyway when I say we're still not going, so I load the parking meter and we get the tube to Piccadilly Circus.

Throngs of European schoolchildren who really should be at The Natural History Museum clog the doors like evacuees from a sinking ship who didn't pay attention to the safety demonstration. An overpaid enthusiastic toy demonstrator in a red t-shirt makes me duck out of the way of an acrobatic aeroplane, and within seconds I've lost Jack. Clara tells me she wants a make-up set and I tell her she's too young, but apparently I'm wrong about that. Jack reappears with a Fortnite backpack that might as well be made by Mulberry for how much it costs. I spend ten minutes in the queue for the one open till to consider my purchases behind a family of four, clutching arms full of toys like they've just won Supermarket Sweep.

Tube back to South Kensington.

Drive down the Fulham Road, left onto the Kings Road, over Wandsworth bridge and we're home. Having the children back in the house they grew up in is odd to say the least. They seem comfortable with it, but I'm finding it too awkward. As arranged, Claire had been while we were out and taken what she considers hers. Apart from the obvious gaps on the wall where her favourite painting has been removed, it's not initially obvious what she's taken. I can't describe the painting to you, it's abstract, mostly blue and cost us £2000 her Grandfather gave us as a wedding present. Her clothes and shoes have gone, obviously. As I mooch around I spot gaps until recently occupied by the bits and baubles of life – candles, carved animals from our honeymoon safari, decorative china, christening silver. Other than the painting, we hadn't agreed whose was whose. The Apocalypse has rendered me impotent. She has done what all good

Generals should, destroyed my power to resist, waging the battle on her terms. First she abducted our children, now she's carting off her spoils.

But I've got the children tonight and we're going to make popcorn and watch movies, Claire won't let them see. I'll put them to bed way past their bedtime, forget to tell them to brush their teeth and read them a story and kiss them goodnight like everything is normal. One marked difference is they've both started saying 'I love you' at every opportunity. They never used to. I suppose that's a victory.

I had been a journeyman cook before I met Claire. She rarely let me in the kitchen once we were married. The kids are in bed, and in a moment of madness I've decided to make a large batch of Shepherd's Pie. We'll have it for lunch tomorrow and I'll eat the rest once they're gone. I never get bored of Shepherd's Pie. I fry the mince and onions, then fabricate a tangy stock, from culinary detritus lurking in the cupboards. Worcester Sauce, Bovril, garlic. Pleased with myself, I peel the potatoes, boil and drain them. Then I look for the potato masher. Where is the potato masher? Where's the bloody potato masher. SHE'S TAKEN THE FUCKING POTATO MASHER!

I could have used a fork. But to anybody who's been there, it's the tiny things that send you over the edge. Two bottles of red wine later, sitting on the floor I shovel cold mince into my mouth with my fingers.

The potatoes are turning yellow in the colander, hardening at the edges.
Ready for the bin.
I hope the kids are still asleep.

Chapter 5: THE INVISIBLE MAN

"Life is to be lived, not controlled; and humanity is won by continuing to play in face of certain defeat."

Ralph Ellison

"I think the children are just awful," says Veronica.

"I agree," says Martin.

Marcus snorts.

"Is it a talent to be able to write the children as so dislikeable?" Asks Ian.

"It made me dislike the book," says Marcus. "If we weren't reading it for Book Club, I would have given up."

"They did get better towards the end of the book, I thought," says Veronica. "It was Tyler who bugged me. He was so needy."

"A completely misnamed character," says Marcus, making a rare contribution.

"His name was explained," says Veronica, "wasn't he descended from someone?"

"Most people are," says Marcus.

I'm sitting next to Orla tonight, with a lady called Katja to my left. She didn't say anything last month, and she doesn't look like breaking her duck tonight. She's in her sixties, with white blonde hair cut short at the back, her eyes hidden by a sweeping fringe that would suit a fourteen-year-old boy in search of his first fumble. She's wearing a blue knee-length dress, with a velcro collar, like a dentists' smock. Oli is opposite me, sitting next to Aude. I can't see if he has bought a belt yet.

"I usually enjoy her books, but I found it very irritating," says Jenita.

"I agree, I didn't really like any of the main characters except Rose's sister, Prue, the only one who wasn't totally self-absorbed," says Veronica.

"What about the son? Awful," says Aude.

"The son! He made me want to throw my Kindle across the room," says Marcus.

"Kindle?" Questions Ian.

"Are Kindles allowed Ian?" asks Orla mischievously.

"Well, they are allowed, but I find it such a shame. You can't turn down a corner or tuck a bookmark in a chapter, or flick the pages to see how far you have come and how far you have to go."

Veronica agrees.

"What I don't like," says Marcus, "with an e-book, if I can't remember something important I can't find it again and scribble a note on the page." He opens his notebook and scribbles something to make his point.

"You're such a bore Marcus," says Jenita. Marcus doesn't react, as if his contempt for his wife, out-contempts her contempt for him.

"I find it sad you can't pass a good book on to a friend or post it through my neighbour's door," says Veronica.

"I prefer the feel of actually turning pages," offers Aude in her lilting French accent which immediately conjures the image in my head of her turning back the bedsheets in a Paris apartment on a sunlit Sunday morning when a little light-reading, coffee and croissants and sex are on the menu. Oli looks like he's having similar thoughts.

Orla says, "I like the scent of a new book."

So, I've got Orla in Irish on my right talking about the smell, and Aude in French opposite me talking about feel, and I'm marveling at the female of the species ability to make me think inappropriate thoughts when an Eastern European voice to my left bursts my bubble, saying, "I get headaches reading from a screen." It's Katja. Well, at least she speaks.

"Okay, Okay," says Ian. "so we're not fans of e-readers. Sorry Marcus."

Martin waves a dismissive hand in the air. Ian says we should get back to the book. The conversation returns to Rose's strength and Tyler's capitulation and Rose's burgeoning independence and how the prose is polished and astute and the characters well-developed and genuine and troubled, but still awful. I am still tuned into the concept of padding barefoot around Aude's Parisian apartment on a Sunday morning, but Oli is on the same wavelength and I'm sensing a war lost without a battle fought. Now a conversation about second-chance romance is building a head of steam. Perhaps it's the average age of our group that is connecting with the concept of late-in-life love. Of second chances. Of sex, when sex belongs to the young, but old is the new young and sex after the children have grown and left home may be better sex that the hurried coupling that made them in the first place.

"What do you think, Tom?" asks Ian.

"About what?" I say, returning from my conversation with the sex-fairies.

"About second-chances."

"Well, I'm single," I say, which is a fact I think Aude needs to be clear on. I tell them my theory about dogs being for Christmas (and fifteen or so years) and marriage being for life and how I never thought I would be in a second chance situation, but how I had to admit, apart from not seeing my kids, it's an attractive prospect. Veronica points out Rose and Tyler had fancied each other at school and asks if there is anybody from my past I had been thinking about. I say there wasn't, but I'm not entirely sure that's true. I talk about a piece I'd recently written in my book about women who stand at the altar knowing they are not in love with the man to whom they are about to say I do; and how it takes a brave woman to marry a man she doesn't truly love and an even braver one to run back down the aisle. Everybody seems to agree, and tacit nods roll around the table like a Mexican wave. Except, of course, Marcus whose raison d'être seems to be to disagree with everything and shakes his head with a snort.

"How is your book coming along?" asks Ian.

"Ok," I say, "it's mostly essays. I don't seem to have found a story yet."

"Well, we await with baited breath," says Ian. "Do you find yourself delving deep into the human psyche?"

"I guess so," I say.

"And what have you learned so far?"

"That none of us really has a clue when it comes to marrying the right person and then knowing how to hold a marriage together?"

"That's for sure," says Jenita

"That's so sad," says Veronica. "I've been happily married for thirty-five years."

"What is your secret?" asks Aude.

"That would be telling," says Veronica with a smile I fear might be lascivious.

I'm standing at the bar, with Orla. Aude and Oli O are talking animatedly a few feet away and I am straining to hear what they are saying while pretending to listen to Orla. Ian had wrapped up the meeting dismissing Trollope into a corner of literature marked pulp, and introduced with a flourish his much-trailed new choice - A Gentleman in Moscow by Amor Towles. Apparently its central character is a man of supreme intelligence and wit. It's difficult not to imagine Ian is imagining himself as having similar traits. I'll read the book and let you know if they compare favourably.

In the way people rotate like fairground Waltzers in a close-quarters social situation, Orla is now talking to Aude and I'm talking to Oli. He comes across as a good bloke with few airs and graces and who really does need to buy a belt for his jeans. Or smaller jeans. Orla, love her, has steered her conversation with Aude to require my contribution. It turns out Aude had wanted to get into journalism and did an internship at The Guardian, and surely we have mutual acquaintances. We don't and didn't cross paths at the Kings Cross headquarters by a number of years, but it's a nice thought. Then Aude asks about my book.

"It's still very much work-in-progress," I say, "full of typos and plot holes."

"I'd like to read it," she says, "if you'd like some feedback?"

"The more the merrier," I say.

"I'd love to," she says.

"You live close by," says Orla, "Aude lives in Earlsfield."

"Oh," I say, "whereabouts?"

"Brocklebank Road."

"That is close," I say, furiously thinking I know where it is, then that I have no idea.

'You should meet for coffee," says Orla.

"Err," I say.

"Why not?" says Aude, "are you free on Sunday morning?"

I check my mental diary which has absolutely nothing in it, and say yes I should be free and I better get working on my book.

"Thank you babe," I say to Orla as soon as we step outside.

"You're welcome," she says with a smile, "don't fuck it up."

Spurred on by the prospect of Aude reading my writing and burying my frustration at not seeing the kids, I'm attacking my book. I write best in the mornings. I keep up a diet of Beck's Blue and Netflix and Silent Witness on Tuesday night and Luther on Wednesday. Becks Blue, if you don't know, is a non-alcoholic lager. The bottles are almost identical to their more damaging brethren, and the contents as near as dammit the same on my taste buds. The payoff is you don't get drunk, fat or hangovers. You smell the same if you're in mind of breathing over a traffic officer and trying not to act smug when the breathalyser reads zero. It's the alcohol equivalent of the blow-up doll; does the job with none of the consequences. I wonder if they make wives?

So far this week, I've been up twice at 5am. It's still almost two months until the clocks go back, and it's been properly dark but I'm feeling motivated to thrash out as many words I can before starting proper work at 10am. I'm making progress in wordcount terms, but don't know if it's any good. I think it is, but am I being too angry or bleak? Who would want to read it? I have sworn to myself it's not a book of blame or character assassination. I'm trying to get to the bottom of the travails of marriage. I'm putting myself through self-torture watching Rom-Coms on Netflix as research. Every film makes me cry, even the shit ones. I make notes on the pad in the brown leather binder Claire bought me. Every storyline I watch resonates like it's me on the screen, except Jake Gyllenhaal and Chris Pratt and Jamie Dornan are all impossibly handsome and quick-witted and when they go home to their real lives, they're millionaires who can afford someone to come and fix their front door. Every beautiful girl, and they are always beautiful, makes me wistful and hopeful and horny and angry and oh my god, what am I doing to myself? It's all for the love of the art, I tell myself. Nobody gets to be an author without angst and rejection and self-doubt.

> *"Utterly disgusted with myself and all the editors, I went home to St.Paul and informed family and friends that I had given up my position and come home to write a novel. They nodded politely, changed the subject and spoke of me very gently."*

Guess who said that? Only the chap who wrote The Great Gatsby and Tender is the Night and dozens of others - F. Scott Fitzgerald. Clearly, I will never trouble the same stratosphere as he, but we all start somewhere. I love that gag about some poor English teacher once having a young Shakespeare in his class. I am loving writing and if I can get a few sentences down, my mood lifts.

Dyfed and I are watching his daughter, my goddaughter, play Lacrosse at a tournament south of Guildford. Both buttoning our coats against the autumn chill he asks me how I am as hundreds of rosy-cheeked teenage girls wearing ski-masks fire hard rubber balls at each other like petulant bank-robbers.

I say, "to be honest, I'm just bloody lonely. Nobody really calls to ask me how I am anymore. I get it. It's a question which could lose them forty-five irretrievable minutes of their life. So, they don't ask. Or if they do, I can see them praying for a succinct answer without my usual vitriol and latest theory on what was really going on in Claire's mind."

"I get that," he says. "I'm as guilty as the next person. I know I don't reach out to you as often as I should. We've all got busy lives and I guess we think you're doing Okay."

"I know," I say, my voice breaking. "You've been awesome. Without you and Mum and Dad and Orla and Annabel, I don't think I'd have made it this far."

He clutches my arm and asks, "how were the kids?"

"They were great," I say, "but it's horrible. Every time I see them it feels like we take a little longer to reacquaint ourselves. In my worst nightmares, they forget me altogether. Or don't recognise me, like they've got early onset Alzheimer's."

"They will never forget you," he said, "they love you to bits."

"I know," I say, "seeing them off was awful. Claire was there with huge bags stuffed from all the things she took from the house and then had a complete paddy when the check-in girl said her bag was overweight. She was effing and blinding in front of the kids and the other passengers. Fairplay to the check-in girl though, she stood her ground."

"She's always had a way with words, your wife."

"Ex-wife!"

"Ex-wife. What had she taken?"

"I'm not sure really," I say, "you know that blue painting that was in our sitting room?"

"Yep," says Dyfed.

"And the potato masher."

"Jesus. First the kids, then the potato masher. Has that woman no shame?!"

"None whatsoever."

"Next you'll be telling me she took the lightbulbs and curtains."

"I don't know," I say, "I should check that."

"You should," says Dyfed, "she's a tinker that one. How did the kids react?"

"More embarrassed than anything. Jack particularly. I managed not to cry when they walked away, then collapsed in the lift. A Japanese lady thought I was having a heart attack."

"Well, Claire had taken your potato masher."

"When I'm alone, My mind starts catastrophising. I fear the worst. I'm too scared to call the children. And then all I want is a drink."

"You're doing better with your drinking aren't you?" he asks. "You should be proud of yourself."

"Thanks," I say. "Yeah, I'm liking what the lack of booze does for me. Becks Blue is my saviour. I just need a lucky break. Something to happen in my life. I've got a date tomorrow with a French girl from Book Club."

"Ooh la-la," he says, because he's Dyfed and retarded and, well, Dyfed.

"I'm looking forward to it."

"Is she fit?"

"Yeah, in that way all French girls are fit, even if they're not super-pretty, they're French. You know the score."

"I do mon brave," he says, "I've always enjoyed a touch of the entente cordiale myself."

I suspect at this point Dyfed has exhausted his repertoire of French, beyond Champs-Elysées and Déjà Vu. I'm wrong, he's suddenly shouting, "Allez Bridget!" And then he catches himself because he sounds a twat, "Look up Bridget! Pass Bridget!"

Dyfed's daughter is Lara, not Bridget. He's on touchline first-name terms with Lara's team. "Bridget!!"

"Orla is my rock," I say. "When she is down and snotty, I'm usually fine. When I lose it, she is up. She texts me. I text her. We're the perfect Yin and Yang"

"She's great," agrees Dyfed.

"We spend hours on the phone lying in bed talking each other up or down," I say, "or off the ledge. Ha! Ha!"

As Dyfed hyperventilates over a wasp called Saskia dropping the ball in front of goal, I watch and wonder how many of the girls come from broken homes. How many have a parent or other, up to no good. I look at a pair of touchline Grandparents and think I've got twenty or thirty years left on this planet. Doesn't sound much, but I guess it's long enough. Worth doing something with. I want Jack and Clara to be proud of me, but already I sense them seeing me as a failure. I failed my marriage. Failed their Mum. Somehow the brunt of that burden is on my shoulders. I am the man, I am weak.

"Olivia! Olivia!" shouts Dyfed, "get your team to push up."

Then he says without taking his eyes off the match, "you've got so much to offer. I know you need a lucky-break, but the harder you look for it the longer it will take. It will only come when you don't expect it."

"I know," I say. "I'm saying, I know, a lot. Chats like these are an exercise in repeating the obvious until I actually hear what I already know. I'm so tired of picking myself up again and again and again. But I've got no bloody choice."

"You will get there fella, I promise," says Dyfed

"I know," I say again, "at least I'm getting better at standing up when I get knocked over."

At this point in the movie, a thundering lacrosse ball will smack me in the head and Dyfed will look round and wonder where I've gone.

Chapter 6: STARDUST

"She says nothing at all, but simply stares upward into the dark sky and watches, with sad eyes, the slow dance of the infinite stars."

Neil Gaiman

"How old are your children?" asks Aude.

"Ten and Eight. Boy and a girl. Do you have kids?"

"My daughter, Yes. Rachel."

"How old is she?"

"She is six," she says, "what are they like, your children? Do you have a good relationship with them?"

"Err, wow, well, they are wonderful. I adore them. Clara is a grown woman in an eight year olds body - she looks out for me, well, she did. She would remind me to do things my-ex would want me to do. It was like she protected me from her. Jack is quiet, and introspective but remarkably astute. The things he comes out with sometimes are startling. What can I say, I love them unconditionally. Are you not with Rachel's Father?"

"No," she says. "I moved here from France when I was pregnant. He left two years ago, and I couldn't bear to take Rachel away from her friends and her school. So we're still here."

"And her Father?"

"What about him?"

"Do you see him?"

She shrugs and says no, but she says she watches out for him on *Crimewatch,* which I take to mean she doesn't get out much. I would give anything to watch TV with my children, rather than steak for one at The Alma.

Aude had arrived at the coffee shop wrapped in a black cape over breezy culottes and sandals and a just-had-sex hairstyle that French girls pull-off, no matter how they spent the night.

She sat starting into her phone while I queued for twenty minutes, shuffling along the long glass counter while lycra clad bike-jockeys and first time Mum's in yoga pants had their bagels toasted and baby milk warmed and asked if there were nuts in this, or sugar in that and if there was any Soya milk.

"What about you?" she asks. "Where is your wife?"

"She lives in Ireland."

"With your children I assume?"

I don't reply, just look her in directly in the eye for the first time and give a non-smile smile.

"It's tough, really tough," she says.

"To be honest, I feel suspended in disbelief. I don't know how I got to where I have got to. To not be with Jack and Clara every day."

"Life is very cruel."

We both reach for our coffees in agreement.

"What do you do? I ask.

"I run a creperie on the High Street. Crêpes and galettes and red wine. People seem to like it. It's very French."

"That can't be easy. Running a restaurant and being a single Mum."

"I have a lot of good friends. People who look out for me and Rachel." With a flourish of her hands and injection of energy from her well-mined reserves, she adds, "and once a month I have Book Club."

"I'm not sure that's much consolation."

"It's my one night out a month. I like it."

"You have a lot of plates to spin I guess."

"You don't have to be married or a couple to bring up children, but I'm sure it helps."

"I can't imagine what it's like. But then Claire… my ex, is a single Mum. But she lives with her Mum. I guess it's not easy for anyone. And not easy for the children."

"Voilà."

I ask where Rachel is now and she tells me she's with a friend and has to pick her up in forty-five minutes and so now I know this really isn't a date. Shame, I think, it's not like we've been flirting but I'm finding her mildly intoxicating. Her vulnerabilities feel both different and the same to mine. And she really is very French. Falling into bed, just because the bed was behind us, even if it were on the cards, feels as equally attractive as inappropriate.

"How do you manage? She asks. Not seeing your children."

"I'm not sure I do. I don't have any choice."

"It is strange. How did you let them go?"

"Err, well I didn't."

"Could you not stop her?" She's sounding angry. She pauses. "Désolé. I shouldn't ask questions like that. It is very personal."

"No, It's OK."

Though it's not great.

I'm now glad this isn't a date. We're hardly involved in foreplay here. Similar to married people at dinner parties only talking about house prices, the divorced can only talk about the injustices they can't get past.

"So," she says, "your book."

"Ah, yes my book. I only have four chapters with me. It's very rough."

"It's not a problem. It's not like I have anything better to do."

I could take that one of two ways.

"How do you know Orla," she asks.

"I've known her forever. She was part of the Gang we all ran around in, back in the day."

"Is she married?"

"Not anymore."

"Plus ça change."

"Ain't that so."

"Does she have children?"

"Two boys."

"What happened with her marriage?"

I tell Aude the abridged version, about how she was always in love with Chris, but when didn't Chris step-up she looked elsewhere and came up with Nick, a nice enough guy, but he was different to the rest of us and how on more than one occasion she had said, *I know he's different, but he's my different.*

"What's wrong with being different?"

"Oh. Nothing of course, it's just he didn't really fit with the rest of us. It was always awkward when he was around."

"It sounds like you and your friends were the problem."

"No, it wasn't like that honestly. He was just weird. He owned a metal detector and did military re-enactment at the weekend."

"Why is that so bad?"

"It isn't. I don't know. It just didn't work."

"For you or Orla?"

"Well," I stall. "All of us really, but obviously most importantly Orla."

Aude's silence let's me know what she thinks of my answer.

"Why are you so interested in Orla?" I ask.

"I think she is beautiful."

That's a turn up for the books.

I'm now wondering which border I am failing to communicate across here - the English Channel, gender or sexuality?

"I find the female form so much more beautiful than men."

"I'm with you on that one."

"I'm not gay if that's what you are thinking."

"Err, no. Well. As you say, us men aren't so easy on the eye. I get that."

"When you take your clothes off."

"Exactly."

A cluster of young Mum's decide to simultaneously leave with their collection of expensive prams, peeling onto the pavement like a chapter of Hells Angels turning onto Route 66. A path to two vacated window comfy seats opens up, so we grab our coffees and run crouched to claim them before anyone else spots them. We giggle at the stupidity at all. Perhaps this *could* go somewhere.

"You are like my husband," she says.

"I look ugly naked?"

"Pah! You look ugly dressed."

Harsh.

"I'm just teasing you. Non. You don't look after your children."

Well, she's pushed the bruise there. Thrown salt on the wound. You name a way to set me off - Aude has just found it. I'm hoping because English isn't her first language, she didn't mean *exactly* what she said there.

"It's not that I don't want to look after my children," I say with as much emphasis I can add without raising my voice.

"C'est ça," she says, turning to look out the window as a yoga mum lights up a smoke and presses her backside against the glass. "My husband doesn't give a fuck."

She bites her lip.

"I love my children more than anything," I say, which are words I can't say or type without my face cracking and tears appearing at the corner of each eye.

We sit in silence while we both let the pain slip back beneath the surface, then the yoga-smoker bends over to tie the lace on her pristine trailers and I say, "at least the female form is a beautiful thing."

Aude turns and smiles weakly at me. If we were still allowed to smoke in cafes we would both be either stubbing one out or lighting one up at this moment.

Whether on dates or not, conversations about broken marriage, and shattered dreams and failed parenting are the world's most rubbish aphrodisiac. Like trying to draw a close on a business meeting with small talk of plans for the weekend to which nobody cares for the answer, I ask her where she is from in France. She says Beziers, which I tell her I once stopped at, on my way to get an aeroplane. I don't tell her I was with Claire and the children, because even though we're not on a date, talking about happy memories with another woman, is never the way to the next woman's heart. I tell her my visit was the morning after some sort of festival and the Grand Rue was littered with semi-conscious bull-runners and rugby players and pensioners listening to rave music while having the mornings first Pernod and how I had always wondered what it would have been like to go back there with the boys and sample their unique hospitality first-hand. I'm clearly trying a last minute flirt as if she'll suddenly be overcome by the tyranny of single-parenthood, spot the spark in me she had previously overlooked, and fall into my arms. But she has no idea the point I am making, so I change the subject and wonder out loud if there are any toilets I can visit before we leave.

Dyfed texts me to ask how it went.
Wash-out, I reply.
Bad luck mate, he sends back - *plenty more poissons.*

Aude and I had parted with a moi-moi-moi, followed by protestations to see each other again at Book Club, and she promised to read my four chapters and text her thoughts. Dyfed is as right as he is annoying. But he's had countless affairs and is still married and from where I'm lying right now, life doesn't feel very fair. I scroll through my contacts and ponder who to text next. Problem is I don't really like myself right now. It's not a great foundation to throw myself at others. Imagine suddenly being on your own after a decade waking up next to someone. Do you remember the first time you slept in a double bed as a child, how big they are? You get me? Imagine no sticky-fingered children leaving the fridge door open or the loo seat up when you come down in the morning. Every joint decision, now for you to get wrong on your own. Pick up your phone and imagine only being called to discuss compensation for the recent car accident you weren't in.

That's me.

I think I've exhausted my bank of goodwill with Orla and Dyfed for the time being. I search for Graeme in my contacts. He knows what this feels like. I type a message and press send and turn off my bedside light, trying not to let my feet stray onto Claire's side of the bed. I lie and think about what to do next with my life and just as I feel sleep coming, my phone wooshes with the sound of my text to Graeme finally heading towards Hampshire. I have no idea when sleep will come now.

Chapter 7: LONDON MEMORIAL

"And meanwhile time goes about its immemorial work of making everyone look and feel like shit."

Martin Amis

I mentioned before being stranded on the moon. Three months in, lunar abandonment couldn't feel more apt. Autumn came before summer had been properly packed away, and quickly assumed a credible cameo of Winter. Standing in my dank garden, I'm literally turning on the spot, then turning again and turning again and thinking to myself in a melodramatic way, I don't know which way to turn. And then trying not to cry.

I go to Tesco, and do that thing people do every year – marveling at how early the Christmas decorations are put out. I know the subject of Christmas is going to be a major challenge for me. Will I be with Jack and Clara? A tiny ping rings out in my pocket like the very last note of a symphony played on a Triangle. Graeme has replied to my text. It's the best kind of text I can get - an invitation. Invitations are golden, each one a winning ticket. He's asked me to stay for the weekend. He says his cottage is tiny but the sofa will be fine. He broke up with Lesley a year ago. One of the last conversations I recall with Claire was about Graeme and Lesley. We had discussed their nightmare over wine and bits of cheese one evening after the children pretended to go to sleep.

"It's not my fault she turned out to be a nutcase," said Claire.

"I'm not saying it is," I said.

"Yes you are."

"No, I'm not." I said. "I was merely asking where she came from as in Australia or New Zealand. I genuinely forgot it was you who introduced her."

"No you didn't," she said.

"Yes, I did. I asked where she originally came from. I meant what country, not who her sponsor was!"

Graeme's cottage is somewhere in North Hampshire. I put his postcode into my Satnav and it's need-to-get-out-more female voice takes me down the M3, off at junction 5 for Hook then on a merry dance around an uncoiled rope of country lanes. I drive through villages called Upper This and Lower That and Somewhere-on-Something until she announces I have arrived at my destination. Unless Graeme is living as a free-range chicken, this seems a gross generalisation. I left phone reception at civilisation, so I get out of my car and walk up and down the same damp lanes enough times to sap my will to live. I'm considering heading home when Graeme's Labrador Betty finds me. I've never met Betty before, but she seems convinced I'm the Londoner she's looking for. Like a Seventies TV animal star, she summons Graeme with a single bark.

"Having trouble?" asks Graeme appearing from nowhere, breathing a breathy grin.

"Where the hell do you live?"

"There," he says, pointing at a bush less than fifty yards away. The bush, if you possess the instinct of a Native American tracker, you would know conceals an entrance. I wonder how the Amazon delivery guy ever finds him.

"I don't get Amazon deliveries," says Graeme. I must have been thinking out loud. Graeme's cottage is indeed tiny. It feels rented. The red brickwork needs repointing and window frames are in desperate need of replacement. The latches on the doors are heavy and ill-fitting letting draughts merge with draughts to form breezes bellowing the only obvious heat source, an open Inglenook fireplace already earning its keep at 10.30am. The furniture is ancient and ill-matched. It could be beautiful, with a few thousand spent and a woman's touch. No offence Graeme.

Graeme asks me to make coffee as he and Betty disappear out the back door. Even the mugs are cold, erupting in steam with the addition of boiling water from a kettle that must have survived The Blitz. I watch him through the kitchen window going in and out of his garage, putting away tools and a hose and winding up a pressure washer. He looks so much older than he is, like he's given in to his fate - his life in the endgame. I remember saying to Claire, Graeme should never have married Lesley. She replied he was pussy-whipped, in that brassy way I never knew whether to admire or recoil from. Originally from New Zealand, Lesley's family had emigrated to the UK when she was a teenager. She was small, dark and as it turned out, poisonous. She loved money. Or rather, loved spending it on things. She liked things.

"It's all a bit different now, eh?" says Graeme reappearing with a long-dead animal in a tin foil sarcophagus.

"It's great," I say, meaning it, but unable to imagine living like this, or come to think of it, surviving the night.

"Dad doesn't live too far from here."

"Where's that?"

"South of Alton."

"That's the next junction down the M3, but yeah, not far. Have you seen him?"

"Have I? Yeah, I went for a walk with him the other day. He pulled! He never changes."

"He pulled on a walk?! Pulled who?"

"The local landowner, whose land we were trespassing on."

"Wow. Respect."

Graeme suggests the Dukes Head for lunch. Apparently we're in Duke of Wellington territory. Everything from the menu holders to the peanut bowls are shaped like a boot. When I go to the toilets to expunge beer no.3, I expect to pee in an old boot, finding a long metal urinal that reminds me of school and resonates the urgent stream of my urine like a kettle drum.

We tit about Claire and tatt about Lesley, swapping anecdotes like a game of divorce one-upmanship. She did that, and I know, oh really! - mine did that too, but worse. Betty, a regular at the Dukes Head, lies at our feet like part of the furniture she has evidently become. The blonde barman skittles around the otherwise empty pub with the flair and flounce of a waiter who once served at the Café de Paris.

"We all knew Lesley liked shopping," I say, "but I had no idea..."

"Oh yes," says Graeme. "A new handbag to her was like oxygen. She couldn't live without it."

"What about your cars?"

"Ha! Yes! Every time the annual registration rolled over, we had a new one. She wouldn't be seen dead otherwise."

"How did you afford it?" I ask.

"We didn't," says Graeme.

The next question didn't require asking.

"Lesley came from money. Her old man was minted. You know that," he says.

"He was a city boy?" I ask

"Sort of. Oil." clarifies Graeme. "He got bored of the travel and cashed in at fifty for the good life. It rubbed off on her like a moulting dog." Betty looks up expectantly, then rests her head back down with her signature depressed Labrador look.

"What I love now," says Graeme, "is when the kids and I do anything we take packed lunches. She never ate sandy homemade sandwiches from tin foil on a beach."

I remember when Claire first introduced Lesley to the Gang. And yes, it was Claire. Striped-tops were Lesley's uniform. Tight, striped-tops perfectly contouring over her breasts like a geological survey. We were all hypnotised by the fall and relief of her chest, but Graeme got it bad. She also had a predilection for peeing on the floor when drunk. She couldn't explain why, other than she was drunk. Like having an incontinent pet. Graeme said years ago how living with Lesley was a frustrating business. But Graeme is one of life's kind people. He treated her uncontrolled bladder as a quirk. A kink in her otherwise perfect contours.

We order another round of drinks. I wonder if Graeme is planning to drive his Land Rover back to the cottage. I suspect such considerations carry little weight this far off the beaten track. In the muted interior light, Graeme looks plain and handsome, his face kind and powdery. I suspect the barman would think so, but the barman is meticulously polishing his bar as if anticipating the arrival of the matinee audience. I would never describe Graeme as an alpha male. Every group needs a Graeme. He was a vital ingredient in our equilibrium. Put too much of one personality type in any group, the imbalance will lead to trouble, one way or another. Life to Graeme has few extremities, everything is soft and rounded in his world. He used to get drunk like the rest of us, had his requisite share of encounters with the opposite sex. Lived his life well. But when push came to shove, he was never at the front of the queue. When the Police arrived; when opportunity knocked, or disaster loomed, Graeme was in the loo; or had gone home early; or hadn't come out in the first place. Too tired. Broke. Having a quiet night in.

His relationship to Lesley was at first incongruous, but opposites attract. Like groups of friends, relationships need balance. He was the counter balance to Lesley and her avarice. Their odd coupling made them an attractive couple in the beginning. His quirky kindness, an appropriate antidote to her spikey abruptness. She had few weapons to deal with him beyond full frontal assault. He circumvented her bluster with calm reason. Had she married her own alpha type, they would likely have killed each other before the wedding marquee had been taken down. But Graeme was different. He diluted her.

Graeme earned a good living. She worked too. In the scheme of things, they were well-off. Just not well off enough to fund her retail nicotine habit. Not well off enough to live up to the way her father expected his daughter to live.

The Professors and pundits say, behind infidelity, money difficulties are the number one cause of marriage break up in the UK. I beg to equivocate the point. It is becoming clear to me, money problems, like infidelity are a symptom not a cause. At the bottom of it, if you can get there, will lurk the enzyme that kicked it all off. Money worries, if you can't openly discuss them, are a symptom that become a cause with hindsight.

"We never talked about money," says Graeme, "or sex."

"We were the same," I say. "I guess money chat isn't high on the agenda when you first meet someone. And then before you know it, it's too late."

"Too late motherfucker," says Graeme, running his finger round the tip of his glass trying to produce that sonic whine that always worked when we were younger, but doesn't anymore.

"So what actually happened?" I ask Graeme.

"I'll fill you in at supper," he says, "I need to be very drunk to tell you. It's embarrassing."

I think we've only had four pints each when Graeme drives us home, Betty in the footwell, her head in my crotch like a comforting countryside airbag. Graeme gets me clearing leaves for two hours to take the edge off the beer. Wearing borrowed wellies and a shooting jacket I'm rather taken with my country look. Tea at four-thirty, gin at six, we eat supper in our socks, our boots prised off and slung by the back door for Betty to negotiate on her way in and out.

"What is this?" I ask Graeme as politely I can muster. "Pheasant," he says, "or possibly pigeon. They all look the same plucked."

"How is it not seeing your kids?" asks Graeme. I use the extraction of a gun-pellet sized piece of bone from my teeth to send back the racing tears that follow questions about my kids when I've been drinking.

"Shit," I say, adding, "I've learned not to cry until I get to the car when I see them off at the airport."

Enough said.

"So, come on tell me. What actually happened?" Graeme lets out a long sigh and pushes his chair back.

"She bet the farm and blew it."

"I take it you weren't aware?"

"Well it was all a bit grey," he says, "would you like some more potatoes?" I would, I'm finding his pheasant-pigeon a tad gamey.

"She got involved in a scheme buying multiple properties off plan and selling in a tax efficient way."

"Efficient or evasive?"

"Both," says Graeme, "but as things wore on it was increasingly of the evasive variety. It went very well for a while, she borrowed off her father and the bank and me and Uncle Tom Cobley, and for a while we all got our money back and she got more handbags."

I can see where this is going.

Back then, they seemed to have it all. Lesley was known for being extremely generous, lavishing gifts upon friends and relatives, over-demonstrating her thoughtfulness. They holidayed in the best places while Claire and I had been demoted to staycations thanks to my income drop when I went freelance. Claire wasn't pleased, and I was jealous of Graeme. We were all mighty once. Oh how we fell. Lesley liked things just right. Everything they had was new and shiny and perfect. Hers was not the dusty, creaky country house. Hers was modern, sharp and crisp in metal and glass and white leather. And, as it's turning out, hers was increasingly not hers.

"She installed me as a Director of a number of companies," continues Graeme, "I just signed bits of paper. I'm an architect for god's sake, what did I know? I did get nervous when I saw these large sums of money flowing between the companies, but she assured me everything was cool and above board."

"She was robbing Peter to pay Paul?"

"Sure, but she was also robbing Paul to pay for our lifestyle and nobody was getting paid back."

"And then the property market tanked?"

"And us with it."

"And now you're here."

"Oh no," says Graeme, "it had to get a lot worse first."

"Top up?" I offer, giving Graeme an out if he doesn't want to talk about it.

"She found a text on my phone," he says. "Do you remember that night we were all out in London and we met those foreign students?"

"In Covent Garden?"

"No, it was on The Embankment," he says.

"Oh that night."

"Yes, that night."

"You remember the Danish girl Dyfed was chatting up? Agathe?"

"Brown-haired, tall, pretty?"

"That's the one. Well, even though Dyfed was all over her, she slipped me her number on a piece of paper. It was like being back at school. Anyway, that night on the train home, I texted her. Why not, right?"

"Indeed."

"She texted back, nothing consequential and that was that. I forgot all about it."

"And then?"

"And then six months later, when Lesley and I were in Sardinia with the kids, ping!"

"And Lesley found the text?"

"No. No not at all. That was months later."

"Did you meet up with her?"

"Once."

"Did..."

"No. not a thing. We just met for coffee and then exchanged a couple of texts after that. That was it. God's honest. Not that I didn't want to. But I didn't."

"So where's the problem?" I ask.

"The problem is, at that point Lesley was facing bankruptcy. She was having all sorts of discussions with lots of unpleasant people. The walls were closing in around her, and then she found the texts on an old iPad. Apparently infidelity trumps bankruptcy."

"But you weren't an infidel," I say.

"I know, but that's not how she saw it. No matter what I said, I had been unfaithful in her eyes. It was her way back onto the moral high ground where she happily filed for divorce. It wasn't as if she gave it a great deal of thought. That was just that."

"Fuck."

"Yeah. There's more. When I eventually realised I was on a losing wicket, I needed a solicitor. I got this awesome Indian lady called Aditi."

"Aditi. OK."

"She was a terrier. Except what she discovered was I owed four hundred and thirty grand on three properties I didn't know I owned."

"Fu.....!"

"Yep, the mortgages were in my name."

"How did you not know?"

"I don't know. I still don't get it," says Graeme, his fork pushing a potato through gravy trying to drown his shame. I top up his glass and refill mine. Betty ambles off in search of a story she hasn't heard before.

"Aditi said it wasn't my debt. I had been coerced or duped. Debt or credit is shared at the end of a marriage, no matter. For a while we reckoned we had her banged to rights. She was a fraudster."

"Right..."

"So I met her in Costa, I didn't want to do the cross-table solicitor thing, it terrified me," he says. "I told her she had another thing coming if she thought I was taking on her debt. Except she did think that. Very much so. She said I should go bankrupt. I said no way, she said, well then, we'll both go to prison."

Plates and dishes left uncleared on the kitchen table, we sit by the fire in two old armchairs like a pair of weeping buffers in a Gentlemans Club on Pall Mall without the arthritis, or tales of being forced to surrender at Arnhem. In the cocoon of his cottage, we let it all flood out. Come morning, we'll be buttoned up men again, for the next few hours we are boys lost. We talk about Claire and how though I get it, I don't quite get it. How things had got so bad without me noticing and how I still couldn't fathom why she just upped and left. We talk about sociopaths and the sense of right and wrong. How Lesley was like Narcissus, in her mind she could actually do no wrong. She cared nothing for her actions. No concept of consequence. Perhaps that was why she pee'd on the floor, we laughed. Graeme and Lesley never made it to court. They got close, her Father stepped in and paid off her half of the debt. Apparently, she now lives in a huge house with her new hedge fund boyfriend.

I push Graeme to admit under his breath, splitting up from Lesley, was probably a good thing. He's grown to love his little rented cottage and his new simple life. In a year or two's time he hopes to raise a small mortgage and make an offer on it. Just beneath the surface, I can see he still loves her. Somehow, he emerged as the guilty party – that bloody text message.

Graeme fills his port glass and then mine. The slurry of sediment filtering through my teeth suggests we are at the bottom of the bottle. He asks, "have you heard about Charlie and Pete?"

"No." I say.

"They've broken up."

"No way. Really? Why?" I say a little over-enthusiastically, adding, "when?"

"Over the summer apparently."

"Jesus, I thought they were so happy. Do you know what happened?"

"No idea, I just heard they were over."

"Fuck."

"Yeah."

It's late and I'm drunk and our hearts and guts have already been spilled, so I say, "you know I've always had a bit of a thing for Charlie?"

"Ha! Of course I do."

"Do you know how much of a thing?"

"I know you shagged back in the day."

"How do you know that?!"

"Everybody knows Tom. But nobody says anything because of Pete. And Dyfed of course!"

I don't know what to say to that, so let me fill you in on a few details. Firstly, Charlie is Dyfeds cousin. Yes, awkward, I know. Secondly, Pete and I were mates back in the day. We had an odd meeting of minds on the sidebar of the Gang. I think we sensed in each other similar unspoken vulnerabilities buried beneath the Gang's machismo. In a peculiar way I was closer to him than many of the others. Right until he hooked up with Charlie. As far as I was aware, he had no idea of my feelings for her. How could he? They were my guilty secret. Though from what Graeme has just told me, not so secret. Anyway, pretty soon I was with Claire. Once Pete had won Charlie over, he wrapped her up and shrunk away. He works in Formula One marketing. They bought a house as soon as they were married, in Tring, Hertfordshire to be near Silverstone and Brands Hatch. Most of us sensed a hidden agenda to take Charlie out of circulation and distance himself from the juvenility of the Gang. He saw his marriage as incompatible with anything we had all once been.

Charlie single, eh? Wow.

Shivering in the middle of the night as my hangover kicks in, the fire is dead and the lumps in the sofa are conspiring with the inadequacy of the blanket to make me feel utterly miserable. Claire pops into my head, which she has a habit of doing when I simultaneously hate her and need her the most. Then I think about the Charlie conversation and I know what I'm about to do before I've agreed in my head I'm going to do it. My right hand drops to the floor beside the sofa searching for my mobile phone. Its light makes me squint as my tired, middle-aged, drunken eyes focus on the text message I am typing. I re-read it five times, then press send. There is no reception and the message hangs on the screen. Perhaps that's a good thing.

Chapter 8: MIDDLEMARCH

"We mortals, men and women, devour many a disappointment between breakfast and dinner-time."

George Eliot

It's gone midnight and I'm reading Amor Towles. It's beautifully written and the main character, Count Alexander Rostov, is indeed a man of intelligence and wit. I'm pleased to say he bears no resemblance whatsoever to Ian. Sentenced to house arrest in a posh hotel by the Bolsheviks, he potters and ruminates about how things were before the revolution. I'm not sure where the book is going or what its purpose is. It asks on the back cover, can a life without luxury be the richest of all? Perhaps, but it sounds boring. I press on, but the book is refusing to get a hold over me. If I'm honest, my concentration is wavering with thoughts of Charlie. She hasn't replied to my text and I have at least three active scenarios playing out in my head as to why that is. Two of them are not good scenarios at all.

Right, a brief trip down Memory Lane if you'd be so kind. I first met Charlie at Dyfed's house when she was ten years old. Which would put me at twelve. I'll never forget it. At least, I'll never forget the red wellies she was wearing. Her mother was loudly admonishing her for wearing them inside the house. She had rain-soaked, matted hair, somewhere between blonde and red. She wore drainpipe blue jeans, a glistening wet blue mac, and those red wellies. I was twelve years old. As I recall, though I may have been unaware of the signals, my prepubescent radar didn't blip. She was plain, naturally androgynous, and given her sodden appearance, not presented in her best light.

Fast forward four or five years. It was Dyfed's Mums fiftieth. I was anchored to a mantelpiece for fear of having to engage in adult conversation. A girl walked in with short, boyish hair on the red side of blonde, cropped at the back with a sweeping, layered fringe shadowing her nose and freckle-sieved cheeks. Despite the masculine hairstyle, there was no danger of leaving the observer in any question of her gender. She was wearing the tightest, shortest dress I had ever seen. Blue elasticated material clung to her like a paper bag in a wind tunnel. These days it would be classed as age inappropriate. Large, flesh revealing port holes punched through each flank, teased a peak. Before she put it on, it couldn't have been much larger than a sock. It took me a few moments for the penny to drop.

It was the little girl in red wellies.

It was the moment a love of Lego and Star Wars figures evaporated like spilled diesel from hot tarmac. The moment my much-loved Yoda poster was tugged from the wall above my bed, along with pats of solidified blue tac and inch-wide flakes of magnolia paint.

It was the final drift of airplanes and clouds across the wallpaper, now hastily obscured by busty cut-outs of Pamela Anderson and Victoria Principal.

A hand-scrawled No Entry sign appeared on my door.

The suddenly adolescent-me, at last knew what all the fuss was about.

Why I was on the planet.

Not to leave it as a spaceman.

Not to police it as a policeman.

To pursue the barely-hidden promise of Charlie's dress with teenage futility.

I spent every frustrated moment that evening, checking where she was, who she was talking to. Towards the end, my opportunity finally came. We talked the awkward talk of teenagers, in limbo between the loss of innocence and the realities of adulthood. I flirted, as best I could flirt. I was terrified of her beauty. Terrified she was my best friend's cousin. I had no idea how I could cross her Rubicon, or if in a million years, she would let me embark on the journey. It was not the sort of party to end in lights down and drunken dancing.

By 10.30PM all the guests said their goodbyes. I can only imagine I looked somewhat wistful in the back seat as Mum drove us home.

As school dragged on for another five, long years, I saw her exactly three times – always accompanied by a different, impossibly hunky hunk on her arm. It was the era of all-American love-ballads conjuring audible mirages between my acned cheeks and the chance of laying my head on a soft breast. The vista of eligible girls at school was rich, but most hopeful glances returned unrequited. Even as awkward school dances began to bear fruit, French kisses and wandering hands, Charlie never faded from my view.

Fast forward to the early Nineties and I arrive home from work on a Friday evening to the flat I'm sharing with Dyfed in Putney, and I find Charlie eating Ritz crackers and watching children's TV. Dyfed was away for the weekend with Alice. She explained she was crashing with us while she found a place to live. There's that phrase isn't there - something about the Queen popping in for an unannounced cup of tea? Whatever it is, it was like that. The evening plans I had were forgotten quicker than it took me to recover my composure, say hi, and wish I'd washed my hair that morning. Dyfed hadn't mentioned a thing.

"Do you want to pop out for a drink somewhere local?" I asked, hoping I sounded like the genial host, not actually asking her out.

"Are you asking me out?" she replied.

"Well, for a drink," I fumbled.

She agreed with a look that knew and said she was going to change her clothes. I smiled at the thought of her reappearing in that blue dress. Then I got a mental image of her wearing nothing but red wellies. Then I decided I needed to get a grip. Then she re-appeared having changed, though I couldn't identify which garment. Perhaps her earrings. I found a warm bottle of Chardonnay that became palatable with four ice cubes per glass and we stood in the kitchen making small talk and trying to get drunk cheaply. When the wine was gone,

Charlie produced a bottle of Champagne she'd been given as a good-luck-on-your-move-to-London present. As the Champagne rapidly disappeared, a tide of discarded CDs seeped across the carpet. Taking turns to select songs, it looked increasingly unlikely we weren't going to make it to the pub.

The Boys of Summer by Don Henley was my anthem – it spoke to my inner-Californian and as luck had it, evoked Charlie's love of sun and the wind in her hair. After INXS had torn us apart and a pseudo dance to I'm Too Sexy, in which I could find no danceable rhythm to guide my awkward shape-making, I lost the game of rock-paper-scissors and ran to the corner shop to replenish supplies. On my return Charlie was making like a flamingo and wind-milling to The Communards singing their version of Don't Leave Me This Way. Bryan Ferry's Slave to Love changed the mood. Instantly recognising its clipping beat and riff, Charlie summoned her inner lap dancer. Her interpretation of the artform was a cross between amateur gymnastics and professional entrapment. Whatever it was, the Royal Choral Society took residence in my head and sang the Hallelujah Chorus. To say she was in control and I was hapless would egregiously understate the power imbalance. In geopolitical terms, she was the USSR and I was Wales. Slave to Love was followed by Bryan Ferry's other sex-dripped opus – Avalon. Little doubt remained we were heading somewhere beyond my wildest dreams, still Charlie teased. Avalon concluded with its orgasmic wail, surely Charlie's cue to remove any questions hanging in the air. As she gyrated in front of me, the unwritten rule stating I was not to touch, I attempted to make the internationally recognised semaphore for take-your-top-off. Crossing my forearms, touching my hips intending to lift my arms above my head, I lost all courage and stood frozen, like I was attempting a line dance.

Neither of us was about to change the Bryan Ferry CD. The kiss, when it came, was during Jealous Guy. Its sax and organ breaks and lamenting whistle, to this day, never fail to transport me back to that moment. The kiss was pretty perfect. I have my technique pretty much down pat I think. Well, it seemed to work. We met in the middle and didn't let go. I have wondered how some people can be so bad at kissing - like a wicked sibling had malignly tutored them to put in a gum shield and make like a washing machine.

The sex that followed was movie sex. No will they, won't they? No belligerent zips, no pre-trips to the bathroom. We were going to and we did. I confess we were both drunk and time has erased more detail of that night than I would wish, but I can still remember the general thrust. I can't claim to have taken her places she had never been, but she made an awful lot of noise getting to wherever she went. I've never revisited the places I went before or since.

At 3am we made naked pizza. Eating on the sofa like unabashed naturists, every time I discarded a crust, she picked it up and wolfed it down.
"I like the crusts," she said.
"You complete me," I said.
"Yeah right," she said.
"No," I said, "I mean we complete the pizza. I eat the middle bit and you eat the crusts. We are so compatible."
"I know what you meant," she said.

We left it at that, and I felt like Wales to her USSR again. We went back to bed and had sex again. It was great, but we'd already had our Bat Out of Hell. For reasons of circumstance, geography, timing, perhaps fear of confronting Dyfed with the fact I'd slept with his cousin, we never went further than the following morning. When Dyfed came back we made like nothing had happened. It was an impossible fairy tale. An opening chapter written by a wannabe author with no plan for the rest of the book – the half-baked manuscript left to gather dust in a bottom desk drawer. Everything changed that day. My perception altered. I had tasted a new delicacy I couldn't un-taste. Driven a luxury car for the first time and I knew driving would never be the same again. Despite the emotions I felt, something prevented me from drawing the obvious conclusion.

From unravelling the jumble of inexperience, lust and love. She was just too good to be true.

By the time, I really figured it out, she was married to Pete. I was married to Claire. And neither of us ever had anything close in bed with our spouses than the one-night Charlie and I had. Go figure, as they say.

Things are looking up. Count Rostov has just had sex with a movie actress. I confess, I didn't think he had it in him. My phone buzzes, it's Dyfed. I ignore it for a while, then curiosity gets the better of me, it's late for him to send a text.

He's just got back from Geneva, he says, and it's all kicked off with Alice. I reply asking him what he means and he simply replies, it's over.

I call Dyfed but it goes straight to the answerphone.

Jesus, this is like policemen and buses, I think, suddenly they all come at once. I don't know any detail yet, but given what I know about Dyfeds indiscretions, if Alice has rumbled him, there may be no way back. First Orla, then Graeme, then me, Pete and Charlie, now Dyfed. I can't do the maths, but we must be getting close to the 42%.

"I have been availing myself of drink, drugs and prostitutes," says Dyfed. He's drunk. It's taken three days for me to track him down. We're sitting in the corner of the Thomas Cubitt pub in Victoria, surrounded by well-to-do clientele displaying their well-to-do-lives. Since Claire left, I have become cynical of people's motives. Looking around, I can't hear words, but every moving mouth I assume to be telling lies; every date a triste; every wedding ring a beacon of deception. "So," I ask, "what's happened?"

Dyfed sighs. "You know Tristan?" he asks. You know it was him?"

I didn't know it was him, but I do know him, he's been my dentist for years. I have to confess, I assumed we would be talking about one of Dyfed's affairs. I think he's telling me Alice has had an affair.

Tristan?

Alice's boss?

Surely not. Tristan is rotund. His midriff extends in perfect symmetry from his navel to his spine and round again. He wears his trousers pulled-high, marking the widest point of his circumference. While he administers my fillings, I always find myself imagining him being sawed in half by a stage magician, his belt marking the perfect point of incision. He's got a full head of wavy and black, slightly greasy hair over a round face and round glasses sitting above his symbiotic chin and neck. Every day, he arrives at his surgery in one of a collection of old, but fabulous cars. He's a walking statement of himself, every attribute from his bow tie to his black Labrador carefully garnered with ruffled precision to project his self-image of grandeur.

"Well," says Dyfed, "Alice used to tell me about the mid-procedure banter they had to put the patients at ease. She always used to say he was risqué and often inappropriate. From what I can tell now it was all for her benefit, not the patients. They always used to go to the Fox and Grapes on Friday lunchtimes, that's when I think they started going off-piste. She said to me they never planned anything, it just happened. It didn't just happen. They made it happen."

Dyfed's voice cracks. As I listen, I struggle with the incongruousness of my knowledge of his own infidelities and his obvious anger at Alice.

"It was an email at midnight that flashed across her screen as she shut the lid on her computer too quickly that first got me worried. It gnawed at me. There were so many rational explanations. And anyway, Alice and her boss! Really? She was the most unlikely person to go over the side I could think of. But the email subject line – Lunch – just didn't seem right. She saw him every day. Why email at midnight? Still, I put it out of my head, I dropped it. Forgot about it, sort of."

"Okay," I say, thinking I need to buy another round, even though I bought the first. This is Dyfed's moment.

"You know those dental conferences she attends? The British Dental Association? She always said how dull they were. At the last one she went to, she called me, she said she was just on her way down to a dreary supper. She texted me two hours later to say she was in bed. Cool, I thought and went to sleep." I look at Dyfed as sympathetically as I can, I don't have any words right now.

"I woke up at 2am," he says. "I don't know what it was that twigged my brain. I'd bought her some underwear for Valentine's Day. I'd never done anything like that before, but I couldn't think what to buy her. You know what it's like."

I do.

"Buying women's underwear is excruciating. But that's what husband's do – so I did. She said she liked it. A bit saucy she said, but she appreciated the thought and she would wear it on a special occasion. I jumped out of bed and went through her underwear drawers. It wasn't there. I couldn't get back to sleep. I wondered if she knew about anything I'd done. My heart was going like a tail-end batsman facing Malcolm Marshall. I couldn't figure it out. Then I thought she must have thrown it out and tried to get some sleep. She got back from the conference, as Alice-like as ever. She said it had been one of the better ones. And then I had to go to Geneva."

"And then what?" I ask.

"When I got back, the underwear was back in the drawer, and that," he says, "is the end of our marriage."

I want to day, dude, it wasn't all her, but that isn't what he wants to hear right now. We drink our beer and drink another and eye a group of girls out-numbering two guys at the bar and wonder if we could shave off a couple for ourselves. Inevitably we get back to the subject, the alcohol nudging Dyfed nearer some truths.

"In my heart," he says, "I know my own shit [he meant his affairs] were the cause of my own distance. I subconsciously avoided getting too close in case I rumbled myself. I get it, but now the tables have turned, I don't like it one bit. As far as I know, she has no idea of all the shit I'd got up to, what goes on tour stays on tour and all that."

"So did you confront her?" I ask

"Not straight away, I needed to be 100% sure," he says. "I got all James Bond on her. I got into her computer, it had copies of all her text messages in it. Tristan was just the tip of the bloody iceberg. Turns out she's got Goldilocks Syndrome."

"What's that?"

"She's been sleeping in all the beds, with all the bears."

"What?"

"Yep. My delightful wife. Quiet, circumspect Alice had been bloody at it for years with all sorts."

"Like who?"

"Oh, y'know, passing tradesman, colleagues, you name it."

"How do you know?"

"I read her bloody emails and texts!" He says, "it was all there in bloody black and white."

There is only one course of action available to us.

We're going to get very, very drunk.

There are hangovers and then there is this hangover. This one is Olympic. Had Oliver Read, Elizabeth Taylor, Peter Cook, Emperor Nero and Princess Margaret been at Oscar Wilde's wake, on the evening the Germans rolled their tanks onto Leicester Square, they just might have had a hangover to rival this one. In years to come, wandering minstrels will sing of its epic scale and skeptical ears will disbelieve and angry mouths will boo them from the stage. Non-believers will dismiss their words as artistic licence and reason no hangover could be as extreme as the one currently racing me to the bathroom every twenty-minutes to throw up what isn't in my gut anymore. There's a difference between getting drunk and getting drunk. Getting drunk, the former, is the consequence of a long evening of drinking when by the end of it, more has been consumed than the mind and body wanted or needed. The latter getting drunk, is when one aggressively pursues the endgame in as short a time as possible by drinking the largest amount of neat spirits the body will imbibe before it starts rejecting them, or you simply can't connect the glass with your mouth. Dyfed and I were afflicted by both. As far as I know he is in my house somewhere. I'm pretty sure I'm in it too, but the thought occurs to me all the houses in my road have similar layouts and I could be in the bedroom of the Passmores at number twenty, or the Baldwins at number eight. Now I'm thinking that's a stupid thought because A Gentleman in Moscow is on the bedside table and neither the Passmores or Baldwins go to Book Club and I'm pretty sure on the last vomiting trip, I wiped my mouth on what was almost certainly my dressing gown. I'm trying to concentrate thoughts on my book in the hope it's cathartic powers are a substitute for the Nurofen I need but don't have, but I'm having flashbacks. Being refused entry to a strip bar for being too drunk, and a gay bar for being too gay, and being ejected from a corner shop for Dyfed's full-tilt charge into a wall of stacked cardboard crisp boxes shouting *bring on the wall*. I need greasy food and Frazzles and intravenous Lucozade.

I've tried lying on my left side and my right side and now I'm on my back staring at the ceiling wondering if Alice and Dyfed were in the wrong marriage or if they were both just congenitally unfaithful? And now I'm wondering if those factors are mutually exclusive. It is probably true leopards can't change their spots, but if the lady-leopard is with the right man-leopard in the first place, maybe problems wouldn't arise.

Hugging my pillow into my face, I'm lying on my front and I'm beginning to think the seeds of my failure with Claire were sown long-before we said, I do.

This is a dangerous moment, I'm hungover and feeling sorry for myself. Of course, entirely unforeseeable events can derail a marriage, but we didn't really have any events to point at. Events and facts, I'm thinking, are usually the symptom not the cause. They can be orchestrated or a natural disaster. Claire and I got onto the marriage band wagon and I'm not sure we had the right to be there in the first place. It's such a shame about Alice and Dyfed, for a while they seemed so perfect for each other.

I've just been sick again.

I'm face down on top of the duvet, spread-eagled like my parachute failed to open. I'm thinking about catharsis again and wondering if they sell it in Boots. The second thing people ask me when I say I am writing a book about marriage and divorce is, is it cathartic? Right now, I can't think what the first question is, but the second always involves catharsis and a little surprise they had stored that word in their vocabulary, it doesn't get out much. I invariably reply in the affirmative. If I'm feeling emotional (usually), or wishing I had another bottle of wine (usually, but not right now) or I've just written a passage from which I've wrestled an answer (occasionally), I might go so far as to say it has saved my life. There is no denying, writing this book is unbelievably cathartic, but there is a difference between remission and cure. A difference between indisputable facts committed to ink, and hazy, time-haggard emotions, inked but open to interpretation.

Affairs are facts. Car crashes, Ribena spills on pale carpets, forgotten passports and birthdays are all facts. What the combatants thought and felt before, during and after are subjective and change with time. What I think I am trying to say is writing something down although cathartic, does not set me free.

I'll give you an example.

I never considered the memory of Charlie in my mind having any role in my approach to my marriage. She was neither a physical presence nor a practical consideration. At worst, she was an unchecked lottery ticket lost at the back of a drawer I might one day uncover and check the numbers. Writing that down helps, but it won't stand up in court. On the other hand, given what I now know about Dyfed and Alice, all I see are facts. Evidence on both sides is as abundant as a Harvest Festival. In a low-rent, self-pitying way, I am jealous of their facts. They have so many, I wonder if I could borrow some. At least they have a beginning, middle and end. When I look back at my marriage, all I see is vague moments and a confused timeline. I can't figure out when it went wrong. Dyfed's infidelities are clear and present. Though he doesn't consider them so. To him, they are a sideshow. As long as real life remains separate from his marital amnesia that sets in at 30,000 feet over the English Channel, no harm is done. Meanwhile, his glamorous lifestyle with Alice, was the antidote to the poisonous truth of their marriage. And Alice, it turned out, had Goldilocks syndrome.

The thought I married the wrong person is crystallising in my head.

So is the cholesterol around my heart.

So is the tar in my lungs.

Perhaps it is instructive I haven't met any men capable of confessing they married the wrong woman. Men don't like to admit they were wrong in the first place. It was events dear boy, they say. Events that put paid to their marriage.

Was it events? Or were the seeds of destruction more subtle?

I wonder what Dyfed would say.

If Dyfed is still alive.

Chapter 9: BELOVED

"You are your best thing."

Toni Morrison

Count Rostov is growing on me. It's not just his intelligence and wit, which he exudes in a constant stream like delicious vanilla ice cream, from a delicious vanilla ice cream machine. I'm feeling uplifted by his erudite pontifications on mastering his own changed circumstances, when by rights his aristocratic blood should have been spilled by a bayonet wielding commissar. The Count genuflects at his love for his country and its culture and makes me use words like genuflects, which I swear I have never used before and have just Googled I have its correct meaning. That said, I'm pretty sure I've never used the word erudite before. Am I turning into a novelist or a ponse?

It's four months now since my separation from Claire. It's almost the end of the working day. I'm on the phone, writing a piece on the low take-up of flu-jabs. I can't say my heart is in it. My heart has gone from pretty much everything. Then, just like that, a name slides in from the edge of my screen with a familiar digital plop. It is the Mozart of digital plops. The ailing flame I secretly nurture, bursts into life like a stubborn pilot light on a gas boiler. Woomf!

I'm on the call for a further fifteen minutes, forcing myself not to open the message while speaking. I finally hang up and it takes me a further five minutes to summon the courage. And then there are her words, short and to the point.

Hi Tom, thanks for your message. How are you? It's been a long time. I hear things haven't been great. Would be happy to meet up. Charlie. X

That's it. Nothing given away. No hook, no hint. Every word, poetry. She'd be happy to meet up. Happy? What does she mean by that? It feels noncommittal, like saying someone is nice. Like filling a void in conversation with a banal comment about the weather. I smoke a cigarette to fill the time between replying in not too much of a hurry.

Hi Charlie, how awesome to hear back from you! You have made my day. Claire and I broke up six months ago. It wasn't pretty. Still isn't. But I'm alive! Rebuilding things. Like I say, writing a book. Miss my kids like hell. I wanted to get in touch, but y'know, thought best not to. Anyway, how are you? How's life? How's Tiggy? Tom. X

I reckon this is enough words to garner a reply. I go to the kitchen to make supper for one. What little festers in the fridge is teetering on the edge of past it's should-have-been-thrown-out-weeks-ago date. I make a Marmite sandwich and plaster Colman's mustard under the top slice of bread. I know - guilty pleasure. I deliberately don't check my phone to see if she has read the message. Succumbing an hour later, she hasn't read it. Nor when I check before I go to bed. I check in the night. Nothing. My head conjures all the scenarios.

She's gone on holiday.

Dropped her phone down the loo.

She's trapped under heavy furniture.

I brood all day. And the next. Slowly, I let the dream subside. The fantasies I play in my head wane as I beg for sleep. The happy ending I dream of dissolves into a fairy tale I let drop.

I move on. Almost forget about it. Think seriously about going on Tinder. Then she replies.

Hi Tom,

Sorry it's taken me so long to reply. Things have been terrible here to be honest. Pete and I are at the end of the road, it's a long story. To be honest, I knew all about what happened with you and Claire. Jess told me before Christmas, Your book sounds interesting. I'm coming down your way to see Dad next week (he's spitting tacks). Coffee?. X

Coffee? A COFFEE?!! She can have the bloody coffee factory. She can have a forest of coffee beans. I actually do a dance. I do the Rocky punch in the air and hold the pose. I let out a big woohoo! I collapse on the ground sobbing, my body convulsing like a cat with a stubborn fur ball. I haven't cried in a while. Not this sort of crying. All the emotion of everything bad in my life mixes with the giddiness of hope creating a chimera of emotions, topped with a very big cherry, on the very shitty cake of my life.

Is this really happening? My black and white fairy tale taking on glorious technicolour? Too good to be true? I know the taste of disappointment too well. Soooo important not to get my hopes up.

OMG! I'm truly sorry to hear that. Yes, let's meet. You tell me yours (if you want) and I'll tell you mine. Will you come to my place or shall we meet somewhere?

She replies, she will come to mine in three days time. She knows where I live. In the words of Bruce Springsteen - woah-oh-oh, I'm on fire. Today, I will go for a run, visit Annabel, get my haircut, clean the house from top to bottom, do everything I can to appear together, sane, an attractive prospect.

Annabel is lying in her bath with the door open, I'm sitting on her bed. We often chat like this. To some Daily Mail readers a brother and sister being so familiar may seem a little off colour, but after our parents divorced we drew each other close, we hide no secrets and give no blushes.

"I've been in touch with Charlie," I say, she's coming to see me.

"Really?" She says, clearly pondering the implications as she sticks her big toe in the tap. "What's she up to these days?"

"She's splitting up from Pete," I say.

"Oh dear," says Annabel, not sounding very deary, "they've only got one child haven't they?"

"Yes, Tiggy."

"Another one bites the dust."

"You could say that."

"She's a bit of a career girl isn't she? That will be tough."

Soon after Pete and Charlie had Tiggy, Charlie had returned to work. She is sales director for an International food company whose name means absolutely nothing for me. She works very hard, I know that much, and Pete did more than his fair share of childcare. From what little I know, her work involves a lot of charts, presentations and meetings at all corners of the globe in soulless hotels and out of town business parks. Fast Moving Consumer Goods they call it (FMCG). I always assumed that meant flat screen TVs disappearing from ASDA on Black Friday, but we live and learn. As far as I can tell she sells chips. I may be doing her a disservice, clearly there's big money in chips.

I say, "did you know I asked her to marry me once?"

"You didn't?!" exhorts Annabel, sitting up in her bath like a beast rearing from the deep.

"I did," I say, " well sort of asked, it was more of a mumble."

"When?" she asks, to the sound of the plug being pulled from her bath with an angry gurgle.

"Just after Pete asked her to marry him," I say without giving due care and attention to how the statement sounds. "They had only been going out a year," I follow quickly, as if that mitigates my heresy. "Anyway, she didn't really hear me, and the moment passed."

"How can you not hear a marriage proposal?"

"Well, I don't know. Charlie did."

"What about Pete?"

"I know."

"How come you never told me that?" asks Annabel, standing in front of me wrapped in a yellow towel.

"I'm sure I have."

"I'm sure you haven't."

"I don't know," I say. "I've always felt guilty about my feelings for Charlie. Because of Dyfed. Because of Pete. Maybe I buried it."

Getting into my stride, happy to be getting it off my chest, I continue, "even when she was married, I never stopped carrying the idea of her around. I looked out for her on the escalators, in airport lounges. I used to pick out women who reminded me of her and wish they were her."

"This was when you were married," asks Annabel rhetorically.

"Of course it was. I didn't think much of it, but she was always there."

When you marry, you forsake all others. One person for the rest of your life. But is that it? Some people say marriage is an unnatural construct. They, whoever they are, argue it simply can't work as a format, humans are not built like that. That religious notions originally designed to bind us together are a fraud. That nothing can tame true instinct.

I get it. Unless you marry your first love, you are by definition, marrying a successor to your former condition. You may have loved, or thought you have loved, a clutch of former candidates before making what you hope to be your final selection. Your partner has probably been in a similar love boat themselves. The chances are, some memories of former love, linger for both of you. The poignancy never fully extinguished. Maybe a former love still holds a candle for you. Perhaps the flame you finally marry burns bright enough to eclipse all former significant others. That is the ideal situation. When old flames smoke and flicker in the half-light, a careless draught can breathe life into the tiniest of embers. The threat to a marriage of an unextinguished memory, may be entirely benign. Or a ticking atom bomb.

"I've got it the other way around," said Annabel. "I still think about Rory all the time."

"Of course you do."

Rory, Annabel's husband and childhood sweetheart had got up one morning, said he wasn't feeling well, and died. The autopsy was inconclusive, but an undiagnosed heart condition was framed as the culprit. Their two young daughters had watched through a crack in their bedroom door as two men in green jumpsuits had tried everything to resuscitate him, then carried their father downstairs on a stretcher. It was the last they ever saw him. Try living with that image all your life.

It doesn't seem to matter if love is unrequited or forbidden or taken too soon, the bloody stuff still burns. Imagine reaching your end of days having walked Machu Picchu, climbed Kilimanjaro, witnessed the Northern Lights, raised happy children, won a medal, left a legacy – everything you wanted to achieve, but for one unfulfilled true love. Would you ask for your money back?

If you exclude Charlie, and Sally Field in Smokey and the Bandit, my first love was Philippa. Having squandered our virginities on each other, she dumped me for an older guy, with a tattoo, earring and Ford Capri - sadly that was the extent of his CV. She told me a few years ago, she always regretted that decision. I don't know, a Capri is a fine car, he can't have been all bad. Didn't all Seventies plain clothes cops drive one? I'm sure Bodie and Doyle did, if they didn't it was a gross dereliction of stereotype. Although I did think of Philippa from time to time, any flame I carried was of curiosity to see how she turned out. When she got in touch via social media, between the lines she telegraphed the notion of unfinished business. But I was married. I thought I was quite happily married.

"Are you seeing anyone?" I ask Annabel.

"I've been on a dating website," she says, "but it's awful. I had to do this huge questionnaire, and all it spits out now are countless ghastly, lecherous men. I went on date and he looked nothing like his pictures. I went to the loo and left via the back door."

"Databases are for credit scores, and car insurance renewals," I say. "It's funny how online dating has become so normal."

"So you're going to see Charlie" says Annabel now dressed and combing her wet hair.

"Yep," I say.

"Found a new shag yet?"

It's Melissa.

Timing is her speciality.

Charlie is due in less than an hour.

"No Melissa, I haven't. But I am seeing an old flame tonight."

"Ah-hah," she bellows down the phone. "Beware the soufflé that doesn't rise twice my boy."

"Well, I'm not going on a dating site. So I've got to find them somewhere."

"Ah-yes. It's such a shame we can't smoke in bars anymore. In my view that was the only way to find true love or a shag - eyes meeting across a smokey bar. Still I hear these Apps are a jolly good way to shortcut all that. Why don't you try that one, you could write a feature for me. What's that one called everyone uses, Grindr?"

"Tinder."

"Tinder. Yes, that's the one. Try Tinder."

"No thanks Melissa."

"Well, suit yourself. Just remember, sex makes for an ugly beggar. If you don't think your old flame is worth fluffing, be a smart chooser, put it back in your trousers and have another drink."

"Thank you Melissa. Did you call for a reason."

"No, just checking you haven't topped yourself. Have a good weekend."

"And you."

The girl in the red wellies walks in the door with the matter-of-factness of a delivery man keen to hurry on to his next drop. She says hello and walks purposely past me into my kitchen. I offer her coffee or something stronger. She asks for coffee. She hasn't changed, but there is a weariness in the creases of her cheeks. She had a boyish cheekiness to her face back then, it's still there, but she's a woman now. A mother. A divorcee. I can read the pain in her face as plain as a frown, but she's not frowning.

We step outside to sit in the postage stamp sized garden where I once played with my children. The early evening air is confused with winter warmth. Back in the day, when smoking didn't matter, she smoked. Like me, she hadn't smoked in years. But I guess her Apocalypse has been no less toxic than mine. When threatened with the silent death of radiation sickness, well why not? She takes one of mine like an unashamed smoke of honour.

"Life is shit," she says. "Smoking is the least of my problems."

Though we haven't seen each other for four or five years, it must be fourteen since we had spoken unencumbered by the lives we ill-advisedly wrapped around ourselves. Since we had first and last laid together. The familiarity between us is unmistakable, but common decency requires the distance of time to be re-navigated. It doesn't take long. By the third cigarette, the coffee becomes wine.

"Do you want to talk about it?" I ask.

"We couldn't have another baby," she says. "It tore us apart."

I hesitate and just look at her sympathetically.

"We desperately wanted a brother or sister for Tiggy, but it just wouldn't happen."

"I'm so sorry. Do you know why? Did you go for treatment I mean?"

"We tried everything," she says. "I wasn't producing enough eggs and his sperm were swimming the wrong way. It's a miracle we ever had Tiggy. He blamed my drinking. Called me barren."

"Fuck that," I say.

"He was so cruel, I even let him think Tiggy might not be his."

""Wow!" I say, thinking Christ, that's mean.

"Of course she is his, but it just got out of hand. What about you?"

"Me? God, I don't know. Claire just upped and left, I had no idea."

"You must have had some sense something was wrong?"

"Well, yes, with hindsight I can see almost everything was wrong, but at the time I just thought that was marriage. I thought we would be together forever."

"I thought you made a good couple."

I wish she didn't just say that. I don't want to hear that. Not from Charlie. I want to hear she never thought Claire and I were good together. I want a hint she thinks it should have been us.

"Apparently not," I say.

Seeking happier places, our talk meanders into the outlying skirts of the subjects we want to discuss. We talk of the old days. I think we both know we are going back, to justify going forward. Her body language is opening up. I've touched her hand across the table twice now.

One glass of wine becomes a bottle. The bottle became a brace. The presumption of the kiss is erased by it's inevitability. Awkwardness is non-existent. Sometimes, a kiss is simply meant to be kissed.

"I'm not going to sleep with you," she says. "I'm not divorced, you're not divorced. No way."

It's getting dark. We're getting drunk. It's an honourable protest. One I reckon she is reconsidering as our kiss turns decidedly French. I think it's her hair that is so beautiful. I don't know how best to describe it to you. It's still reddish but darker than I remember. Now it's long and all I can think of to write are words like cascade and waterfall. It just bloody works. It's Disney princess hair. Ha! Yes, that's it. Sitting staring at each other in the dark, stars are re-aligning. Claire, finally heading into deeper, darker, cold space. Charlie hurtling into my universe like an unexpected comet. She asks if she can stay the night, repeating she isn't sleeping with me.

"Of course," I say, trying to sound like she's asked to borrow a pint of milk.

She gets into my bed wearing only her knickers. Now, I don't know where you stand on the ins and outs of provocation, but this is provocative. I get that a little toplessness on a beach in St. Maxine isn't an invitation to make whoopee, but this is SW7, it's dark, and we're drunk and quite frankly I am thinking the eagle is landing. We kiss and hug, and I know you won't believe this, but at some point I think I'm happy with the result and give way to the alcohol and exhaustion and suggest we go to sleep, so we do.

The following morning we hug some more, but she says my breath smells like trainers and we cancel the kiss. I make breakfast and she pads around in my dressing gown. I'm wearing boxer shorts and a t-shirt, everything is comfortable, familiar and probably correct. She says she is due to have lunch with her father, then back home by evening to take over Tiggy.

"Where's Pete?" I ask.

"He's going out on a date tonight," she says.

"Is that weird?"

"He can do what the fuck he likes," she says. "I'm done."

"Are you going to tell him about us?"

"Who's us?" she says, bursting my bubble.

"Well, if us, becomes us."

"We'll cross that bridge if we come to it," she says. Hmm, I think. The eagle hasn't landed, and we're not crossing bridges. Should I ask her about not mentioning anything to Dyfed. No, I think, I've already pushed it. We've got a long way to travel.

She doesn't want breakfast. Rarely eats in the mornings, she says. I want to make her scrambled eggs whipped with cream and sprinkled in chives and a huge mushroom fried in olive oil and garlic. It's all in the fridge. Maybe next time.

We shower and dress and say our goodbyes. It's like no goodbye I've ever experienced. It's full of hope and sadness and regret and her hips pressed against mine. I pray this time, it's not the last time.

Given my way, I would see her tomorrow.

And the day after that.

The last look she gives me as she turns away isn't full of the happiness I am feeling. Something isn't right, but I am not going to admit that to anyone - most of all myself.

Chapter 10: WUTHERING HEIGHTS

"Whatever our souls are made of, his and mine are the same."

Emily Bronte

It's a month before I see Charlie again. A terrible month. I experience some of my lowest lows. Have some of my wildest tantrums. I'm not focussing on my writing and I've just found myself rereading a huge chunk of *A Gentleman in Moscow* I realise I've already read.

I go to Book Club, but Orla isn't here, and I feel out of place. Aude says hi, then moves the name cards so she is sitting next to Oli. Something about their body language is telling me it's much less than a month since they've seen each other. Lucky bastard. I want to contribute to the discussion, but I don't have the energy. In fact, my life is suffering from an infusion of can't-be-arsedness. Marcus snorts his way through the evening like a sarcastic bull. Trying not to get wound up by him, I look across the river and watch a couple stop and kiss. I think that line you think - *get a room* - and then smile to myself and feel happy for them, and then I feel jealous. I think about Charlie and what she's doing. I have no idea what she's doing and don't want to think she's in the arms of another man. There's nothing I can do about it if she is. After last weekend, I elected to walk here tonight. On the way home I can only manage half-pace and it's near midnight by the time I'm wrestling with my front door.

Last weekend?

Ah yes, last weekend, I scraped a concrete bollard down the side of my car from headlight to brake light. Fortunately, my reckoning with a breathalyzer was avoided by the local constabulary being preoccupied with a riot in Clapham and I snuck away under the cover of smoke from a burning launderette.

Yes, I'm doing stupid things again. I can't blame Charlie, she's got her own shit to deal with. But I'm feeling more lost than ever. To experience the taste of the most delicious, long-desired future, only for it to slip from my tantalising grasp, is smarting more than not having it in the first place. It's doubled my anger at the situation with Claire. I've been bombarding her with text messages, moist of which aren't entirely constructive.

I think it's fair to say my experiment with Beck's Blue is over. I don't know how many whiskey's I drank when I got in, but I suspect my weekly recommended alcohol intake is but a speck in my rear view mirror. I'm convinced Charlie doesn't want to be with me, so I'm taking Melissa's advice and I'm downloading Tinder onto my phone. I want to see what all the fuss is about. Well, that's what I tell myself. Perhaps I'm doing research for a piece. I've heard so many tales of unbounded sex between people who hardly bothered to swap names, let alone life stories. I crop Claire out of a picture of us and upload it to my profile. Setting the net to 20Km (Charlie lives 80km away) I set about swiping.

My god, there are a lot of women out there.

Every shape and size and level of desperation. They seem to fall into three categories: The fitness freaky, yoga types who specify non-smoker and the man must be tall; the downright unattractive, but as human as the next person and the putting-it-out there, bikini shot, come-and-get-it's. Ruling myself out of the first group, I make an assorted selection from the other two.

I find the act of swiping so brutal. With a flick to the left a human being cast into the pit of 'nope,' never to be seen again. A flick to the right and intent is declared. The first match I get is an attractive looking woman from Reigate called Andrea, who quickly admits lying about her age in order to get better matches. She's fifty-nine. Still we exchange messages back and forth and for a while, I think I might get to explore the outer reaches of post-menopausal sex.

She toys with me, but a speculative trip to Reigate is beyond the radius of even my pathetic self.

When I wake the next morning there's a text from Charlie. I instantly panic she's seen me on Tinder. Nope, she's asking if we can meet. Yay! My Tinder account is deleted in seconds before I reply. I realise I have to focus on myself. The only way I have of any chance of a life with Charlie, is if I am someone worth building a life with. I really need to get a grip, get fit, get on with my book. I don't know how many false starts I've had so far, but I'm determined to really hold it together this time. The only problem is there's a Halloween Party tonight at Matt and Jess's. How will I not get drunk and make a dick of myself again? Perhaps by not drinking? There's a novel thought. Not sure how I'll explain it to Matt though. Matt likes a drink.

Halloween is an institution in our street. I hate Halloween. I hate it more when it's on a Monday, because Monday nights are for staying in and getting over Sunday. My South African friend Peers tells me I should never use the word hate. He grew up during Apartheid before his family emigrated to Britain. I guess that's where he gets the notion. It would be totally unfair of me to say he's a rare Afrikaans, but his liberal mind always strikes me as unique. Still, I hate Halloween. Tonight our street will burst forth in a cornucopia of plastic spiders, blood and body parts. Small children will be herded up and down dressed like Thriller video extras, clamouring for sweets and Chinese made plastic toys that will break by bedtime.

We did the whole thing a few times with Jack and Clara. They loved it of course. Claire would stay home drinking wine with other Mothers while I conducted the excruciating farce. Matt and Jess don't live on my street, they are a road down, so not truly part of the ghoulish massive, but close enough to be part of the fringe, still garnering knocks from the smart kids who strike out from the main group in search of untapped bounty.

Matt isn't short for Matthew, it's Matthias. He's English-Slovakian by descent, but you wouldn't know it. His accent crosses between a champion horse trainer and a Cockney darts champion. Transatlantic posh with a splash of cheeky-chap menace. Matt and Jess Hares, are as mad as their surname presupposes.

I bang out chapters eight and nine and then cringe at all the errors I have made when spell-checking. As dusk falls I start picking up the screams of sugar-rushed children and barks of exasperated parents. I shower and am disproportionately pleased to find my favourite t-shirt, washed and folded (though not ironed) in my drawer. I really must be getting it together.

"Come in, come in," says Matt, opening the door and giving me a man-hug. They operate a 365-day open door policy, tonight is just another excuse for a party. The house is full of parents like me, avoiding the horror of Halloween. Standing in the garden having a smoke, I chat to an older blonde lady called Vicky. She's wearing a fur coat, which may or may not be part of a Halloween costume. She's taller than me, but doesn't seem to possess the frame to be. I sneak a peek to see how high her heels are, they aren't. Odd that. Anyway, inevitably our conversation finds its way to hinting at my divorce. I don't know why I do that. I always seem to steer towards the conversation I tell people don't want to have, yet clearly I do .

"I've just got engaged," she says, pulling back the sleeve of her fur to reveal a workmanlike engagement ring.

"Congratulations," I say, as you do.

"So I've got nothing to worry about," she says. I'm not sure if she's being smug, mean or kind. I finish my fag before hers. We can't find an ashtray so designate a bush and throw our butts like we just don't care. Back inside I get talking to Vicky's fiancé. He's shorter than me, and Vicky, and most pygmies. Bald, with a magnificent pot-belly, there is no amount of breathing-in could conceal that sucker. He's clearly well-off. I don't know why I think that, there is nothing beyond an expensive watch telegraphing wealth - he's just got that air telegraphing success with a few bodies stranded in its wake. Again, within the minute I have flagged my divorce. The fiancé, called Frank, segues my divorce into his hate of Vicky's smoking.

"I hate Vicky smoking," says Frank. "Everyone who smokes, knows they shouldn't, they know every fag, shaves a few more minutes from their lives. Those minutes add-up and one day, they snuff it. But they still bloody smoke."

Odd, I think, to be brandishing her negatives before they walk up the aisle.

"I didn't smoke at all during my marriage," I say, "only when it ended."

"Both my first and second wives had affairs," says Frank, "everyone who has affairs, knows they shouldn't. They know they are traitors. And, they know they will eventually get caught. But they still do it."

"My wife didn't have an affair," I say, adding, "I don't think. She just ran off with the kids."

Frank says, "every parent says their kids are the most important thing in their lives. That it's all about the children. They will do anything to provide and protect them. Most would leap in front of a flying bullet to protect their kids. I would. But still they smoke and shag people they shouldn't."

Frank is either an arch-Buddhist, who's hidden his robes in his Bentley for fear of being mistaken as a killer Halloween Monk, or a sucker for women who end up running off. Maybe the two are linked. I think working on reducing his circumference might help.

"So, why?" I ask, mining Frank's wisdom, "do those dedicated parents, still stand by the dustbins having a cheeky fag or jump into bed with people they shouldn't?"

"Because they are unhappy," he says straight out. "An unhappy parent is no good at parenting if they are unhappy. An unhappy parent is inattentive and careless. Unhappy parents do stupid things like smoke and have affairs."

He has a point. I can't help thinking of Vicky outside puffing away and wondering if she's already happy with her lot apart from her diamond ring. I tap into Frank's way of thinking and think, smokers and adulterers know their actions are treasonable. Yet the flame flickers. The lungs wilt. The blood rises. I think about Alice. Is she a traitor, or a sex addict? Is Dyfed a traitor, or a serial adulterer?

Oh Buddha, it's such a mess.

And what about Claire and Orla? What is their nicotine? Perhaps they do have men tucked away somewhere. A man, representing what they want in life – whether they admit the fact or not. Maybe just the idea of a different man provides enough lure to reach for the nuclear button.

Vicky reappears and leads Frank from the kitchen like she's taking him to the gallows. It might be the gallows to hang him from, or tie him to and tell he'd been a very a naughty boy. I'm betting on the latter.

Thankfully my dear friend Adrian appears. "Hello mate," I say, slightly too-high pitched, genuinely pleased to see him. "I haven't seen you in ages. Where have you been?"

"Uganda," he says, like he's just got back from IKEA. Adrian is stupidly tall, highly-intelligent and unashamedly independent. He was always the one to buck the clarion of the puerile conventions of our Gang. He was, and is married to Gemma, one of the most awesome women I've ever met. If you mix the selflessness of Mother Teresa with the fortitude of Ellen McCarthur and the sexiness of Heather Graham, you get Gemma. I love Gemma. Their marriage has survived despite the expense of Adrian's nicotine habit – adventure.

Adrian and Gemma aren't the unfaithful type. They just wouldn't. Adrenalin is Adrian's mistress. Her siren call somehow always manages to overpower his love for his wife and kids. Not that he doesn't love them completely.

Adrian spent last Christmas on the side of the Matterhorn. Two Christmases before that, he pulled his crackers on the Great Wall of China. When Gemma was in labour with their first child, Kit, he made it back from the Andes with only hours to spare. The birth box firmly ticked, he missed Kit's first birthday recreating Hannibal's trek over the Alps. It's not that he doesn't love his family. I guess that's the power of nicotine. He puts his family at no less risk than the smoker or the adulterer. Arguably, considerably more. Still, he is lauded and tolerated, while his unscrupulous counterparts are subjected to lynch mob derision. Believe me, I'm not trying to morally equate adultery, smoking and adrenaline-seeking, though arguably their reasons are born of forms of selfishness.

I wonder what Frank would say on the subject, I can only imagine he'd have been verbose. He'd probably say something like, selfishness can be healthy, and selfishness can be evil. To truly understand someone, their selfishness must be held up in the light. If it is the evil kind, why are they doing it? If it is the healthy kind, why are they doing it? Thanks Frank.

"How are things?" asks Gemma, appearing next to her husband. "I'm OK," I say. "I'm learning a lot about me and marriage."

"Anything you want to share?"

"Well, I'm not sure now, who I was. I think that might have been part of the problem."

I wasn't going to say this out loud, for fear of public assassination, but during my marriage, I'm not sure my family and children were quite enough. They didn't quite colour the full picture. I think I lacked a sense of self, without which, substitutes too easily rushed the void.

"And what about now?" Asks Gemma. She's a teacher and asks questions like those annoying HR people, but I can take it from her. Adrian looks on impassively, his head in clouds 10,000 feet above sea-level.

"I think I lost my sense of self, partly because I saw her nagging and bloody-fucking-mindedness as a direct attack on me, not our situation."

"I think that's normal isn't it darling?" She says looking up at Adrian. "I'm always having a go at you."

I'm not sure Adrian is actually going to speak, then he says, "you felt emasculated, right? You need to come and climb a mountain with me. That'll make a man of you. We're running over the Massive Centrale in the Spring. Do you fancy it?"

I can't think of anything worse.

"Yeah, I'd love to," I say, "I'd need to get fit."

"Don't be silly darling, " says Gemma. "he's only got short legs." She is a teacher who is sometimes a little too frank. Where is Frank?

I know Claire felt disenfranchised by my lack of recognition of her efforts to bring up our family and nurture our marriage. It chipped at her edifice. She broke first. Had we both had something to define us other than our marriage, our kids, maybe the outcome would have been different. In the melee of marriage, she felt unable to be her. I felt unable to be me.

Perhaps I should climb a mountain.

"I'm beginning to figure how all this works," I say to Gemma. "There's no point pivoting my arguments around Claire's decision to leave me. I can't blame her, the blame, like everything is mutual."

"It's good to hear you say that," shs says, "but I think you're taking too much of it on your shoulders. Don't forget Claire's part in this."

"Yeah, but say she did actually have an affair, which she might have. I don't know. She left because she was unhappy. For a long time, I stood by my position; I wish she had given me warning. At least the chance to try. And if we failed, to figure out what was best and try and control the fallout."

Everything about our divorce seems so incredibly unfair. I need to find a way through the fog of raw anger, guilt and regret and grasp the fifty-fifty of failure. To be the father I am, but am prevented from being. Our job as parents is to keep unwrapping, like a child's game of pass-the-parcel. With every layer comes a little more truth. It often doesn't feel like the truth. It feels like daylight robbery, a capital crime to which I was wrongly accused of being the perpetrator. But with each new layer revealed, my perspective is morphing. Eventually, after what feels like the world's longest game, we reach the core. Two little parcels revealed - Jack and Clara are the remnants of our marriage. They are the reason I want to build a new life and this time water and nurture it, not leave it on the window sill to wilt in the sun, die in the cold.

I say to Gemma, "Before the apocalypse I was on a trajectory. I did the twenties thing, had fun, got laid. Then I met a girl, said, I love you, let's get married and have kids. We bought a house. The kids went to school, my career went from strength to strength. Then we bought our 'forever' house, a bigger car and just as were settling in for old age and grandchildren and a comfortable descent into senility, wham!"

Gemma looks at me impassively, I can't tell if she thinks I'm talking nonsense or affording me HR style sympathy.

"You'll get there darling," she says.

"I don't know. I really don't know. The only thing I can do is leave my children with as few scars as possible. There are no winners in divorce Gemma. For fuck sake don't get divorced. Look after that man of yours, even if he is always up bloody mountains."

"I intend to," she says, "I intend to."

"Still banging on about divorce?" Says Frank, reappearing.

"Yeah, sorry," I say, "it seems to be my only subject."

Gemma opens the fridge in search of an excuse to step away from our conversation.

"I was like you the first time," says Frank, "but you'll get used to it."

"I don't intend to get divorced again," I say, "or for that matter, married again."

"I hear you're seeing Charlie," says Gemma, closing the fridge door.

"Hardly seeing," I say, "we just reconnected."

"You're seeing a man?" Asks Frank.

"Ha! No, Charlie is a woman. Charlotte."

"Thank god for that," says Frank, "you don't look the type to get the wrong bus home."

"Perhaps I should try men?" I say.

"Perhaps you should," says Gemma.

Chapter 11: WHEN WE WERE YOUNG

"A bear, however hard he tries, grows tubby without exercise."

A.A. Milne

Tuesday is a late start and a poor attempt at writing a piece on why workers should take their full lunch breaks, followed by a pint of Cider of which I manage only half before switching to a bottle of Red to ramp down the effects of Halloween.

Wednesday isn't my fault. It's my pre-planned monthly catch-up with Dyfed. We both have to work the next day and resolve just to have a couple, which turns into a skinful and a curry and a bottle of Red back at mine.

Thursday I don't drink. I think about going for a run, but the thought isn't compelling enough for me to seek out my trainers, and anyway, I really have no idea where they are. I go to bed early with Count Rostov, who is having something of a drink himself. He's got into a wager with a German and a Brit standing at the bar of the Metropol over the merits of their respective homelands contributions to culture. Amor Towles describes how the Count wins it for Russia, leaving me breathless with jealousy at the beauty of his writing:

"For if the Tolstoy dropped him in a barrel, and the Tchaikovsky set him adrift, then the caviar sent him over the falls."

I will never match that level of writing. Where does that poetry come from in a writer's brain? I manage to read a full chapter and make aim for sleep.

Friday, Charlie will be here tomorrow, so I'm cleaning the house top to bottom, removing every festering fingerprint of Claire I can find. It's early evening and the house is looking spotless when the knocker on my front door clatters, the bell has been broken for months. It's an urgent, mean-spirited slap and clatter, as if some stern-faced authority is standing on the other side with an official letter. A reprehmand perhaps. Maybe it's Social Services with a straightjacket. I twist and tug the door open with its usual protest. No, it's Rowan Kinsey. He's a Dad from the school touchline. This is a surprise. I've shared the odd post-match cup of tea with him, but I don't know him that well. "Hi Tom," he says. There is a bottle of rose wine in his hand. He asks if he can come in. I've chatted with Rowan at the odd event. He always seems interested in what I have to say. Despite being nearly a foot taller, he never looks down on me. It's a rare skill that. I invite him in and he casually asks how things are, like you might briefly engage the familiar figure behind the counter at the corner shop. I remember Orla (or was it Melissa?) telling me not to play the victim, so I say, "I'm good."

"Glad to hear it," he says.

I'm suspecting an agenda. He's an emissary for a concerned third-party, about to tell me to lay off the drinking, or take up golf or some such pointless life hack to keep me north of insanity. "Where's the corkscrew?" he asks. I know reverse psychology when I see it. Perhaps his plan is to get me so drunk I will swear afterwards never to touch a drop again. We rearrange two chairs to face each other down the same side of the kitchen table. He pours, we toast and drink, and before long we laugh. No agenda manifests. No speeches. It seems he's just being company. If I want to talk about Claire and the kids, that's fine. If not, that's fine too. I can hear my words, but there's a background dialogue going on in my head - disbelief we're even having this conversation; overwhelming gratitude for Rowan's presence. I'm not far off tears. I fight back my falter with a question, "did Claire and I make a good couple?"

"Yes," he says with a little too much emphasis.

"Claire said we had a terrible marriage, that she'd been unhappy for years," I say. "I know you didn't know us that well, but from what you saw of us...."

He nods and half-smiles and raises one eyebrow, like the sympathy emoji.

"Now I can't remember if we'd been happy or not. Or when we stopped being happy." I say.

"No-one suddenly stops being happy and starts being sad. Unless..." he says.

"...unless someone gets caught having an affair?" I say. "Did Claire...?"

"No, thank god, or at least not that I'm aware."

"The problem is," muses Rowan, "I have realised, no-one thinks it will happen to them, until it does."

"You're right, it's like the normal people in a Police press conference on TV, pleading for the return of their abducted child, or cat, or Porsche Cayenne, saying, stuff like that doesn't happen around here."

"And then you end up suspecting...."

"Ha! Yes always. You always suspect it's one of the people at the press conference whodunnit!"

Given how little I know him, and despite I keep interrupting him, Rowan's visit feels the single biggest act of kindness I've received yet. Glasses refilled, he lets me talk. I talk for fear of stopping and my tears filling the silence. Company that asks for nothing in return is chicken soup for people like me. If there is a pause he tips in a gentle question and immediately I'm back at some point of my concentric thesis, inescapably revolving to a shrug and conclusion - *it is what it is.* Eventually I remember my manners and ask how he is. His response reminds me I'm not the only shit-show in town. He's been through his own messy divorce. After four kids, Jules, his wife of ten years upped and left for a younger man. He, like me, like all of us, was devastated. He tells me, people used to cross the street rather than talk to him. Not out of malice, or even because they didn't care. They just didn't know what to say. Up to now, I've considered some of the people I thought I knew to be the most heartless bastards ever encountered. Not a single call. Not a text message. Let alone an offer of a drink or supper. What he's telling me is the people who, in my eyes have abandoned me, in reality, simply don't know how to engage. He equates it to a line up at a funeral. He says, how many people can say to the bereaved, I'm so   sorry   for   your   loss?

"My friend Orla has made me join a Book Club," I say, "to get me out of the house and meet people."

"That's a good idea," says Rowan.

"I don't think it's for me, it's full of weirdos and not really my comfort zone."

"I think it's the best thing you could possibly do - get out of your comfort zone. You should stick at it."

"I know you're right," I say, "I'll do my best."

The evening ends with half a bottle of Port, and at some point Rowan let's himself out, but I have no recollection of that.

Saturday, Charlie arrives with two bottles of Pink wine, saying she isn't sure how naughty we were being. Naughty, I confirm, putting one in the fridge next to the bottle of White chilling nicely. On the side, a bottle of Red stands in reserve.

We talk and talk. I'm making supper, but it's a sideshow, I just want to talk and drink.

"I love our talks," says Charlie.

Taking this like a bull takes a red rag, I talk more. She listens. I pour more.

The pork hasn't turned out quite as I hoped. The chops have shrivelled and taken on a grey tinge. The fat hasn't crackled, it's shriveled. I've over cooked the broccoli and the packet gravy I've disguised with onions, garlic, black pepper and sea salt, tastes like it's from a packet.

I'm chewing on a piece of pork and it's refusing to go down.

Oh shit, this isn't good, I have a terrible feeling I know what happens next. The sick rises in my mouth like a trapped air bubble finally released from the deep.I try to hide it from Charlie, but have to run to the bathroom clutching my face, spraying putrid vomit as I go.

This is not my finest hour. Returning sheepish from the bathroom, Charlie takes it in her stride, like she does everything. But I know I have screwed up, this is far from good.

The evening continues until I can't remember the evening continuing and we go to bed and don't have sex. The sex-ban is still in force. I don't think we even hug.

I wake up to find Charlie already dressing. She has to get home to watch Tiggy play a match, she says. I guess that's what's called a wake-up-call. How can I stop drinking so much? I'm convinced I'm not yet an alcoholic. I know all alcoholics say that, but I had Thursday off, right? That said, I've never been sick in my mouth during dinner with a girl. I need to find the secret code, map, antidote, potion, magic flower or ancient artefact that will unlock my internal riddle. Unlocking internal riddles doesn't seem to be my forte these days.

Right now, I can't get past drink not being the problem, it's the solution.

It stands to reason (doesn't it?) when the Apocalypse went off, drink became the opium of my ransacked life. My home, ruthlessly robbed of everything I once held dear. My children. My wife. My hope. Our potato masher. Everything but regret, anger and injustice had been stuffed in a swag bag and carried off. In the detritus of life's burglary, drink was the anesthetic of choice, to be administered in copious amounts.

Alcohol softens the hard edges of my empty shelves. It masks the shadows left by the stolen paintings. It cares nothing for the stinking dishes in the sink, the soiled clothes on the floor. For the stupid decisions I make or the text messages I fired like indiscriminate artillery. Dangerous things, drunken texts. Sent in haste, screen-shot into perpetuity.

"Melissa?"

"Yes Love."

"I am an alcoholic."

"No you're not."

"Yes, I am."

"No, you're fucking not."

"Jesus. Isn't that supposed to be the hard part. Admitting it?"

"Perhaps Darling, but you're not an alcoholic. And you're not depressed either. You are drinking to drown your sorrows, like we all do. Admittedly you are pushing it a little right now, but that is understandable. And when you go on a bender for a couple of days it takes at least three days to get over it. You wake up on the first day feeling depressed. On the second day, you feel depressed, but a little less depressed and by the day you are feeling a lot better and feel like you could have another drink again."

"So, I'm an alcoholic."

"No! Are you putting vodka on your corn flakes in the morning?"

"No."

"Then you are not an alcoholic. Listen my old cock. I have known alcoholics. I've worked with enough broken hacks, swigging vodka out of water bottles in the toilets with their cocks in their hands. My father was an alcoholic and violent and brutal and would stop at nothing for another bottle of whiskey. That is not you."

"But surely there is a road to alcoholism?"

"Yes there is. But I know you. You are a romantic. You love your children too much. You are too attached to the idea of a happy ending to rob yourself of the chance of getting there. You know Fraulein wasn't right for you. I knew the first time I met her. You are not going to become an alcoholic, because you aren't going to give up."

"I don't understand where the lines are."

"That's my point. Actually you do. Have they put you on antidepressants?"

"Well," I say. "I was, but they didn't really do anything."

"Exactly. What fucks me off is everybody in this day and age is so desperate to rush to put a label on things, which then gives people license to live up to that label. Sure, you can say you're an alcoholic, you can say you're depressed. Knock yourself out. But you're not."

"But…"

"But nothing. Look I'm not making light of alcoholism or depression, both of which are really serious and really exist all around us. You went to your doctor, said you were feeling depressed so he gave you some pills and said come back in a month. They give them out like smarties at a paedophile convention. I feel for you, I really do. I can't imagine what it's like, because I don't have kids. But I'm old enough and ugly enough to know this is the toughest fucking battle you have ever fought. But if you give into those convenient definitions, those labels, then that is what you will become."

Monday morning, it's a month until Jack and Clara come over pre-Christmas. Anybody can get their act together in a month. I'm taking Melissa's advice to heart. I don't know if she's right or dangerous, but she's touched a nerve somewhere in me.

I need to do this for the kids. And me. Not for Charlie. I've got Book Club in two weeks, so I need to find out how the Counts story ends. I will finish the book tonight.

I'm out of fags and I genuinely think I don't want a drink today. I really am going to go for a run. I know exactly where my trainers are, I was just pretending before. I'm nervous about running, I enjoy it but haven't pounded the pavement since before the Apocalypse. God knows what has taken residence in my lungs since then. I stretch as best I can but any former elasticity has shriveled up and resists every bend. I put my phone in my old rugby shorts pocket, figuring if I have a heart attack, I may be able to call 999 before I pass out. I slam the front door and take up a slow pace down the hill, game the lights and dodge the traffic at Wandsworth roundabout and head over the river. My intention is to head up the embankment and back over Albert Bridge. That should be plenty far enough.

I find the going remarkably good.

My lungs aren't protesting.

My legs are working.

I try and look like I do this every day to passers-by.

When anything female approaches, I pick up my pace.

Everytime I'm overtaken by another runner, I assume they are in advanced training for the marathon. Good on them, but it's not for me, thanks.

Townmead Road is much longer when I run it than in the car. I emerge from Imperial Park into Chelsea harbour wondering if I've bitten off more than I can chew and I'm trying to calculate whether turning back is quicker than keeping going over Albert Bridge. At the end of Lots Road where the nightclub Crazy Larry's used to be, I get a spurt of nostalgic energy. I think of the hundreds of nights we spent there in the nineties and can't remember a single specific one.

A group of school children has been corralled on the north side of Albert Bridge as I finally arrive and I am determined to not let them see an overweight, nicotine addicted, near-alcoholic divorcee. It would hardly be a good example. I suck in my stomach and pick up a quicker step I sustain to almost the other side of the bridge. There's no turning back now, I'm not in the home-straight but I'm on the home leg and I'm feeling knackered and leaden-legged, but good. Perhaps long dormant endorphins are emerging from their extended hibernation. If that's what they are, it's good to feel them.

The Thames is now firmly on my right shoulder and I'm doing the speed above fast-walk past the glass and steel apartments and trendy cake shops and converted wharfs housing trendy-looking workers who know who Dua Lipa is, and drink tea out of recycled jam jars.

In the last 100 yards I find some of my old vavoom. A heart attack isn't feeling likely, so I push the pace to the front door in case any neighbours are watching. With one hand on my gatepost, I gasp for breath and smile at the irrigative powers of sweat leaving my body laden with toxins. This doesn't feel good, but I know it will in a minute. I've achieved something. I take the app out of my pocket and it says I've run 5.2km. Wow. I used to be able to run 10km with little problem, but this is something, really something. My app asks if I want to share my run on Facebook. For the briefest of seconds my thumb hovers over the blue button, but I haven't told you how fast I ran 5.2km. I think the world can wait for news of my incredibly slow triumphs.

I'd like to report I am now in the sunny lowlands. I am, but they still serve booze and fags here, just not quite so much or so many. I'm averaging three runs a week and have added sit-ups to my daily routine. I feel like I want to give-up smoking, and I know from previous experience this is the beginning of the end. Now all I have to do is recognise the moment to grasp.

Claire has decided she will stay in Ireland with the children for Christmas. I can have them at New Year. Apparently this is a fair division of spoils. She tells me Christmas is just another day. What a fool I've been, all those Christmases I could have worked and earned triple time.

Gemma has invited me to spend Christmas at their house. It's an incredibly kind thought I instinctively think I will turn down. Then I consider my options. I still have two parents I could spend it with, though not under the same roof. I haven't had a perfect Christmas with both my parents since I was a small boy. Perhaps that is why I have become a little inured to the day, though not this year. If I spend it with Mum it will be emotional. With Dad, emotional. It will be for different emotional reasons, but I don't fancy emotions. I fancy a beach bar somewhere, where nobody knows my name.

A beach bar isn't going to happen is it?

I'll go to Gemma's.

And try not to cry.

Meanwhile, I've just thought of a plan.

Claire hates technology. More precisely, she hates it in the hands of our children. They have iPads of course. She limits their use to two hours at weekends. I find her completely draconian. Mean. But then, mean is all I see when I see her these days. Or think of her.

We have always been worlds apart on the technology subject. She took to heart the internet safety lectures we attended at Jack's school. I figure all we can do is attempt to lock down the dark and fleshy parts of the internet and prevent erroneous purchasing of power-ups, level-ups and boosts. But technology will win in the end.

Children will be children.

Children will outsmart their parents.

Children will become teenagers.

We're screwed.

My plan; to buy my kids mobile phones. To construct a digital bridge to Ireland. To have a daily transfusion of lifeblood in the shape of a text message or call. Claire will not be pleased. She'll say they are too young, that we can't afford it. Given half a chance, she'll close down the idea like a steel shutter on an Off-Licence.

I used to buy everything on iTunes. Used to buy pretty much everything Apple sells. Now, I reason, buying Jack and Clara cheaper mobile phones, cheaper than Apple, would be less incendiary to Claire. Like the provocation of buying a new car when still arguing about money is just not worth the fight. My SAAB is twelve years old and pulls violently to the left when I hit the brakes too hard. Cheaper Android phones will somehow pull less to the left.

I call Vodafone UK who say I need to talk to Vodafone Ireland. I redial and speak to a kind lady who understands the situation, sympathises, but without a local address – I'm not going to give them Claire's and alert her - plus the young age of my children sets the hurdles too high.

I need Plan B.

Plan B is Lucas. I haven't spoken to him in years. He's the husband of Lisa, Claire's best friend in Ireland. Sadly, Lisa plays no role in this story other than being Lucas's wife. Sad, because she is seriously beautiful and effortlessly kind. Tall, lean and blonde with shadow-casting cheekbones, she is, to my eye, the perfect example of femininity. You might think I am being disloyal to Gemma, who I have described in similar glowing terms. But, trust me, Gemma and Lisa are different. Gemma has an inner and sometimes outer Tomboy. Lisa's steel is layered in silk. If they make the movie, Robin Wright must play her, or Lena Headley.

Lucas is Lisa's perfect foil. He matches her elegance pound for pound. Tall, slim, perfectly coiffed and succinctly, expensively dressed. They don't have children, for reasons I don't know. If they had, their progeny would spawn from the most perfect gene pool. Boy or girl would be tall and beautiful and impeccably mannered. Such a shame they have not been able to contribute to the human race. Only good could come of it.

I send Lucas a message on Facebook. I'd seen his posts from time to time. My message summarises the situation. I hope he is well; it has been a long time; as he must know, Claire and I are getting divorced; I need to ask a favour. Etc. Etc. Blah, blah. He isn't the first or last old friend I've re-established contact with after the Apocalypse. Isn't it funny and sad, how marriage and the pressures of family and children provides the excuses to not stay in touch?

Asking someone for a favour, I haven't spoken to in years feels awkward. A little churlish. His reply returns in moments. Of course he had heard; he's seen Claire and the kids seemed okay; he is so sorry he hasn't been in touch; he didn't know what to say; of course, he would do me a favour; anything.

I well up a little at that. Little acts of kindness carry disproportionate power at the end of the world. Taking my cue, I elaborate a little further. I tell him how horrendous it has been; how much I miss the kids. I need his help to buy them mobiles which will work in Ireland. I don't know if he's particularly religious, but he sends me this:

The people dwelling in darkness have seen a great light, and for those dwelling in the region and shadow of death, on them a light has dawned. (Matthew 4:16)

Then he writes:

The valley of the shadow of death wouldn't have a 'shadow' if there isn't also a light source. Let me know what I can do. Name it Buddy.

I smile as I read his words in my head, imagining his thick Irish accent. *Name it Buddy.* Then I get what he means by the shadow cast in the Valley of Death. And burst into tears, I really have got to stop doing that.

Lucas is a legend. Within a day, he's bought two reconditioned Samsung mobiles. When they need more airtime or data, I can top them up online. He sends me the link and log-in details. Claire won't need to know any of the ins and outs. The phones are legal, functional and paid for. Father Christmas (Lucas) will deliver them on Christmas Eve. I will be able to speak to Jack and Clara whenever I like. They can call me when they need me. No free man can be denied that.

I go for another run.

I text Charlie.

I'm communing with Count Rostov when Melissa calls back.

"Still alive?"

"Yes."

"Excellent. I want you to do a piece on single men and cooking," she says. I'm to interview men like me on how we navigate supermarkets and kitchens; how we feed our children when we have them; what we cook for new women we are trying to woo. She wants examples of men who can't boil an egg, through to those who grasp their liberation with both oven gloves and cook their way to happiness and the hearts of single ladies.

I readily agree, I need something meaty to distract me from the dread of Christmas hanging over me. My initial digging shows most single men have one signature recipe they perfect (usually involving mince) and everything else involves the freezer or the microwave. I've emailed Graeme for his pheasant-pigeon recipe. Research I uncover shows most married Mum's only have four or five dishes they constantly cycle in between ready meals and take outs. Worrying the premise of my piece being only about single Dads might be innately sexist, I ask Orla for her take.

"I can't cook," she says. "I have meals delivered three times a week."

"What about feeding your kids," I ask.

"They eat some of the meals," she says, "but mostly chicken nuggets."

I write down my recipe for Sea Bass surprise. I have never written a recipe before. Channeling Jamie Oliver I find myself writing drizzle, bosh, splash and Bob's your uncle. I write down the recipe for Pizza Wraps I learned from Claire – tomato paste, handfuls of spinach, ripped Mozzarella, cherry-toms cut across their equator, layers of Prosciutto, fresh thyme, fresh chillies and a glug of olive oil. Then I decide to add stories to the recipes to give them colour. How men repurpose ready meals pretending they've cooked them; how they dress a kitchen like a set and act the part of chef; which music is the best for loosening blouse buttons. Apparently nobody relies on Barry White anymore. Who knew? I begin to think about a career pivot, becoming a food writer. Or writing a cookbook for single Dads, now there's an idea.

I patch together periods of at least two hours without thinking about Jack and Clara and bloody Claire and bloody Christmas, though their presence is never far beneath the surface.

Visiting local independent Delicatessens and talking to the owners I learn about ingredients and shortcuts and how to cook above your weight. I email Melissa and say everything is coming together, but need a few more days. I call Dad, he's single.

"Can't boil an egg Tom," says Dad.

"Exactly," I say, "that's why I need to speak to you."

Chapter 12: LES MISERABLES

"Even the darkest night will end and the sun will rise."

Victor Hugo

Charlie hasn't replied to my text of two days ago. True closure seems to be an ever-moving mirage. I'm beginning to think this whole sorry mess is going to take at least three years to wash through and arrive at a new normal. Things aren't so bad, I'll see the kids in two weeks time, they will get their mobile phones at Christmas. I send my cooking piece to Melissa and she replies it's good, it will be published in the New Year - just after the traditional spike in divorce applications in the first week of January.

I'm feeling fitter than I have in living memory, though I'm still smoking, I can almost justifiably class myself a social smoker. Perhaps I'll become an ex-smoker in the New Year. It's Charlie really. She is rock, paper, scissors - a thirty-three per cent gamble over which I have no control. She has her own situation to deal with. Her own guilt at failure. At first the unexplained radio silences bugged me. I can't figure her out, until I figure it out. I already know it isn't all about me, then I realise it's not even all about us. Time spent together, will be a rare luxury for months and years to come. We must stand in line behind the innocent casualties of our wars, children requiring constant care. There is no way to avoid a brick by brick rebuild. Infrastructure must be reestablished and short-term goals and long-term dreams reset. Time, time, time will be what it takes. A lot of time and patience and strength. And less booze and no fags. And it's Tuesday, so Book Club.

We're at the table waiting for the full jury to arrive. So far it's just myself, Orla, Veronica, Jenita and the oleaginous Marcus. And, of course, Ian, who fills the space by reminding me I was going to give my thoughts on The Quiet American. That was months ago and nothing insightful is springing to mind so I say, "the thing I liked about it was its size. It's less than two hundred pages, so it wasn't threatening. It's almost a pamphlet."

"Unlike For Whom the Bell Tolls."

I ignore Ian and say, "the truth is The Quiet American is one of the first fictions I had read in a long time. For years I had become obsessed with factual books. Also, due to my work I have a lot of background research to do on the places I was reporting on. So when I came across The Quiet American, which of course centres around a foreign correspondent, it was kind of like research, I found it an easy read. I loved it."

"So some books are just too long?" asks Ian. "To be a classic does a book have to be long? Bell Tolls? War and Peace? East of Eden?"

"The Quiet American is a classic," says Marcus, "I agree with Tom."

Which is a surprise.

"The thing with some of these classic books," I say, "is it feels we are supposed to be drawn along by the writing without necessarily knowing where the story is going. And when that's five hundred pages, it's a big commitment. I'm certainly finding it with A Gentleman in Moscow. It took me a long time to get into it, but then it pulled me to the end."

Marcus picks up his copy, flicks to the back and says, "four hundred and sixty-two."

"Are you saying books should follow a formula?" Asks Ian. "A problem, followed by hope, followed by hope dashed, followed by happy resolution? Like films?"

"No. I'm just saying, sometimes the writer asks a lot of the reader."

Thus, the conversation continues as the others file in. Oli and Aude come in together, they are definitely an item. We talk about factual versus fictional, and what one remembers from a book after the back cover has been closed for the last time, and the blurb on the back reread to see if it lives up to what has just been consumed. I recount one of the last factual books I read was all eight hundred pages of Antony Beevor's Stalingrad and isn't it bizarre I could only remember a single fact from the entire read - General Paulus was in charge of the final retreat of the Fifth Army before it was forced to capitulate.

"It was the Sixth Army, and Paulus was Field Marshal," corrected Marcus, just as I was beginning to consider he may have hidden qualities beneath his European missense of fashion. Nope.

When everybody is assembled we return to Moscow and everyone delights at how Sofia, Count Rostov's ward, became his de facto daughter and isn't it odd he had a relationship with Sofia's mother when she was just a child and skirt into dangerous waters of old men and young girls. Ian seems to like it when we drift off topic. The psycho-analyst in him prods the conversation like an annoyingly inquisitive child, thinking we can't see what he is trying to do, and thinking how smart he is we can't see it.

My phone is vibrating in my pocket. It stops, it must be a message. I hesitate to take it out (Ian doesn't approve of phones at the table) but curiosity is having none of it, and text messages are for me, heaven sent - unless it's from O2 telling me my online bill is ready. It might be Charlie.

It's Matt.

Any chance you can come over mate? Serious trouble at mill. Wouldn't ask, but urgently need someone to look after Mandy. Can you come?

Matt needs me. All I have done since, well, you know since when, is need other people. To be needed feels great, even though the reason I'm needed doesn't sound good. The chance to do something for someone else immediately pulls me to my feet and an apology as I exit, mouthing *crisis* as I make eye contact with Orla.

I've got the Uber app, but don't know how to use it so hail a good old-fashioned black cab on Hammersmith roundabout and say Matt's road name to the cabby with enough bark to convey urgency without being rude. I feel like the cavalry racing to the rescue, but the driver has opted to go down the North End Road when I would have gone south of the river and there are roadworks he swears weren't there yesterday.

We edge forward behind a modern double-decker bus with one of those engines that cuts out every time the driver takes his foot off the accelerator and vibrates back to life when he touches it again. I text Orla, explaining Matt and Jess are having a crisis. I add a second message, typing I'm off to the rescue and add an exclamation mark. While we've got a minute, I'll tell you a bit more about Matt and Jess. I've been spending more and more time at their house, taking their open-door policy to literal levels – I know where they hide the spare key and no longer bother apologising when I let myself in. They don't seem to mind.

When they first got together, each brought a daughter from their former lives. Jess read History at St. Anne's College, Oxford. In her first year she got pregnant by her tutor, a serial cruiser modelling himself on a young Michael Caine without the good bits. Fair play to Jess, she stayed on, brought up her first daughter (Shelley) while continuing her studies and got a 2:1.

Matt was born to be a salesman, he forged a successful career straight out of school and moved in with a girl called Kathy, the love of his life at the age of twenty. Their daughter, Bella was the apple of his eye. She was four when Kathy told him he wasn't the father. Kathy's plan, if she had one, didn't go to plan. She eventually abandoned Bella to Matt whom he had never stopped loving as his own. To the world at large, they are father and daughter. A bit like Count Rostov I suppose. I can see Matt as a Count, I think he could inhabit those shoes, he is, after-all, one of life's philosophers. One evening I found the courage from my own situation to ask Matt if Bella knew she wasn't his daughter. He replied, she knows, and left it at that.

We're over Talgarth Road and stuck in more traffic leading up to the mini roundabout on The Fulham Road. I text Matt to say I'm getting there as fast as I can. The real cavalry never have to do this, they just appear on the brow of a hill and whoop their way into battle.

We're crawling through the streets we used to stagger through when we were the gang and single and unencumbered. Matt was encumbered, but in my memories he was always there. He always carried kudos in the Gang being a father - that wasn't - at such a young age. It was like he'd lived a lifetime, when the rest of us were still trying to get laid. Matt and Jess built their love story around the hook and crook of two daughters with dubious provenance, then they made Mandy together. Mandy and our Clara were best friends. Before Claire left, I would often take or collect or babysit Mandy.

When Matt is drunk and out of female earshot, he summarises his trio of daughters as a step (Shelley), a whole-hearted (Bella) and a thoroughbred (Mandy). Despite, or perhaps because of living life so young, he and Jess are the most together couple I know. They have each other, they have money, they have a pile of shit behind them, yet always seem to be on the yellow brick road to even more happiness. And they've been there for me every hop, skip and fall-on-my-face of the way. Matt and Jess both come from large families and have unlimited friends, acquaintances and contacts. If you need a hitman, billionaire, plumber or minor royal, just ask Matt and Jess.

Okay, we're turning onto Wandsworth Bridge Road. Almost there. I run through a mental checklist. Nobody needs to know where I am, because nobody cares. I can be at Matt's all night if need be. I've got work tomorrow, but I can grab my laptop and work from their place if whatever this is, spills on.

"It's Bella," says Matt. He's standing at their front door as Jess pushes past me without acknowledging me.

"She's bleeding."

I look at Matt in a way I hope conveys I understand, but don't understand.

"A baby," he says.

Then he shouts, "Fuck!"

And then he says, "please can you just look after Mandy. I'll text you as soon as I know what's going on."

And they're gone, Matt's Audi TT racing down their road like a Top Gear Special.

Mandy is standing in the hall looking at me with pleading eyes.

She asks, "is it a problem with the baby?"

"Errm, I don't know love," I say. "I'm afraid I don't know what's going on." I'm being honest, I don't know. Surely Mandy is too young to be pregnant.

"Come on," I say, putting my hands on her shoulders, her face burying in my stomach. "Have you had tea?" I can't help thinking of Clara, she's ten now. I think, because my mind thinks things when I don't ask it, Clara will be starting her periods before long. And Mandy too. And then I wonder whether I should even be thinking such things, and whether such thoughts should just be left to Mothers?

"It's the baby," says Mandy.

I hesitate, but children seem to be born young adults these days.

"Is she having a baby?"

"Yes," she says.

"Oh Lord," I say.

"Oh shit," says Mandy. I struggle to muster an appropriate response. No matter; my friend's ten-year-old daughter is lost to the staircase before I exhale my next breath.

I sit motionless in the kitchen, listening to the creaking first-floor floorboards. The thump of Victorian pipes clanging in wall cavities. It sounds like Mandy is running a bath. Normality In catastrophe, a sibling going about her routine. Me, the impromptu babysitter in the vacant kitchen, unsure what to do next. In the absence of anything better, I Google pregnancy and bleeding and see a million results with the words miscarriage and ectopic in bold blue letters.

Poor, poor Bella.

Poor Matt and Jess.

My phone rings just after 10pm, it's Matt. He tells me details are still unclear but Bella has lost four pints of blood. She has lost the baby. No baby can survive such a traumatic bleed. He is matter-of-fact, emotion bubbling-under like a pot of soup on an unattended gas ring. He asks if Mandy is in bed. I say, she is, though I'm not sure. Matt thanks me and says he'll be home before midnight. Jess is staying in hospital with Bella overnight.

Mandy had appeared earlier wearing pyjamas, after what seemed a very long bath. We watched an episode of a teen sitcom on Nickelodeon together, the post-pubescent actors, wholesome and impossibly quick-witted. Neither of us laughed. As the credits mercifully rolled, I pecked a kiss goodnight on her forehead, muttering she should brush her teeth. A pointless act of pseudo-parenting under the circumstances.

My mind keeps turning over the terrible time Annabel lost Rory. We will never get over it. Least of all Annabel, to be cruelly robbed of life in its prime and so full of promise is simply too much for a human being to fully-process. My problems are feeling properly inconsequential in comparison.

I don't look at my watch when Matt walks in. Don't want to look like I care what the time is. He keeps saying he had no idea she was bloody pregnant. As if his forced ignorance is somehow to blame. As if he could have saved the baby, had he known. He doesn't mean that, but in the absence of anything more insightful, little else seems worth saying.

Matt pours two oversized Brandies. Handing me a balloon glass, he sits on the sofa beside me. The first sip scorches my lungs on the way south. Subsequent sips slide down with encouraging forgiveness. Staring blankly at nothing in particular, we trade muttered expletives - carelessly coded transmissions for feelings we can't process. I clasp his knee, physically connecting our emotional impotence. He doesn't flinch.

More brandy.

"How come she was bloody pregnant?"

Matt isn't after a biology lesson. Under normal circumstances he'd have been incandescent at the boyfriend for getting his daughter pregnant at seventeen. Now the baby has gone there is no place to be angry.

I find myself with the awkward sensation of relief. Or something like that. For the first time in as long as I want to remember, the drama isn't about me. Other people have bigger, meaner, nastier problems. This is true life and death. A life never to be realised. I spy the futility in my own self-pity.

My phone buzzes. It's Charlie. Hallelujah! Christ, she picks her moments. I don't want Matt to think I'm texting news of their misfortune, so say I am going for a pee, close the toilet door behind me and read her text with the hand not otherwise occupied. She's in town on Friday, asking if she can come to stay.

I reply, *does a horse piss where it pleases?*

Then I delete that and type, of course she can, it will be lovely to see her.

And add a kiss for good measure.

X

Matt's phone rings. I brace for more bad news – as if it could get any worse. Politely tuning out, I try to lip read the TV News Reporter, reporting some political shenanigan from Downing Street. The reporter drones on, oblivious we have the volume turned-down. Oblivious Bella has lost her baby.

Then Matt shouts "Twins?!"

Oh god, I think, she's lost two.

"Twins?!"

Matt falls to his knees crying uncontrollably. I am gutted for him. Sod my divorce.

He is trying to tell me something. Then I sense a turn of his mouth conveying hope as he grabs my hand.

"The baby's there," he blurts.

I must confess, we get so drunk in the ensuing few hours, the subsequent few minutes are lost to me forever. To this day, I don't know if Bella had officially been diagnosed as carrying twins, losing one. I do know, in the frenzy of an all-hands crash situation, the duty Radiographer pronounced Bella had lost the baby, declaring such blood loss untenable for a foetus. A Consultant had appeared, intervening and overruling in a flurry of calm, unequivocal authority.

Two days later, the dust still settling, Bella is home from the hospital in time for Christmas, filling in some details. She says it was the closest thing she could imagine to an earthly intervention by an angel.

Clutching her sizable bump with interlocked fingers, she says, "I will never forget what the Doctor said - lie still, I am not going to say anything for at least a minute. Do not read anything into that. I just need time. I was rigid from terror. Like, being buried alive in my own nightmare."

I stare back thinking I know a bit about what that feels like.

"A minute later," she says, "the Doctor broke her silence saying; there it is. Legs, abdomen, head. All perfectly normal. Do you want to know what sex it is?"

"My ears, eyes and brain and body were completely discombobulated," says Mandy. I think discombobulated is a strange choice of word for Bella – like it is a made up word, when actually it is perfectly apt.

She says, "I saw smiles, heard annoyingly matter-of-fact confidence, felt the tears streaking my face and trickles of warm liquid running down my bum. Then I heard the consultant say again, it's Okay Love. Do you want to know what sex it is? I couldn't think straight. I couldn't remember if Tim and I had discussed knowing the baby's sex. So, I said no. I still didn't truly believe the baby was alive."

Bella's baby is in at the end of the month. Secretly I hope it comes early, on Christmas day, so I can somehow get involved in the excitement and take my mind off not being with Jack and Clara. Don't want another drama though, probably best if it hangs on until New Year.

It's Friday again and Charlie's here. It's three days to Christmas and the last time I will see her this year. She will be spending Christmas week in Suffolk, shuffling Tiggy between Pete and his new girlfriend and his parents. It sounds ghastly to me, so I don't ask much and try to come to terms with the fact I won't be spending New Years Eve with her. My poorly hung decorations are an embarrassment seeming to entirely miss the Yuletide point as we sit in my kitchen with a bottle of Red wine and a packet of Walkers Sensations. I think about putting them in a bowl, but Charlie seems happy picking from the packet.

I can't explain definitively to Charlie what happened with Bella, the baby somehow hanging on. I'm not sure anybody is entirely clear. Charlie doesn't press, she understands the horror of it all.

Other than that, our conversation is floundering.

Charlie fills every lull in our chat commenting on how sorry she is for Bella's nightmare. She must have said it a dozen times already. How are we running so low on things to talk about, so soon in our relationship? Something else is amiss. We attempt to mull over the cruelty and joy of life, the take and give. We speak in metaphors of our own situations. I try to interpret the subliminal messages she might be transmitting. The dot-dot-dot and dash-dash-dash of her narrative is sometimes clear, often contradictory. I gently nudge the conversation this way and that, baiting the odd hook to see if she will bite, only for it to resurface, glistening and clean. The bait washed away in the current of conversation.

Lying in our unconsummated bed, we get talking about our exes, trying to open windows into their souls and figure out why, and how, and what-the-heck?

Charlie says, "Pete wants to have Tiggy 50/50."

"OK," I say.

"I'm going to lose her," she says. I can only see her out of the corner of my eye, but I know her face is cracking. I have seen that crack appear on so many people in the last year. The crack that starts at the chin, splinters across cheeks and untaps tears.

"Don't be silly," I say, " of course you aren't."

"I am," she shouts with all the melodrama of Vivien Leigh to Clark Gable.

"Darling, you're not," I say firmly but kindly. "At least Pete wants to stick around. Some Fathers I could mention just piss off and leave their kids to high days and holidays. He's a good father and Tiggy needs him too."

Despite my logic being flawless, thank you; when it comes to their children, mothers operate on a level us men will never fully compute. We already know women are from Venus and capable of random acts that defy comprehension - which is perversely why we keep coming back, like Pavlov's child grabbing a cupcake wired to the mains, Ouch! Ouch! Ouch!

Mystery is part of a woman's allure. That and boobs. But add children into the mix and all bets are off. We all know about Mama Bear and Mama Tiger and never to threaten their cubs. Women are as maternally vicious as any bear or tiger, with the added capacity to add what looks from the outside like irrationality. But what do men know? Pete is fighting for what is rightfully his. I've said it before, children are the greatest casualties of divorce.

I lie there thinking Charlie needs to find her own conclusions. It's not for me to be part of the debate, so I shut up, close my eyes and look for sleep. I can see my simple existence dangerously colours her narrative. Are we together too soon? Should I give her more space? It hurts as a thought, given my own fragility. Imagining time without her is not an attractive prospect. But if we are meant to be, we are meant to be – that's what people tell me - don't rush into anything.

As ever, those people are usually right.

But who wants to listen to people?

We, the dispossessed, are on the frontline. Normal people are rear echelon staffers poring over maps, interpreting figures in dispassionate sanity behind the lines of good life.

We are deep in the muck and bullets.

Chapter 13: A ROOM WITH A VIEW

"Choose a place where you won't do very much harm, and stand in it for all you are worth, facing the sunshine."

E.M. Forster

I pick up Jack and Clara from Gatwick on the 28th.

I've survived Christmas by spending a lot of it sneaking away for walks - or taking myself off, as it has come to be known. I became very conscious of becoming a burden on anyone during the Festivities. Christmas day with Ade and Gemma and their extended family swallowed me up by the sheer volume of people and alcohol. I cried of course when I spoke to the children on their new phones, but tried not to let anyone see that. Boxing Day lunch was a walk with Mum and that evening a very drunken supper with Dad, punctuated by a visit from Mary the landowner and Old-Man-bed-companion. He refuses to call her his girlfriend, because he's too old for that or partner, because he says, that's what people who live in Milton Keynes say and he warns not to get him on the subject of my *better/other half.* So, she is just his friend to which I want to add, *with benefits,* but despite being a dick half the time he's still my Dad and I was brought up not to take the piss out of one's elders.

He's still a dick.

I take the children ice-skating at the rink outside the Natural History Museum and they love it, then Jack hates it because he falls over and breaks his wrist (it's not broken) and loses his confidence. We drink hot chocolates buried in marshmallows and buy gingerbread men that only get half-eaten at the market on the South Bank. They show me their toys they got for Christmas and Clara parades around with her mobile phone in her back pocket like she's three times her age, waiting for a call from her husband to say he's racing home from his international trip. I mentally transmit to her to be careful what she wishes for.

On New Year's Eve I tell the children they can stay up until Midnight, because Grandma didn't let me do the same until I was fourteen. And because there is no way Claire would let them stay-up. We wrap up warm on what is a bitterly cold night and make the short walk to Matt and Jess's which is of course full of people, most of whom don't know each other. There is no format, just people standing around drinking and nibbling and going outside to smoke without coats and coming back and explaining loudly, *fuck me it's cold*. Kids run between adults like Victorian street urchins and old people with Grandparenthood status lurk in armchairs hoping they'll see out another year.

"Hello Tom."

It's the woman from Halloween with the fur coat and engagement ring. I can't remember her name, but I do remember her husband.

"Hi, I say. How are you? How's Frank?"

"Frank doesn't do New Years Eve," she says before she confirms she is well, but Christmas with Franks Kids was a nightmare and she's not sure they will ever get married now and she really needs another drink.

I still can't remember her name.

Jess has organised an overly-engineered children's game which is a modern take on pass the parcel design to teach children the maxim we all know is rarely true, that size doesn't matter. Jack picks the biggest and heaviest parcel which, after much tearing and delving in confetti Jess will be picking out of her carpet at Easter, reveals a brick. He doesn't cry, but he feels really stupid and for now, he has learned size does matter. Fortunately the jolly mood of the evening propels him on, until Clara unwraps a pink Swatch Watch and he decides life really isn't fair.

Matt being Matt has put all the clocks forward an hour in the house so we can celebrate New years Eve an hour early, put the kids to bed and get on with the real business of celebrating New Years Eve.

Talking of populars maxims, children aren't stupid and having milked all they can get out of Midnight-minus-one dissappear upstairs in a feral pack of we-know-the-parents-are-too-pissed to care miscreants.

"Are you any good in bed?" asks the woman in the fur coat who might be called Kelly, but I know that's not right.

"Come back after midnight, and I'll let you know," I reply because I'm pissed and happy and I can't be bothered to be shocked by her presumption, which I assume is the point.

Vicky!

Vicky, that's it. Well, I'm glad I've got that sorted.

We kiss at midnight, Vicky and me.

And I kiss everybody else.

And everybody kisses everybody.

And most of us get facial herpes, probably.

As the New Year opens up, Charlie and I press on, meeting when we can, but the significant time-lapses hiccup any true sense of continuum, the gaps between our meetings are seeming to lengthen. January and February are dull as they usually are, but Melissa is keeping me busier than normal. I suspect she may be flouting procurement rules in giving me so much work, but I'm sure she could plead exceptional circumstances. Time apart from Charlie feels like decay in the baby teeth of our relationship. I rationalise my brain is not my own. It has other squatters - chemical stimulants, stress, exhaustion, sadness and guilt. How can I possibly be thinking clearly? Neither of us is yet divorced, our relationship is physical but unconsummated (well at least since the first time around, and that no-longer counts). The hundred miles separating us feels like it's physically feeding our emotional distance. We both need time and space. I need change, a ticket out of the rut.

The ticket comes like a serendipity-soaked aspirin handed to me by my godfather, Anthony. Until recently, he was the Chairman of one of the world's most well-known Advertising Groups and now is about to replace his millionaire status with that of a bankrupt. The hubris of his existence has taken its toll – the long lunches at Club Cinquante Cinq in St. Tropez. The Monaco apartment. The statement cars. The statement models, turned wives, turned ex-wives. His chips have been called in. Dad tells me his game is well and truly up.

One of Anthony's remaining assets is a 'Black House' on the Isle of Lewis in the Outer Hebrides. Worth so little in the grand scheme of his debt, he neglects to mention it to the insolvency officers carving up his empire. A dedicated fisherman, he has hung onto this unglamorous bolt hole as a reminder of who he had been before the bling had blung. Hearing of my predicament via Dad, he kindly offers me indefinite stay. I take all of a few seconds to accept. It seems the perfect solution. I can work from anywhere. It could be the perfect place to finally unravel my riddle of answers and questions. To finish my book. To clear the air before breaking ground on the foundations of my reconstruction.

Charlie understands when I tell her. If I'm honest, I think she is relieved. Life for both of us is simply too full of shit to yet imagine a perfect future together. Our future, if there is to be such a thing, will have to wait. A hiatus. A moratorium. If I'm honest, the sex ban is beginning to wear thin. She's made her point, it's not as if she has to stick to it. Had I wanted to give up sex right at the point when it is theoretically available for what feels the first time in a decade, I'd have joined the priesthood or become a physics teacher. Had that plan failed I could have moved to somewhere devoid of attractive female life. I'm thinking of writing Swansea city centre on a Saturday night, but I'd get lynched the next time Dyfed and I go drinking down the Mumbles Mile, so I won't.

A little over a week later I steer my under-powered, and unsuitable for the terrain, hire car across the treeless landscape of Lewis. I had flown to Glasgow with EasyJet on a packed plane from Gatwick the day before St. Patrick's Day. I mention this because I'm surprised at how many Scots rush home in honour of the Irish Patron saint. Perhaps it's the two for one deals on Guinness on Princes Street. At the check-in desk, a normal girl turned Shylock, in a suit made from orange carpet, demanded reparations for the additional kilogram of luggage I attempted to smuggle on board. £65 plus taxes later I had doubled the cost of my trip.

I only flew EasyJet once with Claire, we were going to Dublin to meet her parents for the first time. She almost got me murdered by a Traveler family whose teenage son was threatening to light a cigarette. All the other passengers knew the correct drill of pretending to study the duty-free magazine, but Claire decided to take vocal offence. Heaven knows what a Traveler family was doing on an airplane, perhaps their horses were in the hold. I pity the check-in staff trying to charge for that.

Claire and I never flew EasyJet again yet there I found myself alone and fuming and thinking Claire had been right. I stood in the haphazard queue to board next to a Mum, Dad and two boys with matching tattoos and velour travel wear, everyone jostling for position prior to the charge-of-the-flight-brigade to secure seats. The boys looked like twins of about ten years old, both wearing heavy, black-rimmed glasses which I know has got you thinking they looked like The Proclaimers. Shame on you.

Then the Shylock reappeared, unhooking the security barrier, like a games mistress setting off a stampede towards a tray of sticky buns for match tea. Elbowing my way on-board I spotted an empty seat over the wing and handed off a junior Proclaimer like I'd spotted the posts in the dying seconds of the Calcutta Cup. He was no match for me, especially given how I last saw scrabbling on the nylon carpet. Someone had knocked off his glasses. The man who crashed into the seat next to me didn't seem interested in my life story, but then he didn't seem interested in very much. He did manage to tell me he was a nervous flyer in a successful attempt to shut me up. Perhaps he was worried the Guinness might run out on Princes Street.

Driving through Stornoway, I'm disappointed by the normality of it all. I had imagined a more primitive, rustic landscape, but everything seems worryingly familiar. Apart from the road signs in dual English and Gaelic, I could be in Surrey. After a brief trip to Tescos, which is identical to every Tescos I have ever visited, I head away from suburbia and the landscape starts to chill into a wind beaten heather of hills, unforgiving stone houses and bewildered sheep. This is more like it. Not a picture postcard, but evocative of former beauty in aged faces. Every rock, stream and valley stands sodden with strata-deep secrets. A tiny leap of imagination conjures kilted warriors wielding broadswords and wenches, marauding from punch-up to piss-up and back-to-battle again. Shaggy and splendidly-horned Highland cattle stand unmoved by my car slicing through the icy mirrors puddling the road. Following the vague email instructions, a determined right turn heads me towards what I assume to be the coast, though I can't yet see the sea. Emerging from a three-mile long cutting heralds my first glimpse of pure white sand at low-tide. I would have missed the sign to my destination had a sheep not been standing under it, staring at me like I had landed from the sheep equivalent of Mars. The name of the village I am questing is incomprehensible, as if typed by fist on some primitive Gaelic keyboard. Deciding discretion is the better part of translation, I christen it Wham O-Bamo in my head.

There are nine houses in the Wham O-Bamo, imaginatively numbered 1-9. My cottage is No.3. In between numbers 2 and 4 I find a track tilting precariously from the main road, dropping out of sight towards the beach. I immediately know it will be non-negotiable in my little car when snow or heavy rain come. Grinding to a steep halt in what I take to be the appropriate place to grind to a halt, I apply the handbrake as if my life depends upon it. Heaving the car door open, I am at the top of the world – or near as dammit. The scene greeting me outclasses every cropped and edited image I've ever seen selling holiday delusion. The beach is deserted of human form or legacy, from East to West, hill to horizon. No litter, no graffiti, no neon, no seaweed, no plastic.

Hectare upon hectare, mile upon mile of perfectly rippling sand - clear, clean water temporarily abandoned in its furrows until the tide returns.

I scan the skies hopefully for the Sea Eagles I'd read about in the seat-back brochure on the Logan Air flight into Stornoway. I see huge black crows waltzing in air-to-air combat, infinitely more majestic than their grimy, peasant cousins in the parks of London.

The sea air rushes my nostrils like opium, instantly emptying my head of the detritus of a year of hell. My lungs plump up like sea anemones, sucking in the good and pushing out the bad. I know immediately I have made the right decision to step out of the ring. To do what once successful sportsmen do when facing a bad run of form – go back to basics. Recall what they were good at, leave out the fancy stuff. Regroup and start again.

The email tells me the cottage will be unlocked, the keys inside – a novel form of security, I think. Leaving my bags in the car, I heave open the gate dividing the dry-stone wall and gingerly walk the short garden path feeling like an arranged bride meeting her future husband. The cottage exterior is harsh, but functional with enough architectural features to distance it from a box and put it on the right side of quaint, if quaint is possible when withstanding the annual terror of Hebridean weather.

The front door, once green, now greenish, opens with rattling protest. Inside, original features mix with touches of modernity in what an Estate Agent schooled in bullshit might describe as sympathetic juxtaposition. It feels work-in-progress, I sense the hand of Anthony, attempting to modernise the Cottage reminiscent of the finer surroundings he normally frequented. The kitchen is stubbornly seventies in gloopily varnished pine surrounding the old fire place still open for business on the back wall. The bathroom is on the ground floor, sending shivers down me, long before I brave taking off my clothes and dousing in water I assume will be on the freezing side of tepid.

Three uninsulated bedrooms top the house. In each, I find a made-up bed, puritanical furniture and a vase of heather. I think of Jack and Clara stirring asleep in the beds as I stand protectively over them, replacing their covers and kissing them gently knowing they won't wake. At the front of the house a large window is punched through the heavy wall. The view is high-definition widescreen beauty. Would they like it here? Would the lack of civilisation and computer games render them sullen and bored within hours of arrival? I have no idea whether they will ever see the place. I haven't spotted a TV yet. I dare not think on the subject of WIFI though I have been promised it. Trotting back down stairs I prise open the back door. The beach is endless; the horizon, ruler straight; the sky absolute in its infinity. If ever I am to find recovery, this is the place. I have checked into my own rehab. I want to be here, no need to lock the door to prevent my escape. No need for straitjackets, medication or group therapy. Puffed with pure oxygen, at last I think, I've done something really smart. Then I jump out of my skin.

"Hello," I blurt, my heart racing into the red zone where it might well stall. "I'm Tom. Pleased to meet you. You must be Mrs. Carlisle." I sound in my head like I've just stepped from a Charlotte Bronte novel. The email had informed me, the housekeeper, Mrs. Carlisle, lives at No.4 Wham O-Bamo..

She emerges from the armchair of her ambush like a giant turtle taking its first laborious stride up the beach. Eventually appearing to be standing, somewhere on the shy side of five foot, she reminds me of the cartoon Inspector Clouseau in the opening credits of the Pink Panther films. She is all nose and eyes over a medieval bosom. Whatever is holding her chest aloft, must be industrial in constitution. Her ginger hair looks to be 100% nylon, clamped to her head like a 1960's open-face motorbike helmet.

Communication doesn't appear to be her thing. She responds to my leading questions with a nod, grunt, or on special occasions *"aye"* spoken like a drunk offered something suspicious. Suggesting she might give me a tour of the cottage, Mrs. Carlisle shuffles behind, her tiny feet at odds with the basic physics of her top-heavy frame. I ask and point. She nods, grunts, says *aye* or remains silent until a reframe of the question induces a nod, grunt, or *aye*.

"This is the kitchen," I say rhetorically. She nods.

"Does the fire still work?" I ask, pointing at the blackened hearth. She grunts her affirmation.

"Should I use coal or wood?" I ask.

"Aye," she replies.

Pointing at the modern, shiny Brabantia kitchen bin, I immediately regret asking about recycling. It's all I can think of to ask, which is as about as relevant as asking if there is a Waitrose nearby where I can pick up some Asparagus.

Silence.

"Where should I take glass?" I ask, hoping specificity might elicit a response. Silence.

"Is there a pub nearby?" I ask, changing tack. "Aye," she says, though not sounding convinced.

I decide not to ask for details, a full sentence in response seeming a churlish weight to place upon her already strained shoulders. Conducting the rest of the tour in relative silence, I nod, grunt and mutter *Aye* to myself, sticking my head around doors, opening and closing cupboards, pointing out this and that to no-one in particular.

Arriving back at the front door, Mrs. Carlisle lets herself out saying *Aye*, as if to communicate: *have a nice stay; call me if you need anything; the hot water geyser is temperamental, but you'll get used to it.* I get the message. I'm on my own.

I'm on my own and I like it. Deciding not to succumb to bachelor bad-habits, I collect my disturbingly small amount of luggage from the car. I unpack, fold and hang my clothes. Line up my toiletries in the bathroom. Store the suitcases in the cupboard. This is home. My first home as a bachelor – since being a bachelor before Claire.

There are no photographs of Anthony or his family anywhere to be seen, as if the cottage had been his anonymous safe house. I discover a folder of literature, suggesting it had at some point been rented out. Most of the dog-eared pamphlets feature the crown jewels of the local tourist industry, the standing stones of Lewis. An advert for a 'Scallop Shack' catches my eye, I make a mental note to seek it out. Charlie loves scallops, she would be jealous of the freshly harvested Scottish variety. There is no mention of the pub, but in a yellowed visitors' book, I read numerous entries referring to 'Dodd's Castle' and how it seems to have resulted in more than the odd sore head.

Over the next few days I play house. Adopting the persona of a loose-cuffed interior designer I rearrange sofas, move pictures, hump furniture up and downstairs and marshall Anthony's books into size and genre order. Discovering a vinyl record player and a stash of LP's I dance around the ground floor in a reverie of my childhood. A gatefold copy of Queen's *News of the World* has me belting; Sammy was low, watching the show over and over again....Then there was Bowie doing *Life on Maaaaaaaaars* and the money shot, Supertramp – DON'T you look at my girlfriend, she's the only one I got.

The cottage isn't mine but for the first time in a year, I feel like I'm building something, and it feels great. In a moment of hubris, I drive to Stornoway and buy a colour printer and run off copies of photos of Jack and Clara and stick them above what is to become my writing desk. I revisit Tesco's and buy the vital icons of mundanity - Colman's mustard, Lea and Perrins Worcestershire sauce, Marmite, Tabasco, Ribena and Heinz Baked Beans. I'm seeing now our house in Wandsworth is a museum to our failed marriage no-one wants to visit. It has to be sold. Then and only then I can find a place where I can start again.

I am Tom. I'm going back to the start.

Chapter 14: THE LORD OF THE RINGS

"Not all those who wander are lost."

J.R.R. Tolkein

It's night three and I'm ready.

With a few hours of daylight in the bank, I strap on my boots which haven't walked in anger for what seems like decades. They feel good, firm and fit for purpose. Pulling on my old yellow ski jacket, likewise devoid of action since before Jack was born, I slam the greenish door behind me, stride down the garden path like I have a clue where I am heading and turn towards the sea.

Hopping over a style, I trot down the steep dune, cascading onto the hard sand at the bottom at a considerably more urgent pace than I start out. Looking back to map my descent, I spot Mrs. Carlisle watching from the end of her garden, her arms folded tightly under her Neolithic bosom. If her arms had been placed on top, she would have looked like she was attempting semaphore. To be round the front, she would need the arms of an Orang-Utang. No, her little arms nestle under her mammary shelf like day-old piglets under the protection of the mother of all sows.

The turning tide is rapidly reclaiming the previously surrendered flats, but I reckon I can round the rocky outcrop before it's cut off. Distances are hard to judge when all there is boundless space. I have never seen a sky so big. Arriving breathless at the pinch point, I gingerly climb through a blow-hole, into a cavity carved by millennia of pounding sea and surely the scene of shenanigans by many a pirate and smuggler. My thighs burning as I safely broach the grassy cliff, the sea slapping disappointedly on the rocks below, I march on and the pain in my legs is receding as I crest the high-point and the scenery opens-up again like the page of a child's pop-up book. More sand, more sea, more miles of unadulterated purity. And a sheep. I swear it's the same sheep who first eye-balled my arrival.

"Evening Shaun," I say out loud. Like Mrs. Carlisle, the sheep doesn't respond. Perhaps they are from the same clan. Shaun breaks into a distressed canter over a hillock to muster reinforcements.

A worn animal trail in the grass leads me to a footpath, eventually leading me to a tarmacked road. I surmise it must have been the one I originally drove in on.

Left, or Right?

My sense of direction tells me right would be in the vague direction of home, so I turn left, simultaneously deciding turning left will become my new mantra, my private euphemism for taking the path less trodden in search of my new life.

Dodd's Castle doesn't seem to advertise itself as a boarding house, or pub, or anything else. There are no signs and it certainly isn't a castle. In the fifteen minutes between spotting it standing lonesome on a promontory and arriving at its imposing door, three cars speed past me. Three cars seems like rush hour. Like the M4 out of London on the Friday evening of a Bank Holiday weekend. I reckon the occupants know something I don't.

Crunching up the drive, the three cars are parked up outside, alongside a collection of weather-whipped four-by-fours and a white mini bus. A line of fishing rods is propped precariously against the wall, suggesting the potential of tourism. Perhaps I might not be the only fish out of water.

There is no signage indicating I'm not about to walk unannounced into someone's front-room, I turn the brass door knob fixed to the door by the flagging-will of two soon-to-retire screws. Peering inside, striding towards me is a man in his late thirties wearing a kilt, tightly buttoned waist jacket, cropped black beard and fierce glare. "Hello," he says, with what I hope is a growing smile, "how can I help ye?"

"Hi," I said, "do you have a bar? I was hoping to get a drink?"

"Do we have a bar?" He retorts as if I'm asking if the Pope is Catholic. "Of course, come in." He turns his slender frame side on, beckoning me down a short flight of heavily carpeted stairs. A horseshoe-shaped bar, on the left of the big wood paneled room is dark mahogany, almost black. Behind it standing an extremely pretty, dark-haired girl wearing a black blouse. She can't be more than twenty. Every fixture or fitting is tartan-covered, dark wood or polished silver. Everything not a thistle is a stag, Saltire or Claymore sword. Like uncovering a lost tomb, I feel part-explorer, mostly interloper. I try to think of our English decorative equivalent; pubs with a copy of A Tale of Two Cities and Fly Fishing by J.R. Hartley on the shelves; damp-aged hunting prints hanging provocatively in wait for North London liberals strayed from the beaten track; the flag of St. George hung large outside East End boozers over opaque doors adorned with stickers advertising Sky Sports, Paddy Power and an absurd plea to drink responsibly. The Scots seemed to have national iconography down to an art us English gave up after we decided fish and chips was our national dish and headed off to lecture another colony how to drink tea and select your cutlery from the outside in.

Faces in gloomy cubby holes are staring at me like selfish zoo animals. I suspect if I rattle their cages I will lose my fingers. In one corner, a small woman is pinned to her chair by a large accordion, playing lamenting folk-flamenco-techno mash-up. She looks Native American, but is probably more likely Romanian. How she has found her way to Dodd's is a conundrum-too-far for my brain. I do often wonder how people end up in places. How does a Chinese family who can't speak English end up in Lower Whimsy-by-Wold serving bean sprouts and MSG to old boys in red trousers on a Friday night? That said, I have no greater claim on Lewis than the next interloper. My mission is to unpack marriage, who says exporting a unique brand of retro-modern accordion is any less valid? We're all world travelers now, assuming you've paid EasyJet for packing an extra toothbrush.

In an accent that could only be French, and a smile I'm really hoping is genuine, the barmaid asked me what she can get me.

"Can I have a pint of something?" I say hopefully, seeing nothing on display indicating the sale of beer.

"Of course. Back-Right or Back-Left?" She offers, indicating towards the rear of the bar. Two beer kegs with wooden taps over Tupperware drip trays, are nestled under the spirit optics, each wrapped in a tartan knitted tea-cosy. Following my new maxim of always going left, I say, "Back-Left please."

"That is the strong one," she says as she plucks a pint jug from a shelf somewhere underneath me with a smile that knows something I don't.

"Good," I say, thinking *oh shit.*

As she pours my pint, I perch on a stool, resting my elbows on the bar trying to look as inconspicuous as any yellow-jacketed Englishman can in a Scottish time warp.

The pint of thick liquid she places before me looks so dark brown and peaty, it could be siphoned from the nearest stagnant loch.

"That is two pounds," she says firmly in her delightful French accent. A price of two pounds means one of two things. Either life in the Outer Hebrides is going to be a fundamental reset of my value system, a million miles from my indulgent London existence, or, the beer really is siphoned from the nearest stagnant loch.

Pausing a moment, feeling like Neil Armstrong with his hand on the door handle of Apollo 11, I tip a meaningful gulp into my throat and take one giant leap for Tom-kind. Heaven itself has just slid down my throat, like drinking marshmallows that can get you pissed, it may be I have just found the key to life. I smile approvingly at the French girl. She smiles back, turning quickly to busy herself elsewhere. I take another gulp to check my first impressions aren't a case of mistaken identity. They aren't and in that moment, another coin of my new life, plunks into my piggy bank. Whatever happens next, it is going to be good.

What happens is somewhere between 50 and 80 years, and five foot five and five foot seven. His chest is all barrel and his white beard buzz cut. His ten-gallon white Stetson prevents me from seeing if his hair matches his beard, or if he owns any. He is wearing a heavy checked shirt with blue jeans held aloof by a thick leather belt and over-sized, ornate buckle. On his feet are spotless, white, Nike trainers – like he'd turned up late at the fancy dress shop on the day of the annual Hoedown, only to find all the cowboy boots had been hired out.

"Hullooo," he gravels, "I'm Eddie," his face illuminating at the sound of his own name. "Hi," I said, "I'm Tom."

"Please to me ye," says Eddie, "have ye come a long way?"

I wanted to say I'm from just up the road, but knowing I can't attempt the Gaelic for Wham O-Bamo, I bottle and say, "yes, from London."

"I thought as much," he says, without declaring his thought process. "I'm Eddie," he says again, "I'm in a band. We're pretty good."

"Good," I say, not wishing to sound like I'm questioning his claim, "what sort of things do you play?"

"Och, just covers mainly, we're pretty good."

"What's your band's name?"

"Arrived on Foot."

"Good name."

"Aye," says Eddie. "I canny drive and Dexter isn't allowed t'."

A second man appears at Eddie's shoulder looking like a walking homage to the disgraced American music producer Phil Spector, his explosion of blondish hair, a tribute to the anarchic majesty of static electricity. "This is Dexter," introduces Eddie.

"Hi Dexter," I say. Dexter is looking preoccupied.

He asks me, "did you see the Melbourne Grand Prix result?"

I confess I hadn't.

His accent is less Scottish than my Mum, which is saying something as Mum sounds like Hyacinth Bouquet.

"Tenth of a second in it," he says. "In my opinion, Rosberg switched to the wrong tyres."

"Really?" I feign, channeling my inner shock at his freak hairstyle until I realise he is utterly cross-eyed. I remember Dyfed once referring to a cross-eyed baby we encountered on the Fulham Road as having 'home and away' eyes. One looks home and one looks away, Dyfed had explained, as we giggled our way down the pavement.

I can see now why the band had arrived on foot.

Dexter is talking about the merits of grades of racing fuel. Eddie is looking hopefully at his empty glass. "Did you grow up around here?" I ask.

"No," says Dexter. "Basingstoke."

Well, that explains a lot.

"Another?" I ask.

"If you insist," says Eddie rhetorically. "Back-Right will do me. "Dexter?"

"I'll have a Back-Right too," he says, "the stuff on the left would have won Schumacher his eighth title." Not wishing to dent my national pride in front of La Mademoiselle, I opt for one more Back-Left and two Back-Rights for my new friends.

Being the new boy in town, I figure I smell of fresh meat, fair game, virgin territory to be trodden. I discard my yellow jacket, thinking it might as well have *head-butt me* writ large across it's back. Next to join our happy throng is Abigail, a thirty-something Aussie on the plus-size. She doesn't need an invitation or introduction, she is among us like a flash summer hail storm when the crockery and glasses had just been laid on the garden table. She tells me she is a blogging-journalist for a travel magazine, sent to report back to her countrymen the delights of the other edge of the known world.

Her accent is as Australian as Eddie's is Scottish. While her final syllable always rises to incredulous heights, Eddie friends viciously clips his. Imagine your best Australian accent, and say GlasgOOAW. Then do the same in Scottish - Glasgi. The conversation is a metronomic tennis match, messing with my head as much as the Back-Left.

"What brings you here? Eddie aske me.

"Um. I've come to sort my head out," I say, "find some space."

"Aye. The Back-Left should do that for you."

"Women troubles?" asks Abigail.

"Marriage troubles."

"Shit mate," she says, "I've been married twice. It sucks."

"Half of marriages end in divorce," says Dexter.

"It's 42%," I correct a little too quickly. "I'm one of them."

"You got wee ones?" asks Eddie.

"Boy and a girl."

"How old are they?" asks Abigail.

"Ten and eight," I say. "Cheers." I hold my glass up in front of me to close off the subject.

"Slange," say Eddie and Dexter in unison.

"Cheers mate," says Abigail, looking me in the eye offering me a mental cuddle she looks worryingly determined to see through.

Pints three, four and five disappear as my new friends and I jostle and guffaw and curse, discussing the universal truths of love, marriage and rearing sheep. Abigail presses me into conversational corners forcing me to fight my way out with talk of Charlie and my dreams for our future.

By the time I find myself talking to an elderly couple called Aileen and Bean, my five senses are officially subprime. Touch and smell are gone. Sight and hearing are flat-lining slightly above my rapidly deteriorating capacity to taste. Aileen and Bean are local farmers, I assume of sheep, but to be frank, I am beyond the business of Curriculum Vitae. I don't recall how or why we joined their table and I have a sneaking suspicion it may be the beginning of my end.

Aileen and Bean are as old as the hills now invisible in the pure ink of far northern night-time. They have something to do with brewing and we are drinking their home brew. Why Dodd's Castle allows corkage, I have no idea. I can't say it's Whisky, I can't say what it is. Something akin to Port and a bastard cousin to Sherry. Whatever it is, we drink it from glasses slightly larger than the average shot glass. It isn't a drinking game as such, just a Magna Carta of conventions to be broken at our peril. Conversation rambles and bounces and tumbles like loose luggage on the roof of a car careering down a rutted farm track. Australian, Scottish, English, meld into the universally loud vernacular of completely pissed. Anyone who takes a drink is duty-bound to to finish it while holding someone else's eye and hailing *Slange!* Every empty glass must be refilled to the top. The more we drink, the more I'm getting it completely wrong. Not looking someone in the eye is akin to waving your shoe at an Arab, or making oral sex quips in front of your best mates' mother-in-law. Aileen and Bean take it very seriously. Every time I transgress I feel more stupid, and English and wishing I had a sympathetic wife to pick me off the floor in the morning.

It's tomorrow and the only thing I remember of the remaining part of last night is Rocky the Policeman. I wish that was true, I also remember sidling up to the bar and trying to engage the French barmaid in chat and her telling me after only mild interrogation she was called Marine. What a gorgeous name, I thought.

"Do you believe in marriage?" I asked her, my conscious brain trying to extend my marital research to the younger generation, my inebriated subconscious flirting like a successful conclusion with a twenty something French girl was a matter of life and death.

"We have only just met," she said with Anglo-Saxon deadpan. Perhaps it was Celtic deadpan. A French deadpan would have tossed a garlicky response saying (in French) something like, "I will only marry a man who will make love to me in the champagne aisle of a supermarket at midnight on a Saturday night."

"No," I said, " I mean, will you ever get married?"

"I have not met ze right person," she said, trying not to sound German.

I took her use of the word 'person' to mean she was a lesbian, or better still bisexual, which (and one shouldn't generalise) all French women are, or at least in all the movies I've seen.

"I'm getting divorced," I said.

"I know," she said, " I am so sorry," sounding like she meant it. I don't know how she knew I was getting divorced, but then I do recall overhearing two old boys in the Gents talking about some English twat who'd fucked up his marriage. As far as I could tell, I was the only Englishman within fifty miles. News travels fast on Lewis.

One of my qualities, which is a short list involving some of the fingers of one hand, is knowing when to cut my losses. Marine was beyond the definition of lovely. If I were driving through the American Midwest I would pass through the old-ranch town called Horse, stop for a coffee and pancakes in Hope, speed through the retirement village full of Irish exiles called Diaspora and pull up in a palm tree lined resort called Lovely, and there she'd be sitting on a park bench wearing pop socks, a tight top and pencil skirt with red neckerchief and I'd ask if there was anywhere I could get a bite to eat and she'd suggest a place called Marine's where we'd drink Espresso and hold hands until the cattle were driven home. But I was drunk, and I didn't know when to cut my losses, so I asked her if she'd like to come back to Wham O-Bamo and drink a bottle of wine.

"I don't drink wine," she said, which is an odd thing for anyone of Gallic lineage, and I took as a rebuff the French are famed for, when they're not making love in midnight supermarkets.

Anyway, back to Rocky. It had dawned on me somewhere between *Slanges*, getting home in the dark was going to be a challenge for which I was not equal. I needn't have worried. Worry I did when I saw the familiar blue flashing lights of a Police car outside. To my utter astonishment, the arrival of the Law heralded a zombie-like shuffle of clientele into the car park, unashamedly getting into their cars and gunning their engines. Multiple sets of headlights sprung to life like vindictive searchlights searching for escaping prisoners in the distance.

"You better go with Rocky," Eddie had said to me. Being arrested on my first night was not in my planned playbook. "He'll take you home."

Stripped of powers to protest or process, I accepted my fate. Ham-feetedly slumping into the front seat of Sergeant Rocky's Police estate car, my abiding memory is of all the extra toys the Police have on their dashboard, like being at the helm of a flight simulator.

"Alright lad?" asked Rocky, taking his seat beside me and removing his peaked cap. "Yes Sir," I said with no truth and less conviction. Rocky didn't reply. Turning the ignition, he eased up the crunching drive, followed by a faltering procession of dual light beams. We drove at snail's speed followed by a carnival of cars like a haphazard string of Christmas lights, one by one peeling away into this house or that ditch until we were the only car left.

"You're at No.3. Is that right?" asked Rocky.

"Wham O-Bamo," I said.

"What?"

"Yes, Sir. No. 3."

I remember feeling unforgivably English as the inquisition of Rocky's full-beam picked out my pathetic red hire car.

"Take care son," he said, "see you again."

Mumbling my gratitude I exited Rocky's meat wagon with all the grace of an obese kid at a gym display. Standing alone in drunken incomprehension, I watched Rocky reverse up the track and swing back up the hillside. Had I believed people actually pinch themselves, when they say, *I had to pinch myself,* I would have pinched myself.

The drunken brain is a funny thing. Actually it's not a funny thing, it's a stupid thing. A once glorious organ, reduced to a shadow of its former glory. I saw the gate to the cottage and calculated which side I recalled the hinge to be, thus knowing which side to push and not appear drunk to anyone who was looking. Not that anyone would be looking.

With alcoholic inevitability, my calculation was 100% incorrect. Pushing the wrong side of the gate, finding it with no give, created the perfect fulcrum to propel me over the gate like a broom stick had been stuck in the wheels of my bicycle.

Lying giggling on my back, the stars were like the pinpricks of light shining through the blackout curtain at Clara's Year 4 play. I wished Charlie was beside me, marveling at the heavens of stars, laughing at the wonder of bloody everything. The shadow that eclipsed them was Mrs. Carlisle peering over the gate.

"Aye," she confirmed to herself.

Chapter 15: ROMEO AND JULIET

"Good night, good night! parting is such sweet sorrow,
That I shall say good night till it be morrow."

William Shakespeare

I'm sitting in an old armchair, writing on my laptop and watching the air and waves in the hope they will sooth my head. They are combining into an audible hiss that if I close my eyes could be a distant motorway, but it's not it's purity in motion.

I think about Marine.

I think about Charlie, then find I'm thinking again about Marine..

I think about Aileen and Bean and the 58% of marriages which survive? Which of those are actually happy and what is the secret of a truly happy marriage? What do two bootlegging sheep farmers from the top of the world, have that half of the rest of us don't?

I need to figure this through.

Legally speaking, marriage is binding. Emotionally it is an artificial construct, designed to keep a couple together to create and bring up children in a unified environment. Religiously, it also has many connotations and purposes, but I'll leave matters spiritual under the altar.

For the purposes of children, marriage is not a bad idea. Whoever thought of it should get an award – a medal or chocolate watch perhaps. Like all good ideas, there is a law that applies – the law of unintended consequences. Marriage binds two people together. Two people who can only unbind themselves by the begrudging say-so of the legal system, generally in the aftermath of broken crockery and promises. Intentionally, the unbinding process is not straightforward. It costs a fortune financially and emotionally. It attaches the D-word moniker to the combatants forever. Worse than a criminal record, being a divorcee can never be expunged. There is no chance of pardon. No statute of limitations.

You are a failure.

Or a victim.

Or a victim and a failure.

Or a bastard.

Or a bitch.

You walked up the aisle, said some words, heard some back and sometime later it turns out at least one of you was lying.

My mind is wandering and I pick up the remote and flick through the four and a half channels I can get here, there it is a love bomb of a film about to air. I've got the DVD and seen it a gazillion times, but somehow watching it for free on TV makes it compelling viewing.

Hang on. I've got to finish this.

At some point along the road, you argue. For some, it all kicks-off while still wearing wedding fatigues, as your drunk guests are still busily trying to get-off with each other. Some wait for the honeymoon – or at least the taxi on the way to the airport. Some wait for weeks, even months. But arguments will come. That's natural. Siblings argue. Best Friends. Politicians. Drunks. Everyone's at it. Why shouldn't a married couple argue? Some say they should, *it's healthy.*

The bonds of marriage are both unintended and intended. You can't get away. And.....you can't get away. You can walk out. Go for a drive. Crash at your sister's house. Hide in the pub. But you come back. You must return. Half of everything you have just walked out on is yours. You can't abandon it. And anyway, the Judge hasn't let you off the hook yet.

So, maybe you don't walk out. You go for a bath. Or hide in the garage. Or turn the TV up loud. Go upstairs and read the child a story to prove what an amazing parent you are.

Maybe you give in.

Agree to disagree.

Talk about it tomorrow.

Just leave it.

The film has started, it's Local Hero. This calls for a rescinding of my promise to myself not to drink tonight and a double Scotch and a large bag of prawn crackers. Set to one of the greatest soundtracks of all time, this is Scotland porn. With half an eye out the window as a tempestuous night rapidly draws in I smile at each next scene before it arrives, because I know what's coming. Trudy the Rabbit, Burt Lancaster's lunatic psychiatrist, the village solicitor who is also the village inn keeper and his beautiful wife for whom he has a predilection for *knocking off early* with.

My laptop is feeling warm on my lap.

I guess Claire and I were not alone. When we argued, the words, vitriol and spittle were neutered by the fact we were married. It's not as if we were actually going to resort to fisticuffs. I'm thinking about the usually out-of-nowhere blow-up. Just when you thought everything was going well, a raised loo seat, a spill on the carpet, a forgotten arrangement and suddenly it's World War Three.

No chance of a UN resolution.

Gloves off, send in the troops.

But, but, but…as the first shots ring out, the early border skirmishes, still, you're married. And the kids are upstairs (usually listening).

And anyway, you didn't mean all that you said.

It's been a bad day.

A bad week.

You're stressed.

You're sorry.

Let's have a date night next week – *and we mustn't cancel it this time.*

Within reason, and reason has broad remit in this instance, there isn't much you can say within a marital argument that can't be admonished with a little groveling. Marital arguments are pyrrhic, impotent weapons. Before long, all will be forgotten.

Probably.

The village Vicar in the film is African. He is charged with shepherding his flock while they, and he, are set fair to be made overnight millionaires by the evil American oil company if they play their cards right.

I have a story about an African vicar which I hadn't thought of in years.

Come to think of it, as I just have, it's rather apt.

It's OK, I know what happens in the film, so I'll tell you.

I mentioned Van before – the redhead in my pre-wedding picture. As happily married today as the day she said I do to Griff. He wasn't one of the core Gang, but everyone knew him from around and about and liked him. He was a tough-nut, back row forward, seemingly impervious to pain. We were more than a little surprised when he hooked up with Vanessa. They weren't chalk and cheese, but she was a tad chalky to his out and out cheesiness. Beneath her bouncing red hair, she was on the prim side of proper. She didn't dress conservatively, but she didn't flaunt it either. Beneath the cashmere and buttons, lurked something of a time-share rebellious streak. Her mischievous appeared as infrequently as comets, eclipses and Bob Dylan tours, making it all the more delicious when it did.

We were all at their wedding of course. No-one there ever forgot it. They picked an idyllic church on the South Coast, its fingerprint dating back to Roman times. The sun shone, the bride stunned, the flowers won awards. Picture perfect English syrup.

The resident vicar was on exchange. He and his wife had taken a posting in Nigeria for six months. Their Nigerian counterparts had moved into the

Hampshire Vicarage to tend to the spiritual and pastoral welfare of the small, elderly and deeply conservative congregation. Van and Griff had met the co-exchanges. Reverend Godfrey couldn't be happier to perform the wedding service. The feeling was mutual. Van didn't mention the holy substitution to anyone. She sensed the odd apple-cart may be in for a bumpy ride. She delighted in the thought of it.

In Anglican black-and-whites, dog collar starched, shoes shined like a Sandhurst staff sergeant, Reverend Godfrey's skin was the most perfect, hewn and buffed ebony. His whole being shouted goodness, happiness, love and care for others. He conducted the service as per the words, written and apparently left by the son of the great man from upstairs some two thousand years ago. When it came to the sermon, Reverend Godfrey had more latitude to impart his wisdom on the attentive flock. His wife sat on her own in a side pew, wrapped in yards of bright green, patterned material. They say, if you unravel and spread all the tissue from the human lungs, a tennis court will be covered. When it came to Mrs. Reverend Godfrey's dress, perhaps a football pitch would be required. Reams of cloth wrapped and wrapped around her frame and pirouetted on top her head to dizzying height. She looked truly splendid.

The Reverend got into his swing. He was passionate on his subject: *the beauty and importance of happy marriage.* The importance of looking after one another. And, he said, when it came to arguments, the need to make-up by *making love.* In the thickest, most resonant, East African accent you can imagine, his tenor and conviction rose into the ancient rafters, echoing about its stony frame. *You must never go to sleep on an unresolved argument,* he implored. *If you have an argument, before you sleep, you gotta make love to ya woman!*

We got the point, but he wasn't letting us off that lightly. He meant what he said, and we weren't leaving until we believed him. Truly believed.

"You gotta make love to ya woman!"

Putting it delicately, Griff's grandmother Sylvia, seated in the front row, was from the old school. When, I say old school, I'm referring to the Imperial kind, when the colonies were colonised and Britannia ruled the waves and pretty much everything else. The long pheasant feathers poking from her tightly pinned hat, began to vibrate like she was seated on an invisible locomotive trundling over cobbles.

"If ya argue, you gotta make love to ya woman!"

It looked for all to see, given the amount of plumage in her millinery and the rising steam beneath it, Granny Sylvia might achieve flight.

"So just remember, Gentleman, and Ladies. Never go to sleep on an argument without making love."

Reverend Godfrey was using a little too much hip action to drive home his point.

Granny Sylvia nearly passed out. The Reverend's wife sat impassive. She had heard it all before. Thankfully, from the point of view of her conjugal obligations, her husband wasn't the argumentative type.

It's not public knowledge whether Van and Griff took the Reverend's advice to heart. It may have been impossible not to. With God and the Reverend Godfrey set to a soundtrack of the *best part of breaking-up, is when we're making up*, perhaps the recipe for a happy marriage is simpler than we thought. One likes to think when Griff is feeling horny, all he has to do is pick a fight. God bless Reverend Godfrey, if he hasn't already.

I've drunk quite a lot of whisky now. The sale of the village to the American Oil company has stalled due to "Old Knox" who lives on the beach refusing to sell.

With Claire and I, our fights were simply followed by more fights. We never *made love* to make-up. More damagingly, while I thought the content of whatever dispute had been swept under the carpet and hoovered up by the cleaners (fortnightly), Claire had been building her case against me. Much of the time, she didn't even know she was doing it.

The bloke from Gregory's Girl has fallen madly in love with Jenny Seagrove who plays an oceanic-biologist-mermaid. I can hardly blame him.

Claire possessed an in-built sub-conscious librarian with an encyclopedic knowledge of where each piece of ammunition was stored. When the Apocalypse came, she deployed her arsenal in seconds. Like opposing forces at Waterloo, I was out gunned, outsmarted. I was Napoleon that day. Defeated. Exiled.

If only Reverend Godfrey or the vicar from Local Hero had married us. Perhaps things could have been different. Perhaps the ways of the Lord's moves aren't that mysterious after-all.

Perhaps Freud was right.

It does all comes down to sex.

Slange.

Chapter 16: TO KILL A MOCKINGBIRD

"Real courage is when you know you're licked before you begin, but you begin anyway and see it through no matter what."

Harper Lee.

I'm ready to climb up Philippa.

She will be my first hill. She's not a mountain, but she's not an insignificant hill. I have no map, and nothing is signposted, so I have taken to naming the peaks I plan to conquer after the significant women in my life.

I take the road heading south from Wham O-Bamo and clamber over a five-bar gate that isn't explicitly threatening 'keep-out.' Thankfully, I quickly discover a winding track heading in the vague direction of Philippa's lower slopes. Eventually petering out, I opt for the Roman method of navigation, making a direct bearing for her nipple. The terrain is heather and gorse in unforgiving humps threatening to twist my ankles with every other step. Hidden bogs linger beneath the surface of benign looking moss, determined to hoover the boot from my foot.

The ascent is initially steep enough to require scrabbling hands as well as feet, as I pump my legs to reach a ridge where the incline eases off to a lactic-acid inducing walk. It's early Spring, and the weather is mild. There is not a soul in sight and I sense little danger of stumbling across anyone all day. Before setting out I packed my small rucksack with water and emergency provisions and charged my mobile, though finding any reception seems highly unlikely.

I spot something a few hundred yards away, my eyes focussing in and out on movement across the camouflaged backdrop. It's a herd of deer - their tiny scale indicating they are further away than I originally judge. I pick out the Stag at the head of the herd, hurrying his harem away from my approaching yellow blob.

Another three hundred yards at a steep but manageable incline, the final assault requires a clamber over huge slabs of granite, scattered like cake decorations over the summit. Philippa's nipple turns out to be a cairn. I add a rock to mark my ascent and suck in the air like some modern health conscious brand of marijuana, simoultaneosly expanding my mind, lifting my soul and making me think stupid things.

I extract my phone to take a photo and to my complete surprise, I have four perfect bars of 4G reception. Sitting on damp, springy grass, the sun in my face, I send a text to Jack and Clara; *I'm up a mountain! How are you? Love, Dada. X*

Waiting for a reply, I text Charlie, then Orla the same message without the *Dada* bit. Orla's profile springs immediately into life, *typing....*

Orla is in a terrible state. She tells me Nick has announced he plans to take their children on holiday to France that Summer with his new girlfriend. Orla is apoplectic. *How can he be so insensitive to the children?*

I reply with my sympathies, then call Mum. "Where are you?" she asks, sounding worried.

"Up a mountain on my own," I reply, doing nothing to allay her maternal concern.

Mum doesn't like talking too long on the phone. She hails from an era when telephone bills racked up like gambling debts. She tells me to call her when I'm home safely, makes her excuses and hangs up.

Nothing from the kids.

I fucking hate him, texts Orla.

I take a selfie of myself with Philippa's nipple in the background and send it to Dyfed, then eat two tasteless sandwiches.

No reply from the kids.

The sweat under my shirt is starting to chill, so I retrace my steps downwards, hopping from rock to rock like a yellow-coated mountain goat. I wonder what might happen if I slip and knock myself out. Who will raise the alarm? I guess Mum will eventually. No-one else will register my absence.

Reaching the ridge before the final steep descent, I check my phone again.

No messages.

No reception.

Picking up the guiding compass of a stream, I follow its twist and turn downhill, scanning every bank and mid-flow island for Otters or anything vaguely furry or mammalian. My search for animal life looks like it's going to go unrewarded, but the walk is magical. The stream is guiding me all the way to Wham O-Bamo.

Standing at the back door of the cottage forty minutes later, I'm feeling mightily pleased with myself. I look back up at Philippa. She is a beauty and I have conquered her. On the other side of Philippa is a perfectly shaped hill which just has to be Gemma. I will climb her tomorrow. To the left again, is a bigger hill half-swathed in sunlight – clearly, it's Charlie. Far to the right are twin mountain peaks which look bitches to climb. I christen the smaller one, Alice and the really mean looking one, Claire.

And so, a routine forms. Every day, I clamber up one of my former lovers or favourite females and collect any phone messages at her summit. When I'm on top of Gemma, I get a response from the previous day's message to Jack and Clara. They want to know what I am doing up a mountain. *Walking,* I reply. I figure our conversation is going to be somewhat drawn out.

Holding Charlie back until last, the meaner mountains are beckoning. In preparation for whatever heaven or hell they throw at me, I make a trip to Stornoway to buy more advanced kit. Navigating my pathetically small car around the backstreets, I eventually find what I'm looking for. Blacks of Stornoway is decorated with an authenticity impossible to recreate in an English shopping mall. Above the door, a sign declares its current proprietor as Kevin McMenamin, which I consider an egregious monopoly of syllables.

Much of the shop is dedicated to the circle of life – the buying of dead things, to bait live things, to make them dead and eat them with potatoes. One wall is lined with a splendid array of fishing flies, like vampish earrings in a hemp-smelling stall in Camden Market, sprouting feathers, hooks and baubles designed to lure the unsuspecting into a fatal hook-up. A hand-written sign offers bloody fish guts for chump at 50p a bucket and the prospect of catching big, scary things. A shuffling figure I take to belong to Mr. McMenamin maneuvers into view as I inspect the frozen fish heads.

He launches into a detailed vignette on how fish heads are an irresistible delicacy to any Crayfish or Lobster foolish enough to wander past any baskets recently arrived in their neighbourhood. Then he asks how he can help me.

He reminds me of former Labour Party almost-but-not-quite-saviour, Neil Kinnock, without the ginger hair. Perhaps it *is* an aged Mr. Kinnock, turned white-haired and Scottish as a result of his fall from grace. It could happen.

I explain I am after some water proofs for some serious hill-walking. He grunts something about fish heads, disappearing to a darkened recess leaving me to inspect the honesty-DVD library where everything from *An Officer and a Gentleman* to *Back to the Future IV* sit stacked patiently available to borrow. I think about borrowing one, but that might necessitate form-filling and unnecessary brouhaha when I am on the island with the specific intention of brouhaha-avoidance. Anyway, I reckon I'd seen them all, except *The Goonies* – but it has never appealed. Reading the sleeve of *On Golden Pond*, I remembered it as a lovely film from my childhood. I also suspect it might not have aged as well as Jane Fonda.

Reappearing, holding forth a pair of dark green waterproof trousers, Mr. McMenamin beckons me to pull them over my jeans and try them on for size. Doing as I'm told, I wrestle the impressively rubberised material up to my crotch before treading oaf-like into a selection of pet baskets, suitable for both dogs or cats (they are trans-pet). Handing me the top-half, rather than his hand, I plunge my arms into its sleeves, it's hood flopping over my head. I emerge like a virgin fisherman ready for his first day throwing up on the Briny.

"That'll keep you dry and toasty," he says.

Too embarrassed to ask if I am about to buy gear designed for deep-sea fishing or a touch of rambling, I decide to agree with his prognosis and set about finding some appropriate underwear.

It's the night before my planned ascent of Claire and sleep is nowhere to be found behind my eyelids. I fear carelessly opening my eyes and restarting the going-to-sleep process, which just keeps me awake more.

Don't overthink it, I repeatedly think.

An uncommitted storm grumbles far out at sea with the portent of an impending inquisition in which I am probably the fall guy.

The tinnitus in my ears is skewering my brain like wailing feedback from a guitar amp. Sweat is pouring from pores where I didn't know I had pores. I feel like a nicotine addict flying long-haul with ten hours until landing. The longer I lay awake, the more anxious I become. Surrendering to a bare-footed pad around the kitchen and a bowl of Rice Krispies does nothing to decrease my anxiety. The clock on my phone tells me nobody I know in the western world is awake.

Sleep, when it finally shuffles in, is a series of dreams reminding me if I'm not asleep and dreaming, my life is even more messed-up than I'd credited. Semi-consciousness when I wake is a tussle of veracity between the implausible facts of my dreams and the implausible facts of my life.

I stomach a quarter of the breakfast required for the task ahead. Touching my toes to stretch-off is a feat I haven't managed in years, my middle-aged back throwing in the towel somewhere just south of my knees. Pulling on two pairs of socks is a display of amateur Yoga. My boots are hard and unforgiving, the laces mud-caked and truculent. By the time I'm ready to leave the cottage and assault Claire, I couldn't be in a worse frame of mind. I have the feeling she's beaten me before I start. She's beaten me once, and now I can't see the score settling at anything but 2-0 to her.

The first half a mile, down the dune and across the beach is lacklustre. In sporting parlance I haven't yet turned up. I traipse on, and at some point I sense the leaves of my despondence are lifting and tickling. At first afraid my thinking is wishful, the invisible elixir of Hebridean air teases, then unmistakably manifests and takes my hand and pushes at my back and sympathetically tells me to keep going and not look back. Heading toward the road leading most of the way to Mount Claire, the steroid of the goal ahead injects my thighs, my lungs inflate. My brain seeks out my competitive spirit from a forgotten crevice like an oyster knife. When my boots finally meet the tarmacked road, they do so with the confidence of a salesman's handshake. A life-changing deal is on the table. Win or lose, we are on.

Claire isn't going to surrender without a fight. The further I walk, the more her summit refuses to appear nearer. Each ridge I crest, presents the next like a stripper peeling off layer after layer without ever getting to the money shot. It feels like the mountain-walking equivalent of Déjà vu. Like I'm unknowingly orienteering in circles, each new bit of terrain looks worryingly like I'd been here before. Claire was never one for dragging out foreplay. When she was in the mood, she hurried for the main event. This mountain isn't behaving to type.

Now the clouds are threatened to rain.

Now they are making good on their threat, releasing whipping barrages of water like I'm a raging bushfire in need of drenching. Deluge after deluge slapps into my face like I'm marching between a lineup of fish wives throwing buckets of spent water. Hood strings pulled tight, leaving me a small porthole through which to navigate, I silently thank Mr. McMenamin for his selection of waterproofs. With the exception of the sweat and water pooling in my eye sockets and the dripping tap at the end of my nose, the majority of my being is remaining cocooned and relatively dry.

In the lee of a standing slab of granite, sitting in a well-sprung patch of damp heather I eat a Mars Bar. Looking down the mountainside, I can't believe how far I have travelled. The distant Wham O-Bamo is easy to pick out beneath the weather, like a model idyll on a toy train set. The nine houses are illuminated when there is no source of sun to be seen. No.3 is standing steadfast, fixated on the sea like a warrior's wife long-abandoned to her anxiety. With a gloved hand, I wrestle the sticky Mars Bar wrapper past the Velcro of my waterproof pocket. Time for the next push.

Sensing the game on her hands, Claire upps the odds. Turning the rain to hail, she carpet-bombs me, tiny white balls collecting on the ground like a million exploded bean bags. My rubberised waterproofs are the perfect armour. The hail attack repelled with ease, Claire will need heavier artillery if she is to stop me now. I calculate the plays she has left.

Wind.

Snow.

Sun.

Avalanche.

Earthquake.

Volcano.

Eclipse.

I wouldn't put anything past that woman. All I can do is play the ball ahead of me, which as it happens, is Sun. Broaching another ridge, an oasis of undulating flat terrain opens-up, bathed in cold, benevolent sunshine. For a fleeting moment, it feels like sympathy from my ex-wife. Christ, we had some good times. We had fancied each other. We made babies. Amazing babies. Contemplating the idiocy of our whole situation, my improving mood hiccups. Like hitting the metaphorical wall with six miles left in a marathon, the easiest part of the mountain has become frustratingly hard. The mossy bog is clasping at my feet like clamouring hands.

Eventually finding firmer ground, my thoughts drift to Charlie, the unexpected walk-on in the curtain call of my horror show. I imagine a future with her and that future feels good. I think of Jack and Clara and making them proud. Or at least, being alive for them - if they need me. Surely at some point they will. Everybody needs a Father. I think of Clara one day walking up the aisle. The thought irks. I want nothing but happiness for her. But marriage? How often does that bring happiness? I think of Claire. Stupid, long-legged, horrible, lovely Claire. All I can picture is the vitriol camped in her face as if it settled there centuries ago and took root. I want to imagine her happy side. Her prettiness. Like a double-sided mask, her smile teases an appearance, then flips back to mean. Where has she gone? I know how I could have handled my marriage so much better, but how did we brew Armageddon?

Claire's summit eventually reveals itself as an inverted nipple, flooded by a secret lake of green water, like a spent volcano. There is no obvious place to stand and plant my flag. To declare victory. To take a selfie signifying my triumph. I chuckle. A score draw says it all. Damn her - she hasn't lost, but she hasn't let me win. There are no winners in this game.

My view across the expanse of Lewis is as vista-like as vista's get. I pick out the roads I've driven. The white structure of Dodd's Castle standing placidly where it has stood, probably for centuries. I spot the red square of the postman's van hovering across a hillside as if the road beneath its wheels doesn't exist. I haven't met the postman - surely there can only be one - distributing bills, marketing flyers, divorce papers, love letters, dear-John's and gossip. Is the Postman a Postman or Postwoman? Despite the desolate existence, I am among real people, living real lives. Would living here drive me crazy within months? Or would the lack of crowds, traffic, bullshit and broadband make for a better life?

"What do you think, Claire?" I shout out loud. A pair of branches floating in the green lake reveal themselves as Otters. Sitting up on their haunches when they reach shallow waters, they look over at me, or perhaps they just sense my presence.

"I'm Tom," I call out to them.

They potter off unimpressed, disappearing into their warm holt.

Perhaps it's teatime for their little ones.

They're not interested in me.

Chapter 17: ANNA KARENINA

"He stepped down, trying not to look long at her, as if she were the sun, yet he saw her, like the sun, even without looking."

Leo Tolstoy

My phone rings, which is something of a surprise as recently it seems to have got out of the habit of ringing. The name Mouse is buzzing on my screen.

For your information, there is still one person from my pre-wedding picture so far unaccounted for, and that is who is calling me.

Mouse.

Otherwise known as Rosie.

Still, to hear from her is something of a surprise. A pleasant surprise. We'd talked on text of meeting up in hypotheticals. At least I thought we had. I swipe the green icon expecting one of our long-rambling chats, only to hear her squeaky Scottish brogue announcing without preamble, "I'm at the airport."

"Where are you off to?" I ask.

"I'm here you idiot," she says, "Stornoway. It's Friday!"

It might indeed be Friday. I have achieved the semi-rapturous state of losing track of the borders between weekdays and weekends in three months on the Island. "Friday the 13th," she tells me later. "I never fly on Friday 13th. It scares the bejesus out of me. It was all I could get at short notice."

It takes me fifteen minutes to shower, dress and rid the house of the more obvious evidence of a single man living alone with no expectation of a visitor. Forty minutes later, I'm at Stornoway Airport.

Rosie is Scottish, had married a Scot called Scott, moved from London back to Scotland. Her blood runs tartan. If I were to think what a typical Scottish woman looks like, I don't know what I'd think, but it wouldn't be Rosie. She is a tiny, diminutive, natural blonde. Her eyebrows are almost white. Every curve from her nose to her shins, aquiline. Her moniker of Mouse, in the local vernacular is pronounced *Moose.* It is only when she speaks, you realise she isn't Swedish, or an Elf, or creation of the Disney Corporation. If women were all to look the same, like Meerkats or Pigeons, women should look like Rosie. OK, I'm sure Meerkats and Pigeons look different to one another, but their basic physiology is the same. If the animals were in charge and gauped at humans in cages in zoos, I can imagine a clutch of cute Rosie's staring nervously back through the bars.

Rosie has two kids and sadly, no longer a husband. Three years into her utterly dysfunctional divorce, there is still blood on the road. We stand in the kitchen of my cottage drinking tea, minimally laced to off-black with the last drops of milk I retrieve from the fridge. Having covered the most recent ground of her divorce, our conversation takes on the awkward tremor of frisson and mild embarrassment. We haven't seen each other in years, but have developed a digitised intimacy via text message and shared photos. Now we are in close proximity, physical and alone. A choice of rooms to play in. No one to answer to. No one likely to barge in. Only Mrs. Carlisle has the power to prick whatever bubbles telegraph our unspoken thoughts above our heads.

Inevitably, I suggest alcohol as the sequel to our disappointing tea, prequel to whatever main event might unfold. Ambushed as I've been, I'm not prepared for Rosie's arrival. Three quarters of a bottle of Sauvignon Blanc is all I can offer. Three quarters of a bottle is a tease. It takes the edge off, it does not round the corners. A walk is in order, across the sands to the shop for supplies.

Rosie has come prepared for Lewis's temperament. She layers herself in figure augmenting outdoor wear, the likes of which didn't exist when we were children. Back then, a correctly prepared adventurer facing the fickleness of the great outdoors would surrender suppleness of limb to duvet-thick padding. Trips to the loo were a too close-to-call race between zips, Velcro and elastic and the increasingly urgent protest of a full bladder. Modern Rosie, clad in gortex, lycra and sympathetic fleece could equally be headed to a gymnastics class as a Highland hike.

In comparison, my outdoor gear, courtesy of Mr. McMenamin, makes me look as if I'm preparing for biological warfare. While Rosie is in the loo, I decide risking a soaking is the better part of sartorial valour, discarding my waterproof trousers, I stuff the top-half in my protesting knapsack, breaking its zip in the process.

Sporting an old skiing fleece and jeans, I scan the heavens for signs of inclemency as we head across the sands. The sky is unsettled like a *Monet*, revealing something different each time I squint for signs of rain or worse. White and yellow rays poke from behind irregular cloud formations as if there are multiple suns.

The returning tide pushes our pace across the disappearing bay, our boots fighting the suck of seawater on sand as we reach the safety of the blowhole. Despite her legs being a short trip as the crow flies from heel to hip, Rosie prances up the tumbling rocks with the carefree dexterity of a spaniel following a scent.

Looking back from the crest, to return the way we came is already impossible without a boat or gills. We have no choice but to return the long way by road. Not a bad thing, I think. I'm feeling uneasy about being alone with Rosie. A schoolboy dread of not knowing how to approach the delicacy before me. Charlie's presence is hovering like a butler in the shadows.

We walk side by side, conspicuously hand out of hand, filling the holes in our conversation with vacuous appreciation of the landscape. Making it to the store without bumping into Shaun the Sheep, I'm relieved. I can't face his piercing glare right now. In my mind he has become Charlie's ovine spokesman, her highland emissary exposing the wolf of my confusion - eviscerating that place on my insides where my head, heart and groin meet to argue over the words my mouth should utter, where my hands should wander.

The store, as ever, is further away than it looks. I have walked here a dozen times, but it never gets any closer. Fresh produce lines the shelves, much of which is unlikely to have been grown or garnered in Lewis's soggy peat. An improbable five different species of mushroom tumble for attention next to giant spring onions and bright purple baby beets. Fresh Parmesan cheese and Parma ham. Cockles and mussels and clams. Everything one needs to knock-up a *Jamie Oliver* recipe.

Everything is fresh and tantalising, except the wine. A regiment of unheard of red and white confections squeeze to attention like a row of unfit kids struggling to get picked for a playground football team. Improbably named and sired from grapes not daring to declare their provenance, selecting bottles that might not eviscerate the throat is a lottery.

Of course, we have brought no bags with us. Metropolitan eco-doctrine has made it to Lewis - no plastic bags are available, lest they make it into the ecosystem and gag short-sighted Seals. We buy a 50 pence mesh bag, emblazoned with a long Celtic word and squiggle that could mean anything. Somebody once told me the vast majority of Oriental symbol tattoos on western skin bear no resemblance to what the tattoo artist promised. Countless people proudly display their unwitting invitation to "kick-me" or worse. I wondered if the Celts have a word for fuck-wit.

Taking the long road we start back to Wham O-Bamo. Dodd's Castle heaves into view, and with the inevitability of Pavlov's dog, I suggest we stop-in for a couple of sharpeners. Given it's started to rain with thumping drops of icy water, there is no question of passing by the long drive. The sight of shelter induces long strides past Rocky's Police car and a familiar array of four-by-fours and vans. I have revisited Dodd's Castle countless times since my inauguration. It has become a second home to me. Unlike the transient bar staff in the East Hill Pub or Alma Tavern in Wandsworth, every time I step inside, Marine pulls me a pint of Back-Left before I ask. Each visit the same actors stand in the same places, saying the same lines. I have begun to wonder if I'm in a Celtic remake of The Truman Show, everyone actors except me. A social experiment and I am the specimen, my every move captured by secret cameras. The whole nation, watching from the comfort of their sitting rooms in nightly episodes. Am I the only person in the universe not in on the ruse? Is Claire a guest pundit in the TV studio, offering her opinions on my every rise and fall, steering the story to suit her narrative?

"Hullo Tom," says the Maître d', opening the door with a beaming smile and perfect timing, as if he's watched our approach on CCTV.

"Hello, good to see you again," I say with a little too much projection, "this is Rosie."

"Hi," says Rosie, offering her hand to shake, the tiny word of her opening gambit unequivocally outing her as a Scot. Their eyes meet and transmit unspoken words, as if he is saying, *what are you doing here with the Englishman?* To which she replies, *I know, it's embarrassing isn't it.*

Eddie is in, wearing his Stetson. Dexter is reading the sports pages. The Bean's are drinking at their table. Eddie makes towards me, his thumbs jabbed into the hip pockets of his jeans.

"Hello Tom," he says, "how've you been going?"

"Going? Err, walking mostly," I offer.

A man appears from a shadowy recess that doesn't look like a recess until he appears from it. Wearing blue jeans, trainers and a tightly buttoned white shirt I don't recognise it's Rocky, until he says, "Hello Lad."

"Hello Sir," I say, following hurriedly, "this is Rosie."

"Hullo," he says, smiling at Rosie, "you better watch out for this one," without explaining why or what she should watch out for.

"Oh, I know him well," says Rosie, without explaining what of me she has intimate knowledge.

Rosie asks for a Vodka, lime and soda. We perch on bar stools. I scan for a table and the vain hope of privacy where we might be left alone as a couple of apparent lovers swapping sweet nothings.

My search is interrupted by a new, impossibly good-looking character sauntering onto the stage. He looks over forty, but all the better for it. Impossibly tall and tanned, his sinewy strength, deep-seated and fat-free. He's wearing a perfectly-aged, nondescript blue t-shirt clamped to his torso like the body armour of a Roman Centurion. His hair is tousled, curly brown with the odd artful streak of blonde, his eyes pure blue marble. The tail of a tattoo peaks from beneath his bicep-hugging sleeve.

"Hi, I'm Tom," he says to both of us, directing a high-wattage smile at Rosie, her face immediately illuminating like finally finding the loose bulb in a string of Christmas lights.

"He's Tom too," gushes Rosie in his glow. "Ha! Ha!"

If there are grades of Tom, I am suddenly relegated to the Sunday leagues. This Tom is Premier. I can't imagine a woman in the world who could keep her knees parallel should he be in the business of seeking a little daylight.

Don't get me wrong, he already seems like a lovely guy. Natural and unaffected. He looks me in the eye and seems genuinely interested in my conversation. Eddie and Dexter join in and he includes them with sincerity only someone who has figured out life's balance can muster. Whatever he does for a living, it is never going to involve sales, or a suit or Swindon. Apparently, he rowed for Great Britain. Of course he did - bagging Silver in the Atlanta Olympics. He is on Lewis training for a TV show that will have him walking unaided to both Poles. I really, really want to dislike him, but find nothing to dislike - not a chink or flaw to develop a derogatory view. We are namesakes, but there our similarities ended. Rosie re-christens me Tom One, he is Tom Two. I am subconsciously grateful she gives our friendship primacy.

In all my life, I have never seen two strangers' gel so quickly. Tom Two and Rosie are perfect, complementary ingredients melding in a pan with the natural heat of chemistry. There is no need to whisk, come to the boil or add seasoning. They just work. Every line they utter makes the other smile, or laugh or fervently agree. Their conversation tumbles like fresh fruit from a wicker basket while the rest of us look on like out of date vegetables. If there was to be anything between myself and Rosie, it's just ended here and now. It's truly magical to watch two people who've only just met falling in love before my eyes. Not least, given everything Rosie has been through. Unless of course, this really is all a TV set-up, in which case they are brilliant actors.

"It's stopped raining," says Dexter, looking up from his weather app, staring out the window to confirm his technology is correct.

"I hadn't noticed," says Rosie, without irony.

"That's that terrible line," says Eddie, "from that film." He pronounces the word film, fil-em.

"Four Weddings and Funeral," I say too hurriedly, demonstrating my parochial ownership of the film that defined 1994 for me and The Gang.

"It's so badly acted," says Eddie

"What? That line or the whole film?" I question.

"No, the line," he says, "It's still a good fil-em."

Then he says they shouldn't have used an American actress, as that was a cop-out to sell cinema tickets.

"I think it's a great line. She's just being ironic," says Rosie, unironically.

"The best part of the fil-em, is the wedding in Scotland," says Eddie.

"When Andie MacDowell married the *stiff in a skirt?*" I add, helpfully quoting the fil-em.

Eddie glares at me like he wants to reach for the six-shooter he wishes he was wearing.

"Actually," says Dexter, the Scottish part was filmed in Hampshire, in England.

"No it wasn't," says Eddie.

"Yes it was," retorts Dexter, "in a house called Rotherfield Park."

"I don't believe ye," counters Eddie.

"How do you know this stuff?" asks Tom Two, "you're a mine of information."

"I'm the Scottish Pub Quiz Champion," says Dexter, his obvious pride sending a charge of electricity through his copse of hair.

"You won a general knowledge quiz in 2009," says Eddie spitefully.

"Say what you like Eddie," retorts Dexter. "The invitation to Andie MacDowell's wedding said Glenrith Castle, Perthshire. Want to know where it really was?"

"No," says Eddie.

"Yes," says Rosie.

"Guildford."

Game, set and match to the geek. Eddie looks into his glass, taking a final glug of national pride.

"Bollocks." Eddie slams his glass on the bar.

"Back-Right?" I ask.

"Don't mind if I do," says Dexter.

From the corner of my eye, I see Tom Two locking little fingers with Rosie, like kids building up to a snog in the back of a cinema. Had I brought my coat, I'd have got it. I wonder where Tom Two is staying before it turns out he has a room upstairs.

I drive Rocky home, my festering depression and disappointment alleviated by the thrill of driving a police car. Rocky is drunk, but not drunk enough to accede to my request to turn on the blue lights. I'm drunk enough to ask, but thankfully not drunk enough to find a ditch.

Leaving him and his car on his drive, I walk alone the last mile to the cottage. I can only imagine what Rosie is getting up to. I imagine I'm walking hand-in-hand with Charlie chatting about how far we have traveled without reaching a destination. I realise how I have let her presence validate the person I want to become, but I'm still a long way from being that person. I wonder what role I have played for her. I know I must complete my recovery before I can give her what she needs. That she must find herself before she can reciprocate. If we are to spend a happy swansong together we both have more mountains to climb.

I am Tom. I want to go home.

Chapter 18: THE ALCHEMIST

"When a person really desires something, all the universe conspires to help that person to realise his dream."

Paulo Coelho

Rosie and Tom Two have embarked on their journey and I am staying in bed all day. Oddly, it is the first full-bed day I've had since the Apocalypse. I am so happy for Rosie, but it's only making me feel worse. I suppose it is fair I'm wallowing. I feel sorry for myself. The self-appointed victim. My fevered mind pinging and ponging between Charlie, Claire, Rosie, my children, my career and then for good measure, Marine. There is very little comfort to find other than the glimmer of Charlie. I smile at the memory of driving Rocky's police car home last night. The police car that, under normal circumstances, should have transported me to the cells, handcuffed in the back. But life is not normal. Perhaps it never will be again. By evening I manage a microwave meal. By bedtime, feelings of positivity reappear like nervous animals assessing the danger of stepping out into the open.

When first light shows again, I'm already half way up Charlie's slopes. My ascent accompanied by a few spats of rain and clouds that threaten omens I fear I might take to heart. I'm terrified of being derailed again. By the time I'm sitting in the long grass of her summit, the clouds have pushed far out to sea leaving me to commune with Charlie in the warm sunshine. *It has been a tough time,* I tell her. I have been way below my best, but I'm imagining a future together that surpasses anything I have experienced to date. I'm daring to imagine a life a few years down the road. If she will allow it. If she wants it. A house together maybe? I even wonder if we are too old to have another child. A child of our own. Perhaps a dog? What would we have? A Spaniel? A Dalmatian? A Labrador?

That night, I print a picture from Facebook, folding it neatly and secreting it into my coat pocket. I know what I have to do.

This time, I have Claire's measure. I know her tough parts, I know where the going is good, and I'm ready for her. I understand what she can do to me if I take the wrong step. I'm in control unlike before, climbing her every face with confidence. Standing on her summit, I unfold the piece of paper from my pocket and take a long look. I fold it in half, turn it through ninety degrees and rip it in two. Then four. Then eight. Stacking the squares of paper together until I can't rip anymore, taking each piece, ripped into confetti, then toss them into the water. I recall the day Claire and I married, the joy of the faces that greeted us outside the church. The overzealous photographer attempting to marshal the crowd who wanted champagne, not marshalling.

For a moment, I think the Otters have reappeared as I watch the tiny pieces of the picture of Claire and I floating away like a doomed armada. It's not the Otters. It's debris. Nobody sees me say goodbye to Claire. Nobody sees me cry.

By the end of the week I will be back in London. Back to the reality of life, but I'm not sure what real will look like. The night before I leave, the good people of Dodd's are throwing me a Ceilidh to see me off. At least that's what they've been telling me since I announced my impending departure. It seems churlish to disabuse them of this flattering fiction. Truth is I'm rather enjoying the attention of what is being spoken of as Tom's Ceilidh. It has doubtless been in the diary for months, and has nothing to do with me, but following the maxim of any excuse for a party, I'm more than happy to provide an additional excuse.

My last two visits to Dodd's have brought an undercurrent of mild-ribbing about how I might or indeed might not, survive this event. If it carries a movie classification I'm beginning to think it might be: mild threat, violence, adult language.

Dexter told me he remembers his first time, then failed to elaborate what he remembers, but by the look on his face he remembers somewhere between absolutely nothing and nightmare inducing flashbacks.

Eddie said, "if you don't know what you're doing, you'll get hurt."

When I enquired how I could find out what to do, he simply said I would work it out.

Bean told me if I turn up without a kilt it will be frowned upon. Having been on the receiving end of Bean's frowns, I was in no doubt he is serious, and protested I am English and don't have the right. Aileen countered by saying people from all over the world where Kilts even Sassenachs. And anyway, apparently I'm one of them now which is a red rag to my adopted Scottish bull.

The cottage is all but packed up and cleaned as well as a man who doesn't cite cleaning as his profession can. Having a heavy night drinking before a double plane ride home I am well aware is a heinous error, and I am terrified I will soil myself on my way home. But I have no choice, so I embrace my fate by finishing my bottle of gin before I head across the bay. Feeling like I'm heading to a school prom without a date, I head down the sand dunes, my kilt flapping ungraciously behind me and I know, just know Mrs. Carlisle is watching. At least I have no underwear on, Mr McMenamin had made sure of that fact when I bought the damn thing. He had explained there are cheap tourist kilts, but a proper one costs £300-£400. When I picked myself back out of the pet baskets, he took pity on me and found me a second hand number for £120, which he said was a non-private family tartan so I could get away with it without being lynched.

I walk across the bay with a jaunty falter, it's a perfect dusk of dancing colours and sense tingling nature. I think to myself of the things I have learned, the things I will leave behind and the things I will take home with me. On balance, I conclude my account is in credit. My liver may have not taken a turn for the better but my soul is beginning to feel plump, my head less full and my heart match-fit.

Arriving at Dodd's, it's like walking into a school disco. The chairs and tables are all pushed back and the lights are up, robbing it's usual dark ambience of any atmosphere. Along the sea-facing windows, a group of kilt clad characters are setting up their instruments, all wearing regulatory white knee socks, bound to their calves by tight leather laces sprouting from ornate black brogues. I am wearing my embarrassingly out-of-place walking boots - I had also turned down the Dirk, the Dash and the Sporran Mr. McMenamin had offered me. There is Scottish and there is Scottish and I am neither, but now I'm regretting my half-attempt and wishing I'd stayed full-English and just taken the beating.

A welcome party of my new friends is gathered at the bar, and by the looks on their faces as I arrive, they are waiting for me. Marine is the first to greet me with a kiss on the right cheek, then the left, then we both hesitate in a moment of cross-cultural uncertainty.

"Back-right?" I ask with a smile.

She leans forward and kisses me a third time, just in front of my right ear, lingering long enough to transfer the sense the world wasn't such a bad place after-all.

"Tu vas nous manquer," she says.

I reply *moi aussi*, because I know what that phrase means. I also know how to say I love you in Swedish, but suspect it won't be much help right now.

Eddie says. "You were a broken wing when you got here. I'm not sure you're ready for long haul flight yet, but there is at least wind between your wings. We've enjoyed having ye." He gives me a slap on the back, a *slange* and a belt buckle of the Saltire, without a belt attached to it. I *slange* him back, wondering when I will ever wear such a thing and how I might ever get around to attaching a belt to it, and decide I will do both with pride in my briefly adopted country.

"Are you playing tonight Eddie?" I ask.

"Well," he says, "it's not our show but we'll probably join in later. Are ye ready?"

"I have no idea."

Abigail appears. I haven't seen her since my inauguration.

"Hello mate," she says, giving me a hug violating all of my personal boundaries. I ask where she has been to which she replies, all over the place.

I don't doubt it for a moment.

"I came back for the Ceilidh," she says, "I've been looking forward to it for weeks."

As suspected, this evening isn't in my honour, but I am truly honoured to be here. No matter what is about to be unleashed.

I drink two Back-Rights because if the Dutch know anything about courage, I'm sure taking a leaf out of their book right now.

At the moment I notice the lights have gone down, I sense a palpable rise of anticipation in the air. There must be sixty-people in here which surely is half the population of Lewes. Tartan is everywhere.

Traditional tartan.

Sexy vampish tartan with Doc Martin boots, and breast suffocating tops.

Irish Dancer mini tartan, topping off long black-stocking legs.

Frilly, Bavarian Oompah band tartan.

There are belt buckles straight from Gullivers Travels.

Ball gowns.

Farm wear.

And, of course, a cowboy called Eddie, still in search of a pair of cowboy boots.

A hard press of the accordion by the Romanian woman wedged into her seat is accompanied by the rattle of a snare drum. It is the Highlands and Islands equivalent of sounding the cavalry charge at Balaclava, the moment of terrifying dread at Passchendaele, the first day of the Harrods sale, last orders on Princes Street.

The sky turns briefly black with raining lager and they are off.

And I'm off, though I didn't ask.

Abigail links her arm with mine and flings me onto the dancefloor like she's hurling incriminating evidence into a lake. Another arm links with mine and violently counters my trajectory, sending me off in a new direction from which I am rescued from the rest of my life in a wheelchair by another arm deciding I will have more fun back in the middle. Couples of every gender combination link crossed hands and barrel through the middle of the crowd like demented Dick Van Dykes reprising his famous cockney chimney sweep.

Legs, knees, kick, kick.

Heel, toe.

Heel, toe.

There seems to be no way to exit the throng, every time I grasp for the safety of the edges, I am fired back. The Dashing White Sergeant has no end, like it's composer missed the class about how to end a song without resorting to a fade.

5, 6, 7, 8.

Wooooooosh. I lunge for the bar and hold on like Bruce Willis hanging from a Skyscraper.

"Ca va?" shouts Marine.

"Back-Left," I gasp.

Strip the Willow.

The Highland Fling.

The Macarena.

Circassian Circle.

Agadoo.

The Gay Gordons.

Oops-up-side-your-head.

The dance equivalent of a military-grade fireworks display run by fireproof drunks. And the most fun I've had with my clothes on since Englnd won the World Cup, but I'm not thinking about that, because right now I'm Scottish and proud of it.

And we're doing the Conga.

Down with the English and their King.

It could be midnight, or it could be a week next Thursday, the band seems to have run out of tunes or fingernails or sweat to excrete and Eddie and Dexter take to the stage. After an improbable performance of Prince's *Kiss,* which clears the floor, they play Lady in Red. To my amazement this doesn't start a riot, nor does Marine turn me down when I ask for a dance. We shuffle around the floor holding each other waist to shoulder, not really catching one another's eye, but not avoiding the glances either. It is frisson without anticipation, a beautiful moment of peace to the world's cheesiest song that makes me smile and think about crying and hope I can negotiate to the end without flattening Marine should gravity get its way.

I'm feeling rather embarrassed at all the fuss. Perhaps like pets can sense pain in their owners, my Scottish therapy group has peered inside my fragile exterior and seen the things I still haven't figured out for myself. I will never forget the extra mile they have gone for me.

I open the front door of my Wandsworth townhouse, pulling the worn brass handle towards me, simultaneously lifting and pushing up and to the right with the action of turning the key. I know I need to fix that door. Perhaps my reluctance to call John or Steve or Pavlek to be remunerated at vast expense is a reason for my downfall. Claire always said I didn't 'do jobs' like other husbands. I was happy to settle for the status quo and a stubborn door. It slams behind me. It always slams, even when shutting it gently. It is one of those doors.

Only hours earlier, I had locked the cottage door behind me and got into my hire car. Then got out again, unlocked the door and left the keys on the kitchen table where I'd first found them. I had looked out to sea, deliberating whether to say goodbye to Mrs. Carlisle, knowing what a one-way conversation it would be.

Returning to the car I spotted a sheath of heather bound in a tartan ribbon, perching on the windscreen wiper. Attached was a cheap paper tag, like you find on a birthday present. Written upon it in childlike handwriting it said, *'May the road rise to meet you. Mrs. C. x.'*

What a lovely gesture.

I know the phrase – from an Irish blessing I'd first heard read at Dyfed's wedding. The next two lines; *may the wind be ever at your back. May the sun shine warm upon your face.*

For a brief moment I allow myself to think Claire might be back – in the kitchen, fixing lunch. That the kids are in the playroom, fighting over this or that. There are no suitcases at the bottom of the stairs. Perhaps Claire has changed her mind. Perhaps, it has all been a terrible nightmare. Well, it has, except I have been mostly awake. The pile of mail on the doormat tells me there is no Claire, no kids, no reconciliation. Despite being away for three and a bit months, all the detritus of family life lies undisturbed, each set of keys, device chargers, unhung hangers and crockery on the draining board a reminder of what normality once looked like. The missing painting in the sitting room wall confirms it. No time warp. No Truman show. Despite finding myself on Lewis; despite saying goodbye to Claire and making pledges to Charlie, on the face of it, life hasn't improved much since I left. It crosses my mind to move lock-stock to Lewis, wear man-jewellery and marry a girl who smells of petunia oil. Lewis couldn't be that much further from Dublin than Wandsworth. Even as I toy with the notion, I know it's not the answer. I have to face up to whatever life has planned next.

Chapter 19: JANE EYRE

"I would rather be happy than dignified."

Charlotte Brontë

I'm pleased to say, I haven't hit the canvas, or the bottle. In fact, I'm *proud* to say it. Perhaps I am making progress. I'm not quite so proud to say I spent almost £2000 on my credit card before I unpacked my bags from Scotland. I went straight out and bought a new sofa and chairs and a large framed print of French Countryside to cover the gap on the wall. Plus a Nespresso coffee machine, new bedding, four carrier bags full of essentials from Sainsbury's and a replacement fridge freezer I had long promised Claire but never delivered upon.

When I collapsed on my old sofa that evening, I felt like I'd done one of those supermarket shops when you buy bags of stuff, but nothing you can easily constitute into a meal. £2000 down and not a great deal had changed, so I hung the picture, hooked up the Nespresso machine and got high on coffee.

A week later my new furniture and fridge have arrived. They look great. I shop again and stuff the fridge full of good stuff and feel like a man. It would be obvious to say something is missing – my wife and kids, blah, blah. I know that, and I know she is not coming back. So what is it? I text Claire.

I'm going to put the house on the market. I don't think I can live here anymore. And leave it at that.

To my surprise, she responds quickly and kindly. *I think that's a good idea*, she typed.

Ping.

Another message.

How are you? How are things?

Taken aback I am. Flabber-gibbered. She is asking after my welfare and I cant' detect a trace of mean, hidden subtext. For the next two or three weeks we converse by text a great deal. She asks me if I want to see the kids. I say yes, then she obfuscates. She had a point. The kids have four weeks left of the summer term. They will see me in the holiday. Best not to confuse or unsettle them. I suggest I come over for the weekend, she doesn't seem so keen on that. I ask her why, and she avoids the question. In fact, I ask her a lot of questions over the next few weeks. Questions she answers with questions, or swerves or bats sideways. There is something very different in her tone. Something kind. Almost pleading. I can't put my finger on what it is. Her life is completely alien to me now – I have no idea what she does, who with or when. The whole life of the woman I have spent all those years with is closed to me.

I keep up my text conversations with the kids, punctuated by the odd call, following the same format. *How are you? What did you do at school today? What are you doing now? What are you doing tomorrow? Love You.*

Sitting at the dining room table at Matt and Jess's house we discuss my chances of getting a good price for the house. Where I might move to. How I could see more of the kids. We talk about Claire and how, for a while, she had become much friendlier on text. How those texts have now stopped completely. She isn't replying. I'm used to her moods, so I put it down to her moods. Something must be going on with her love life.

Matt and Jess agree I'm looking much better. *Less pinched,* Jess says. I'm not sure I like the fact I had ever looked *pinched.* Hey whatever, pinched, punched, I'm sure I've looked like a B-movie zombie at some points. Matt tells me I'm obviously in a much better frame of mind. We talk of Charlie and how I hope we would all have dinner together soon. *They would love that,* they say.

All I say is *blimey* when the name 'Ian' appears on my phone. That is where the understatement ends. Ian is still technically my brother-in-law. I can't recall when I had last spoken to him. Perhaps his task is made easier by the distance created by the Apocalypse. He tells me Claire is very ill. Breast Cancer has been diagnosed and it may have reached her lymph nodes. Ian himself had only just found out. Claire had made her family swear to secrecy about her illness.

"Are you Okay?" Asks Matt while I'm still listening to Ian.

Hanging up the call, I tell them the news. "Are you Okay?" Matt asks again, reaching for a cross-table man hug.
"I'm not sure," I say.

Let me take things in order. Firstly, she was the woman I married and once loved in an oops-we-got-married kind of way. She is the mother of my children and a human being. On none of those levels can the news be anything but bad. The fact she hadn't told me, confuses me. We have our *decree nisi*, but not yet our *decree absolute*. We are still married by law and I still feel responsible for her. Even once we are divorced, we will forever be bound by our children. And when we are no longer financially responsible for them, there will be graduations, heart-breaks and weddings to co-navigate. To be cut out of such terrible news makes me sad. To not consider the implications on Jack and Clara and by turn, myself, makes me angry. But she is the one who is ill and there is no trumping that, so I settle on sad.

Matt and Jess and I do the only thing we can do, given the hour and open a bottle of red wine. We discuss treatment and remission and cancer survivors who go on to their natural end. Perhaps it is the wine that leads us to a roll-call of lives taken too soon. Everyone knows someone. The super-fit triathlete who never came back from his swim. The lover of life rugby player with the big heart concealing a congenital fault. The mother and two daughters rear-ended by a truck driver texting hookers on the M5.

Mortality is never a good conversation, we all realise it is time to call a halt. I teetere around the corner trying to process the information. Some of the scenarios I conjuree necessitated Claire not pulling through, so I stop that as well.

Sitting at my kitchen table I type a text to Claire:

I've just heard your news. I'm so, so sorry. Bit pissed you didn't tell me though. Can we talk in the morning?

Then I deleted the bit about being pissed and pressed send.

It's past my kids bedtime, but still I text Jack and Clara to say hi and check they are Okay. I have no idea what they know, if anything, about Mummy.

I get hold of Claire the next day, she is upbeat. She is sorry she hasn't told me, it is just something she needs to deal with alone. I remind her of the kids and she says sorry again. They don't know anything. Her next appointment isn't for another two weeks then they will have a more definitive prognosis.

I spend the rest of the day at a loss. Here I am again in the limbo of uncertainty. I can't allow myself to project forward and think what it might mean for me and the kids, but of course I do. I even take Claire's news as another slap in the face of *my* recovery. I know that's selfish, but I can't shake the stupid thought she has somehow contrived this.

I deserve a drink. Two bottles of wine and a curry, under the circumstances. Okay, maybe just the one bottle.

Other than pesto, there is one other thing I really hate. Sorry Peers. It's the double blue tick. When grey turns blue, your message has been read. So, why hasn't the reader bloody replied?! I could go on about when we were young and dating there was no text messages, no ticks and how you waited for a girl to call sitting by the landline and if she rang (which she usually didn't) you let it ring for five rings or if you were cooler than Steve McQueen, let it go to answer machine. If I go down that path, soon I'll be prattling on about vinyl records and photo negatives and allowing twenty-eight days for delivery. You don't need any of that. I'll move on.

The messages I sent to Jack and Clara when I heard Claire's news still have grey ticks. They haven't read them. Did I mention I hate that?

Three days laters and the ticks are still grey and I'm going insane, but Claire finally calls and I answer with wet fingers, waddling across the bathroom. She tells me her Mum, Charlotta had confiscated the children's phone's when she had been diagnosed and they've only just been given them back. I'm desperate to know they are OK.

Claire is outside the hospital.

"It's not so bad," she says switching subjects..

"How bad is it?"

"Nothing in my lymph nodes, we've caught it early. Lucky I've got small tits!" She says. I take that point both ways. "They've given me a good chance of full recovery."

"That's great," I say. I've got no contact lenses in. Naked, I scan the bathroom for my glasses through the Vaseline that smears across my eyes when my vision is uncorrected.

"There's something else," she says.

"What?" I ask

"I'm pregnant."

"How pregnant?" I say, my vision restored by my glasses as I hurry to catch up with Claire's ridiculous revelation.

"How did I get pregnant or how far along am I?"

"Both."

"I got pregnant the normal way and twelve weeks."

"But you've got cancer."

"Cancer is not a contraceptive."

"You can't be treated for cancer with a baby inside you."

"Yes you can. It's not uncommon."

This is classic Claire. She can start a riot over someone stealing her car parking space. She can start a revolution over fishcakes being removed from the school lunch menu. But being pregnant with cancer is *not uncommon*.

"Jesus," I say. "You're too old to have another baby."

"Says who?"

"Says everyone. It's just not right."

"It wasn't planned," she says, adding, "obviously."

"So why are you keeping it?"

After a long pause when I regret what I just said, she says, "I'm not answering that."

Silence hangs, waiting for one of us to say something.

I don't know what to say.

Eventually she starts up again, "my Doctor says I'll have to have a mastectomy."

Note her use of the word, my. This is just another adventure in the world of Claire. I can imagine her flirting with her Doctor, making light of her misfortune. She doesn't cry like the other woman. She is going to bolster her sense of self-righteousness by making the doctor blush and think unprofessional thoughts. There is something else obvious bothering me I didn't want to bring up because I'm pretty sure I don't want to know the answer.

"Who's the father," I ask.

"I'm not telling you."

"You've got to tell me."

"It's nothing to do with you."

"How is it nothing to do with me?"

"It's my life. It's nothing to do with you."

"Jack and Clara are going to have a brother or sister."

"Yes."

"So it's got everything to do with me. Who's the father?"

"It's none of your business."

"Is this the person who broke up our marriage?"

"Nobody broke up our marriage," she yells, "take some bloody responsibility."

"I am taking bloody responsibility. You've never even said sorry."

"Of course I'm sorry," she says, "look, we've got to move on."

"But the Baby? The cancer?"

"Look," she says. "I can't have radiotherapy as it might harm the baby. They are going to open me up and chop it out. Job done. The baby will be fine."

"I don't care about the fucking baby," I yell at the top of my voice. "I care about the mother of my children and my children ending up without a fucking mother." I slam the phone down, scream Jesus at the top of my voice and go hunting for some fags.

I call Matt, "are you working from home today?"

"Yes mate, are you Okay?" he replies.

"Can I come round?"

"Of course mate."

He doesn't ask why. My asking is sufficient to know trouble has brewed again.

Matt has a Nespresso machine.

He is the Emperor of Nespresso.

The coffee pods are stored in a felt-lined presentation case, sorted in strength and colour order. Offering him instant coffee is like offering Chardonnay to Claire. "You look like you need a strong one," says Matt, easing a pod from the 'specials' pod row as if selecting a mercury-tipped bullet from a tray of illegal ammunition.

"Claire's pregnant," I say.

"What?!" says Matt.

"Bullshit," adds Jess, in that way saying bullshit doesn't dispute the fact, but the fact is so incredible it deserves the status of bullshit.

"What about the cancer?" asks Matt.

"She's got that too," I say.

"How can you get pregnant when you've got cancer?" asks Matt.

"That's what I said," I say, "she said cancer isn't a contraceptive."

"Tasteful," says Jess.

"She's having a mastectomy."

"Jesus," says Matt.

"That's what I said."

Matt busies himself sorting the washing. He runs a strict regime of piles according to person, tops, bottoms, underwear and heaven forbid if a sock doesn't present itself with its partner. Inspecting a bra in the light, I assume to match cup-size to the owner's cup, he asks, "what are you going to do?"

"I have no idea," I say. "it's just one thing after another." Clutching my coffee, I stand up and stare out the window, I'm not expecting a reply. Matt is picking washing fluff from his sweater. Jess has her head in a cookbook. I close my eyes and try to find calm. Orla is always telling me I need to find calm as if calm is a place with bean bags and soft-furnishings and quietly spoken nurses bringing you tea. After a long pause, Matt says, "listen mate, it doesn't matter what we think of Claire, what is happening to her is awful."

"I know."

"It's terrible, but you've got to think about the children, more than ever," says Jess.

"I know," I say, picking up a plastic medicine bottle from the window sill above the sink, "but Claire is treating it like she's got a headache. What are these?"

"Homeopathic happy pills,"

"Do they work?"

"I doubt it," says Matt

"Not given his moods," says Jess.

"L-5 Hydroxy Typtofan," I say reading the label

"Catchy," says Jess.

"Oh god, she's going to be on horrendous drugs," I blurt. "She'll lose her hair."

"I doubt it mate," counters Matt. "Not if she's going under the knife, they can't mess with the baby."

"I suppose not."

Had there been an elephant in the room I'd have asked, what if Claire doesn't make it? As it happens, Elephants are hard to come by in Wandsworth and anyway, Matt would never stand for muddy feet in the kitchen. But he does ask who the Father is

"I have no idea," I say, struggling with mental images galloping through my head:

Claire making babies.

Claire in a maternity unit.

Claire holding a newborn infant.

Jack and Clara standing at the christening font with Claire and their new sibling.

Claire and another man looking proud.

"It is someone she's just met, or someone we know?" asks Matt.

"I still have no idea, but now you put it like that, I wonder."

"Surely, it can't be anyone we know," says Jess.

"I wouldn't put it past anyone these days,"

"It wasn't me," says Matt. "I wouldn't go near her with my barge pole."

"That's helpful," says Jess.

"We've got to eliminate the suspects," says Matt. "It definitely wasn't me."

"I'm sure the list is long and distinguished," I say.

"What a bastard," says Matt helpfully.

"Probably," I agree.

Which just about sums it up. We are none the wiser. Claire is fighting cancer she treats like a walk in the park. She is pregnant by someone, who Matt has introduced the concept of us possibly knowing. And my children are blissfully unaware of not one but two more potential Apocalypses about to detonate in their life. I simply do not know what to do, so I ask if it's too early for a drink.

"It's Midday somewhere," confirms Matt. .

Chapter 20: OF HUMAN BONDAGE

"It might be that to surrender to happiness was to accept defeat, but it was a defeat better than many victories."

W. Somerset Maugham

I've missed three months worth of Book Club, which according to high-ways and by-laws of Ian Korf means I have forfeited my position. According to Orla, he repeatedly asks after my progress and by association my book writing. She says I should attend the next meeting with her, which it turns-out, is no different from all those I attended before. Little has changed - almost all the same people. Ian's misplaced dress-sense. Marcus snorting and sniping at his wife doing backstroke in Sauvignon Blanc. This is the first meeting not attended by Aude and Oli, a fact causing some consternation as the Club is now seriously under strength and Ian is perturbed at the strain it may place on the rest of his disciples. The unconfirmed rumour is Aude and Oli have gone on holiday together and they are only going to get a big high-five from me for doing that. I wonder if they have laken little Rachel with them or left her with a friend explaining Mummy is going for some Mummy time. I hope Rachel is with them and they are a happy threesome. I sense Ian is frowning down upon fraternisation between Club members leading to deffection and think he probably needs to consult his inner-Freud on that point.

Veronica catches my eye and trundles towards me like a poorly designed robot, apparently beaming at my return from the North.

"How have you been lovely Tom?" she gushes. "How is your book?"

"I've been great, thank you. A great trip."

"And your book. How is your book?"

'Errm, well, I'm almost there, I think.'

"Oh how exciting."

"Yes, how exciting," says Ian, hoving into view. "As we are two men down tonight, perhaps you might give us an update."

"Aude is not a man," points out Veronica.

"No, Veronica, spot on as always, she isn't," withers Ian.

Whatever I am about to say, I know Marcus will be lining up to shoot me down like the Guns of Navarone. I'm not sure whether to down-play or over-play so I open up by saying, I don't know what to say and then say not a lot until somebody asks me how many words it is and somebody else asks me if it is cathartic, which of course it is, as always, and somebody else asks me how much of it is based on real experiences and then Marcus asks me the smart question, which does, in fairness stop me rambling.

"Who is it aimed at?" I reply, stalling. "That's a good question."

It is a good question.

"A woman who read it says everybody should read it. Another friend said she and her husband had had sex for the first time in almost a year having read it. So, I'm not sure."

"I just want to read it," says Veronica.

"You are hardly target market," says Marcus.

"What the fuck do you mean by that?!" spits Jenita across the table at her husband.

She's pissed.

I think Marcus may need to retrain his guns.

"The truth is," I say, trying to divert attention from what looks like it may be about to become a case-in-point, "it is written from a male perspective. Obviously. But that's the point there are two genders in every relationship..."

"Unless it's a same sex marriage," adds Veronica.

"Yes, Veronica, I meant two people, my apologies. Two people in every relationship, and two sides to every story, and dispute is only resolved when both sides are heard and understood."

Marcus snorts.

Jenita gulps her wine like there may be something precious at the bottom of her glass she needs to get to.

"Should people read it before they get married?" asks Ian.

"I'm not sure they would ever get married if they did," I say, laughing nervously at my own observation, and then thinking it through and wondering what I always wonder which is how to help couples not walk up the aisle who really shouldn't. I'm beginning to feel very uneasy. All the people I'm having the conversation with are in the book. It's not really a novel, it's a journal, but I can't say that.

"Every man and every woman thinking of getting married should read it," says Orla in her let's-close-this-fucking-conversation-off voice.

Jenita isn't listening and decides to add her value to the conversation, telling us all how many years she has spent in marketing (twenty-five) and how it's all about positioning and the why, how, what, who and how book marketing is generally crap and please will someone bring her another glass of wine.

Walking home with Orla, we chat but I'm having a second dialogue in my head. Why am I writing this book and yes, who is it for? How many people will I offend? Should I try and go through the slog of trying to find someone foolish enough to publish it? Dealing with rejection, which isn't my favourite emotion these days. Self-publishing doesn't sound great.

Orla is fuming about Marcus and Jenita saying they shouldn't be allowed out and they are dragging the world down around them and they should be neutered, at least Marcus should. And then we talk about how they probably haven't had sex since Blair was in power and then how Cherie and Tony had sex at Balmoral which Cherie overshared to the world. To round off our happy banter as we near home we talk about Claire and cancer and her fatherless child who of course has a father, but we don't know who it is.

Then we talk about artificial insemination

And spatulas.

And then thankfully we're at my front door, which I really need to fix.

The following morning I make a menu plan for the kids, annotating where Jack and Clara can help in the preparation when they come in the summer holidays.

I guess it's because I'm really enjoying my writing about cooking.

It is the constant creation of something new, rather than my recent diet of picking through rubble.

I bake a cake, forgetting the sugar, creating a cow-pat.

No Biggy.

It goes in the bin and I start again. Somewhere along the line I have gone from every petty failure being a reason to open a bottle, to an inbuilt sense of *que sera.* I feel in my heart Claire is going to beat her cancer. The question remains of the baby growing inside her. A question I can't quite *que sera.*

An abridged version of my single Dad's cooking piece (I had got rather carried away) is finally published in The Guardian on Saturday and the full version on the website, under my byline and the headline "COOKING AND THE SINGLE MAN." Melissa tells me the fuckers upstairs had held it back and she had to fight for it, but now I will finally get paid. It's great to see my name in print again.

I'm staggered by the response. Single men and women email bombard me with recipes, stories and thanks for the inspiration not to be a kitchen loser and by inference the same for the bedroom and life. Feeding off their applause, I decide to throw a dinner party for the people I consider paramount in my recovery. I select a Saturday night a month hence to give as few as possible an excuse to plead diary clashes. My planning becomes D-Dayesque. In my head this is to be my swansong to my life lost and launch party for life Part 2. Time can't pass quick enough, I think about what I am going to wear on the night, paint over the damp in the corner of the dining room, buy a set of ten napkins

Proposed guest list:

Charlie
Orla
Dyfed
Annabel and David
Rowan and Joanna
Peers and Janine
Adrian and Gemma
Matt and Jess
Graeme
Rosie and Tom Two

Including me, that makes sixteen. I can only fit ten chairs round my table plus two non-matching kitchen chairs wedged on the ends. I send an email to everyone on the list, except Charlie who I will ask in person. I assume plenty won't be able to make it. Adrian will be half way up the Khyber Pass, Dyfed will be flogging MRI machines to Eskimos, Rosie and Tom Two will be in a love cabin in Bali. We'll see.

It feels good sending out the email, like I'm re-entering society. I'm not a dinner party fan, this is the one-off, I hope, to end all one-offs. My ointment still has flies in it. Will Claire be Okay? Will the identity of the father of her baby hit me for six, or does it even matter? The thought occupying me most is whether Charlie will come to my party. I hadn't seen her since before Scotland. We have exchanged many inconsequential texts, enquiring after each other's health and happiness and how the children are. Up until now, in each exchange I have held back from asking if we should meet. It has taken Herculean restraint, but I figure the ball is in her court and she has to hit first.

I figure I also need to lay off Claire's baby's paternity question. In life's cruel order, Claire has to come first. One can't exist without the other. She called yesterday after her operation.

"Success," she said.

"Success?" I said.

She told me her surgeon had got it all out.

"That's good then."

"It's great!"

I can't quite share her optimism, cancer rarely plays with a straight bat.

"Is the baby OK?" I asked.

"It seems so," she said, like she was commenting on the weather.

"So, what now?" I asked. She said she had a lot of thinking to do, we would talk soon - which was marginally better than when a woman says she needs to talk. Needing to talk rarely ends well.

The responses to my invitation are coming back one by one. I'm going to need a bigger table. I finally text Charlie asking if she'll come. *No pressure*.

Matt and Jess can come to the rescue (as ever). They have two trestle tables we can line up next to my dining table. They say they have plenty of chairs. I'm working on the menu. Working on Melissa to allow me to do a follow-up piece based on all the feedback I've received. I wait a typically long time for Charlie to reply to my text.

I'm not good around people, she eventually texts in the middle of the night.

You know them all! I reply

She says she will see nearer the time which I take to mean she will come. And then I take it to mean she probably won't. I have learned there are things in life I can't control:

Who is the U.S. President,

Which Eighties pop-bands should and shouldn't stage a revival.

The price of fish.

What goes on in Charlie's head.

I text Claire, *is the father of your child going to be part of your (our) life?* I like the provocation of it. I don't anticipate a reply. She replies in thirty seconds.

No.

Why not? I fire back.

He's not that sort of person

What sort of person is he?

She doesn't reply, but Charlie does. *What time is the party?*

This is Charlie-speak for accepting the invitation. I'm over the moon and then immediately stressed about getting it right. I'm worrying the drunken conversation might go places she doesn't feel comfortable. Worried how people who knew us both with our former partners will react to us being together. To make myself feel better I open a beer and text Claire, *he sounds like a nob.*

She doesn't reply to that either.

The only invitation declined so far is Annabel and her new boyfriend David. They have to attend his younger brother's twenty-first birthday. Twenty-first?!! Her toy boy still has toys. I'm gutted Annabel can't make it, she had been my familial rock throughout it all. Mum and Dad have been great in their own ways, but Annabel and I have a bond I think might be stronger than anything even the happiest of marriages could achieve. Blood is thicker than water, no rocket science there, but siblings forged in the same crucible are made of steel that cuts through the bullshit like no other.

I realise now I have a party on my hands. I haven't thrown a party in years. I'm not sure I've ever thrown one on my own. There is only one thing for it, I have to fix the front door.

I'm standing on the Edwardian tiled path looking at my front door. If you're thinking I'm about to fall for the old lock yourself out while fixing the door gag, don't worry, I have my house keys in my pocket.

This is looking a mighty task, but I'm determined to get it right so I watch a Youtube instructional video posted by a character called Geo who wears a headcam, never revealing face, just his fingers appearing at the bottom of the screen pointing things out like a machine gun in a game of Call of Duty. He has a transatlantic accent with an added hint of somewhere lawless, giving the strong impression he locks children up in his cellar when not making Youtube videos. Having learned little I decide it's the large, brass locking mechanism causing the problem and set about removing it with a selection of screwdrivers, chisels and a bradawl. Attempting to create leverage I crack the stained glass and then the locking bolt thingy falls inside it's own shell, thus rendering the door unlockable. In my frustration I kick the bottom panel which implodes without protest. An outcome which would have been useful had I been attempting to install a cat flap. A trip to B&Q and £650 on the credit my new door will arrive in 48 hrs. I spend the subsequent two nights with the inside door knob lashed to the stair bannister by a rope tied to an extension lead in a moment of ingenuity Macaulay Culkin would have been proud of. The man I pay £120 to install my new door does a good job. I never asked his name, it was probably John or Steve or maybe Pavel.

Chapter 22: THE CHILDREN OF MEN

"We can experience nothing but the present moment, live in no other second of time, and to understand this is as close as we can get to eternal life."

P.D.James

Matt and Jess appear with the trestle tables soon after first light.

"Couldn't you sleep?"

"It's party-time," barks Matt too loudly, yanking the first table up the hall with Jess at the other end, struggling to keep her end up.

"Nice door," says Jess.

Of course, the two trestles aren't the same height as my table. They aren't the same height as each other. Once we have added all the odd chairs round the uneven square, I say it looks like a meeting table of a paramilitary group plotting the overthrow of Wandsworth.

"It looks like a meeting room for Alcoholics Anonymous," says Jess.

"There's nothing anonymous about all the alcoholics going to be in this room tonight eh buddy?!" says Matt, slapping me on my chest.

Ping! Message from Charlie. Oh fuck, she's cancelling.

I'll be there at 7.

We are on, we really are on.

Ping! Message from Melissa. Of fuck, I haven't delivered something.

Good luck tonight. Drink until your eyes bleed and make a tit of yourself!

x

I spend the day chopping and polishing and hiding things behind sofas. I hold off having a drink because I really need to hold it together tonight, for once

I'm going to ignore Melissa's advice. I keep going to the front door to open it and see if anyone is coming, though it's hours to the party. Like walking away from a brand new car and turning back to admire it, I've got new-door-syndrome. Whoever it was who hung it did a really good job. It gently sucks into it's own frame like a cutlery drawer in an expensive kitchen. I feel guilty I didn't do anything about it when Claire was here. But that horse has bolted and I'm enjoying opening and closing the door to my stable. I'm excited about what or who might come through it.

After my shower I stand three inches from the mirror and attempt to cut the hairs growing out of my earlobes with kitchen scissors that refuse to adopt the correct angle no matter which way I turn them.

I cut myself shaving.

I put on my favourite shirt, discovering a suspicious brown stain down it's chest. Four shirt changes later, I have only just finished furiously sponging the stain on my favourite shirt when Orla arrives.

"You've got a stain on your shirt," she says stabbing me with a bottle of Prosecco. "I came early so we could have a drink before everyone gets here."
"Good idea," I say.
"What time is Charlie getting here?"
"Seven," I say, "god-willing."
"How are you feeling?"
"Sick. I've just eaten a whole Double-Decker, I needed some sugar."
"Arse."
"No. Good, I think," I say, "glad it's here. I just want to say thank you to all the people who've been there for me. I guess I'm worried I might be being a tad premature. There is so much still unresolved. Do you think I should change my shirt?"

"I'm sorry old friend," says Orla, hugging me as tightly as a weeping mother on her son's first day at school, despite my wet patch. "It's never over. This is your life now. You can only move forward."

"I guess so."

"I know so. Calm down. The shirt is fine."

Adrian and Gemma walk in.

"Big man," bellows Adrian, giving me a man-hug.

"Hello silly-boy," says Gemma, kissing me smack on the lips like she always does. Claire's Godmother kissed me on the lips on our wedding day. I had never met her before. She sidled up to me during the photographs, introduced herself and following her astonishingly direct kiss, said something into my ear. I was never sure if it was, "you've picked *the* right one there," or " you've picked *a* right one there." I think I know now.

"We got here early to have a drink before everyone gets here," says Gemma. "Nice door by the way."

Soon everyone will be here early, arriving on time is becoming rude. Anyone arriving late is running the risk of a dry bar. Orla opens her Prosecco, which isn't part of my highly-detailed plan. I protest and say Champagne is the first drink, but a full glass is shoved into my hand before I can resist.

"Slange!" I shout.

"Cheers!"

"Cheers!"

"Up your bum."

The evening is underway.

The Prosecco evaporates, then the hall is suddenly full of eager people, the hall funneling their progress like barrier tape in a nightclub. With the exception of Rowan and Joanna, everyone has known each other a lifetime. The noise levels rocket. Charlie is last to arrive. She looks utterly lovely in jeans, boots, a simple white shirt with loose cuffs and a double string of beads. It takes her a while to make her way to me as she reacquaints herself through the crowd. "Hello," she says with a smile that seems glad to be here; glad to be out in the world again; glad to see me. She kisses me on the cheek, squeezing my hand.

I pass round plates of grilled chunks of salmon wrapped in bacon splitting itself between mouths and the kitchen floor. I haven't stood in a room of happy people like this for what feels like years.

Notwithstanding my friends at Dodd's Castle of course.

They were special.

They were different.

 A rescue squad.

Whatever *this* is, it feels true and warm and how it should be. By the time we sit down for supper the empty bottle count is alarming.

Filing into the dining room, each guest identifies themselves on the seating plan to which I have put way too much thought. The huge improvised table requires a clamber to a seat and abandoning all hope of an exit for the loo or a fag. I sit nearest the door with Gemma on my left and Orla on my right. For the starter, I serve individual fish pies in white finger bowls I'd found in Tesco. In each I have painstakingly doled out the required number of prawns and a hunk of haddock, ensuring everyone gets a fair bite.

This is good, Charlie mouths across the table, pointing her fork at her bowl. Every bowl comes back empty, we're off to a good start. For main I serve handmade chicken strips in breadcrumbs with rosemary and thyme potato wedges and pak choi. The pak choi turns out to be a mistaken, watery and tasteless attempt to offset any idea I'm serving nursery food. Nobody minds, the red wine is rendering the food a sideshow.

A mass loo and smoke breakout leads to a shuffling of seats and pudding (My Granny's old recipe called Norwegian Cream) an afterthought few will remember. Charlie holds my hand briefly under the table. When I'm sure no-one is looking I rest my hand on her denim thigh.

Dyfed starts a game of *shove, shag, marry* which doesn't seem as funny as when we played it when we were young. Back then, publicly admitting your carnal preferences from three unsuitable candidates carried a piquancy absent now life is real and scars run deep.

"Thank you all so much for coming," I yell, in a plea for silence. I need to keep it short, so I say, "in what has been a very tough year, each and every one of you has shown their true colours. Thank You. I wouldn't have made it without you. I love you all."

Gemma stands up and raises her glass. "Much as Tom would like to make this evening all about himself, we are a great group of friends and true friendship can stand any test. To us!!"

Everyone agrees noisily and glugs their wine. Okay, I think, I get it. Gemma always likes bringing me down to earth.

She hasn't sat down. "Thankfully not me, but too many of us have had a terrible time recently. To all of you I say, life, like Tom and Dyfed, is too short. Never let the bastards get you down!"

Hoorah, and hear-hear and pass the wine!

"That's a great new door," says Janine. "When did you put it in?"

"Oh. A few days ago. Thanks."

"So what next Tom?" asks Peers, in that South African way that bypasses the niceties.

"Well, now you come to mention it. I'm going to sell the house."

"You've just put a new fucking door on!" says Peers, like he actually is in disbelief. Before I can respond, the conversation is no longer mine to own.

"I think it's a good idea." (Orla)

"Where will he go?" (Gemma)

"It's a good market at the moment." (Joanna)

"I think it's the best thing he can do." (Jess)

"How much was the door?" (Peers)

Absolutely nothing (Charlie).

"It's just an idea at the moment," I interject. "But I need to move on. This isn't my house."

"Of course it is Man," says Peers.

"I know what he means," says Jess. "This was their house."

"Where are you gonna go?" Asks Gemma.

"I think I might buy a Campervan."

"You can park it on my drive," says Graeme.

"Thanks mate."

"A campervan?" It's Peers again, he's knocked locked onto this idea.

"Look, I don't know. I have nothing anchoring me here. I just need to get out there and be me, not be a version of me on a dating profile."

"You could be a travelling writer," says Orla. "A Travel Writer!"

"Ha! Yes I could. I've been doing my food writing as well. I could see if I could twist Melissa's arm to commission me. I could travel around Ireland and visit loads of pubs and restaurants and see the kids. Now, there's an idea."

I'm not looking at Charlie, but I can tell she's not looking at me. She's disengaging. Life in a Campervan is not what she wants for her and Tiggy. I have no idea what she wants. When the port comes out, reeling from the failure of his first attempt at getting a game going, Dyfed announces we should play Chinese Whispers, saying something in the ear of Joanna on his left. The words pass from person to person arriving back at Dyfed who announces, "it is cold in Stalingrad and the flowers are coming up."

"What did it start as?" asks Graeme.

"My dogs got no nose," says Dyfed, grinning at me. It is one of our favourite old gags that will never translate into paper. You had to be here.

"My turn," I say, turning and whispering into Orla's ear. She looks at me sideways and turns to Graeme who spins his head to Charlie and passes it on. Charlie looks at me in disbelief and turns to Rowan who turns to Janine who turns to Adrian. Adrian turns to Jess who turns to Joanna who turns to Dyfed who looks at me with a look transcending our years of friendship. He hesitates before turning to Rosie who says out loud, "oh for fucks sake." She turns to Peers who turns to Tom Two who turns to Gemma who announces, "Claire is having twins and Chris is the father."

Somewhere in Wandsworth a pin drops.

We all hear it.

"Sorry Tom," says Gemma. "I shouldn't have said that."

"My bad," pipes up Dyfed. "Chris isn't the father, I was just messing around."

"Why did you say Chris?" I ask.

"I don't know," he says, "sorry I was just being an idiot."

"Is she really having twins?" asks Gemma.

"No," snaps Orla, "she's not."

"But she's pregnant?" Asks Rosie.

"Jesus," says Joanna.

"Has anybody seen Chris recently?" asks Peers.

"I saw him at Christmas on Waterloo, he was pissed after a works lunch." says Adrian

"Chris wouldn't do that," pleads Dyfed, "let's move on."

Mercifully, it doesn't take long for everyone to make an extra effort and restore normality. The volume edges up again in the search for new topics to gloss over the hand grenade I stupidly tossed. Skulking in the kitchen, trying to clear up, Charlie appears and asks, "what did you say?"

"I just said Claire was pregnant. I don't know why."

"Why didn't you tell me?"

"We haven't had the chance," I say. "It doesn't matter, it's got nothing to do with me."

"Of course it's got something to do with you."

She seems genuinely concerned, openly holding my hand and putting her arms around my neck. "You do pick your moments."

"I know," I say, "I just wanted it out there. What an arse. I wasn't thinking. Fuck."

"Didn't Chris and Claire have a thing before you went out?"

"Yes. They did."

I rarely remember the end of dinner parties, but I've suddenly found myself disquietingly sober. In the hallway there are thanks, goodbyes, man-hugs, woman-hugs and wrangles over taxis.

"I'm sorry mate," says Dyfed on his way, "that was stupid of me."

"No," I counter. "It's my fault."

Everyone but Charlie is gone. She picks up the pre-wedding picture from the table by the old phone and I mumble something about water under the bridge.

"A lot of shit under the bridge," she says.

"We weren't to know how things would turn out"

Squeezing two fingers of my hand, she says she is tired.

"You go up," I say. "I'll lock-up."

I take my phone from my jean's pocket and text Claire.

I hear Chris is the father of your child.

□ □ □ □ □, comes the reply.

Have I learned a thing?

Chapter 23: THE BEGINNING

"A story has no beginning or end: arbitrarily one chooses that moment from which to look back or from which to look ahead."

Graham Greene, The End of The Affair.

Orla calls and tells me Ian has asked for my number. She says he wants to talk to me about my book.

"Fuck."

"Why Fuck?"

"Well. Truth is Orla, it's turned out to be more of a journal than a book, or a novel. I haven't exactly hidden people, and I'm sure I've been pretty unkind in places."

"I thought you'd changed everybody's names?"

"I have mostly, but really I've just been writing stuff down. I'm a journalist. I report facts. I'm not sure I ever intended this to be published."

"Of course you did."

"I think I thought I'd go back and move things around it a bit if I ever got anywhere with it. It's taken on a bit of a life of its own. I can't let Ian or Book Club read it, they'll murder me."

"Just call Ian, see what he has to say. He's not as bad a bloke as you think."

I say I will and resolve to do the opposite.

She asks me how things ended with Charlie after the Dinner Party and I tell her we are over, quickly following up we are a never ending story, so never really over. Orla doesn't offer much more than a shrug which bugs me. She has an opinion on most things and I can only conclude she isn't giving hers because I won't like what she has to say.

The morning after the Dinner party I lay next to Charlie, my hand resting on her hip. If she wasn't asleep, she wasn't letting me know she was awake. For a while, I had felt good, smiling in the dark. She didn't stir and as quietly as I could whisper, I had asked if she loved me.

The tension eating me, I got up and made scrambled eggs. She appeared, dressed, putting her overnight bag in the hall. We ate a polite breakfast picking over the highlights of the evening. Glossing over the low lights. Though I knew it was coming, to my crushing disappointment, she said, "I have to go." At the door she said, "I can't fix your life, you can't fix mine. You are you and I am me. Let's just hope we can get through this, and maybe we'll find each other."

"I get that," I said.

As I let her out the door, my shoulders slumped. Suddenly I felt like that bloody man on the moon again. She stepped out and then turned. Pulling me into a hug, she said, "of course I love you, I just can't give you what you want right now."

With a kiss on my cheek, she was gone.
I'm not sure she will ever look back again.
Why hadn't I said something more?

A mobile number appears neither me or my phone recognise.
"Hello," says a voice I immediately recognise. "It's Ian. Ian Korf."
"Hello," I reply. "How are you?"
Oh shit.
"I'm good thank you Tom. Now listen, I want to talk to you about this book of yours."

"OK."

"Would you be prepared to let the Book Club review it? I think it would be an excellent exercise all round."

I stall and stutter and explain it isn't really finished or edited, to which he says the Club can be my finishers and editors. So then I say I don't think it's very good but that doesn't cut any mustard so I say, the truth is, it really is more of a journal, a diary of my journey and I haven't exactly been discrete with some of the characters in it.

"Am I in it?" asks Ian.

"Err, yes, I'm afraid so."

"And have you described me as having a big nose and terrible dress sense?"

"Errm."

"And have you said I treat Book Club as a psychotherapy session?"

"Errm. Something like that."

"Well. You are spot on. I do have a huge nose, so that is a fact perfectly observed. I do have a terrible dress sense, but I am not brave enough to change what I have always known. And yes I treat it as a psychotherapy session, but not for you, for me."

"I don't understand."

"Tom, you are not the only person in the world who has problems. Yes, yours have been extreme in the last year, but you are not the only person in town having a tough time."

"I know that Ian."

"Well, I have my problems Tom. And I'm a psychotherapist, so who do I go and talk to? If I saw a shrink it would be like a Busman's holiday, and I would see every technique he or she used before they used it."

"I'm sorry to hear that Ian. I'm not sure what to say."

"It's like being an artist painting a self-portrait. Does he paint what he sees, or what he wants people to see? I am trapped in my own reflection."

"Like Narcissus?"

"No! Not like Narcissus, that is something entirely different. I am simply saying my route out of my problems is hard to find. Like yours is. You have written a book and you are a writer, and from what I can tell, you have a problem creating fiction when all you see is facts. Am I right?"

"I guess so."

"So, our problems are not dissimilar. What I am asking, and I know it's a big ask - please bring your book to the Book Club. Perhaps only read out some selected chapters where you haven't been a little too honest and let's see where we get to."

"I'm not sure Ian."

"I am asking you from the bottom of my heart Tom."

I sense an opening and explain how rude I have been about Marcus in the book and I could never sit opposite him and share my words. We'd end up in a fight. Ian is ready for my parry, telling me Marcus and Jenita have left as their marriage has finally come undone. Apparently Marcus has been having an affair for years.

Go figure.

"Aude and Oli have come back though. They seem to have figured out how to be happy."

"You mentioned your problems," I say. "Is it your marriage?"

"That, if you will be so kind" says Ian, "I will tell you over a beer after Book Club."

Six days later, I make the long walk to Hammersmith on my own. I ask myself again, had I loved Claire? The good news is I had. Of course, I had. Perhaps still do in some residue way. It's a relief. Love is harder to destroy than wedding photos on the fire. Our love wasn't fake, it was flawed. Imperfect. Too imperfect to survive the all-seeing lens of forensic examination. I can see now there are many shades of love. When I first met Claire I fancied her. When we got it together, I was flattered. Proud to be on her arm. I liked the lifestyle we built. I felt positive for our future. Love, therefore, although not showing itself in a ceremony of fireworks and grand gestures, would surely be a natural consequence of our coupling. At some point, we must have decided we loved each other. There was no grand announcement, no press release, no exchange of jewellery. I imagined many people would say they never experienced the thunderbolt of love. That love is a product of nurture and growth. I'm sure that is true in many cases. In the absence of a thunderbolt, to stand the best chance, I believe you need something extra - a hook, a shared purpose, a commonality or experience that forges a strong bond. I'm not sure Claire and I ever had that.

"So Tom, where shall we start?" asks Ian.

I kick off with the first chapter and hear myself reading about socks and sushi and ticks and tocks and zeroes and booms. When I finish Veronica is crying and Aude is squeezing Oli's hand. I skip the chapter about joining Book Club and read the one about my walk with Dad and the one about Dyfed's affair in New York.

After each there is muttered praise and muted claps and attempts to talk about style and tone and grammar then Veronica asks me if I will ever marry again.

"Ha! Ha! I don't deserve to get my hands on the weapon of marriage again. I wish I had never forgotten what the Nigerian Vicar said, marriage is hard work. Granted, it shouldn't be, but it bloody is. The problem with oft-repeated phrases - they grow glib, and dismissible. And that is the challenge I have found in writing this stuff down."

'What do you mean?" asks Ian.

"Writing stuff down is easy.I mean writing stuff that means something. Making it stand up in court or actually fixing something rather than sweeping it under the carpet is not easy. There's a difference."

"So what have you learned Tom?"

"More than I know, I think. Ha! Ha! I wrote down a charge sheet actually," I say, ferreting for a piece of paper I pull from the green foolscap folder I carry the book draft and my notes in. It didn't make it into the book. It's my sort of conclusion."

"Off you go Tom," says Ian, leaning back in his chair.

With a suitable pause for dramatic effect and because I'm seriously thinking of running out the door, I eventually take a deep breath and say, "This is how I plead:

Marrying someone without fully completing due diligence.

Guilty.

Assuming your marriage was fine when it wasn't.

Guilty.

Assuming a good lifestyle was the sign of a good marriage.

Guilty.

Conducting a marriage without due care and attention for your partners grievances.

Guilty.

Failing to establish a working relationship over money discussions.

Guilty.

Failing to be smart enough to provide your children with two parents permanently cohabitating under the same roof.

Guilty.

Giving mental consideration to a third-party during the hours of marriage.

Guilty."

I cough and look up at the eyes staring back at me. Orla knows who I'm talking about.

"Taking an eye for an eye response to your perception of your partner's failures and weaknesses.

Guilty.

Going to sleep without resolving arguments or heeding the advice of the Nigerian Vicar.

Yep. *Guilty."*

And now all I can hear is the sound of silence.

"You seem to be carrying all the guilt for your marriage failure," says Oli finally.

"That's the thing," I say, "that's only my half of the equation. My 50%, Claire had the other 50%. But I don't think we ever filled our collective tank to anything near 100% because I married the wrong person. I'm sure she feels the same. There remained a toxic fume-filled void, volatile to combustion because at the end of the day we weren't right for each other. Whatever percentage we got to, we were driving in the dusk - light enough to drive without lights, dim enough to misread corners and bends. Our engine sparked and propelled us forward, negotiating the twists and turns in a smooth enough ride with our sidelights on, peering absent-mindedly into the distance, until something triggered one of us to switch to full-beam and make an effort or crash. And we crashed."

"Oh Tom," says Veronica.

Sitting alone at the bar with Ian, I ask him if he wants to talk about what he mentioned on the phone. He finds it difficult to talk about himself, but with a little to and fro he reveals his wife, who he has been with since University has told him he has a deep sadness within him that is bringing her down and she is not sure how long can she stay with him unless he finds himself and finds some light. Ian talks of a life unfulfilled. They never had kids. He never became Freud. He was never as successful as his older siblings and never lived up to his parents expectations. The Book Club is a vehicle to try and prise open the lid of his life, but he knows many of the members are laughing at him. He says only by looking through the lens that the members and books bring to the table, can he look at himself.

"Did you marry the right person?" I ask.

"Oh Lord yes," he says. "She is the most wonderful woman in the world, but now I feel I am failing her. She has said as much. And now I, the great listener, don't know what to do."

I feel guilty I have been so dismissive of him. Of course he has problems, everyone does. So I do what I always do, which is try and talk my way towards a conclusion I don't yet see.

"I suppose my biggest take out of all of this has been about finding the right partner in the first place. When you are in the wrong marriage with the wrong person, you bring out the worst in each other. But you say you married well, you love your wife?"

"I did. I do. We've been together twenty-seven years."

"OK. So this has got me thinking. None of the people in my book are bad people (well almost), they became bad in flawed marriages that turned sour. Isn't it strange how one man might describe a woman as ghastly, but the next describe the same woman as the finest to ever walk the earth? If it's all about the initial match, you have done what half of the world fails to do, find her and stay married."

"So far."

"So it's more than that. There's a piece of the jigsaw I've been missing. You know better than most, sadness comes from within. You have done the hard part. She doesn't want you to be sad. How can she not interpret your sadness as at least partially because of her. Yet you clearly love her. So it isn't that. I think probably we've both been looking through the wrong end of the telescope. I know I'm preaching from the cheap seats here, but clearly it's as much about the individual going into the marriage as it is the couple who are in it?"

"Of course you are right, but people never really compartmentalise it like that. For me I think it might be because I always wanted to be a writer, but my parents, my world, my life discouraged me."

"Have you written anything?"

"Yes, two books actually."

"And?"

"Neither published of course. The first one I know is crap, but the second might have something in it. I've been wanting to talk to you about it since you joined the club, but was nervous you would quash my ambition."

"Don't be ridiculous. Can I read it?"

"Well, I guess so."

"What's it about?"

"It's a love story."

"About your wife?"

"Well, now you mention it, I suppose it is."

Walking home I think about my conversation with Ian and his total love for his wife and I think about Charlie and I know one person can't fix another's life. No matter how much we have been eviscerated by life's betrayals the only light that can guide us is the one that comes from within. If only we can find it and let it shine.

By the time I go through my new front door. Ian has already emailed me his book. I read the first chapter and the first few pages of the second. It's good, properly good. Clear and clean, concise and descriptive without crawling up it's descriptive backside. I text Ian a message and tell him I really like the beginning of his book and will read the rest and get back to him. I'm genuinely impressed and tell him that. I hope he believes me and, right now a little bit of light is shining under his door and his wife walks past and notices.

If, and I pray you are not, you are one of the 42%, I wonder which was more difficult - living in a failing marriage or trying to stay alive after its failure? They are on different sides of the same coin. A coin that flips too easily. It was only two months into my Apocalypse when Dyfed said to me, *this is your darkest hour.* I reminded him of that recently and we laughed. It was nothing like my darkest hour. When he said it, I was just at the beginning of my journey into the deepest voids of dark space from which I wasn't sure I would ever make it back to earth.

I realise now marriage isn't just about the match. It's also about what we bring to the party as individuals. If we are not comfortable in ourselves, we have little chance of reflecting that on others.To move forward from here I have to go all the way back - back beyond anything I can lay blame upon. I must travel back in time before any excuses about how my parents raised me or how life's experiences have shaped me or people have disappointed me. I am going all the way back to the womb, imagining upon my second birth, I can stand to attention, give a sharp salute and announce, *right, let's have another crack at this.*

Yes my marriage failed.

But I am not a statistic.

I am Tom.

THE BEGINNING

Aug 28th
self-isolation for 14 days.
nhsvolunteer 08196 3646
can do home tests.

44071540R00144